The Return of Frankie Whittle

Caroline England

A Bullington Press publication
Copyright © Caroline England, 2024

ISBN 978-1-7384448-6-1 (paperback)
ISBN 978-1-7384448-7-8 (hardback)
ISBN 978-1-7384448-8-5 (e-book)

This novel is a work of fiction. Names, characters, businesses, places, events and incidents are either the product of the author's imagination or used in a fictitious manner. Any resemblance to actual persons, living or dead, or actual events is purely coincidental.

For permission requests, please email: info@bullingtonpress.co.uk

Interior layout by Textual Eyes
Design for Print Services

Cover design by Will Templeton

Printed and bound by CPI Group (UK) Ltd, Croydon, CR0 4YY

www.bullingtonpress.co.uk

"A taut, claustrophobic thriller that left me breathless!"

Simon McCleave, bestselling author of the
DI Ruth Hunter series

"An unsettling psychological thriller that taps into our deepest fears."

Paul Burke, Crime Time FM

"An ominous sense of impending disaster from the very start of this creepy thriller. Will hold you to the very end!"

Trevor Wood, winner of the
2020 CWA New Blood Dagger

"An absolute scorcher, infused with tension and menace. A beautiful and insightful slow burner of a thriller."

Chris Lloyd, winner of the
2021 HWA Gold Crown award

"A dark, gripping, claustrophobic thriller with a terrifying premise."

A A Chaudhuri, bestselling author of
Under Her Roof and The Final Party

By Caroline England

The Stranger Beside Me
The Sinner
Truth Games
Betray Her
My Husband's Lies
Beneath the Skin

As C E Rose

The House of Hidden Secrets
The House on the Water's Edge
The Shadows of Rutherford House
The Attic at Wilton Place

Caroline England was born and brought up in Sheffield and studied Law at the University of Manchester. She was a divorce and professional indemnity lawyer before turning her hand to writing. As well as *The Return of Frankie Whittle*, Caroline is the author of *The Stranger Beside Me*, *The Sinner*, *Truth Games*, *Betray Her*, *My Husband's Lies* (the e-book bestseller), and *Beneath the Skin*. She also writes gothic-tinged thrillers under the pen name CE Rose. She lives in Manchester with her family.

To my lovely friend, Deborah Grace,
and her much-missed husband, Jonathan.

Prologue

I peer into the black night. The stillness and silence feel oppressive and, despite the balmy air, I have a horrible sensation that someone is behind me, their bony fingers reaching to drape an icy blanket across my spine. Suddenly terrified it's a stony-faced matron or an inmate risen from the dead, I force my feet to inch around. Only emptiness ricochets off the old buildings and bricks, the walkways and the perfect maze of trimmed green, thank God. Yet my stomach clenches at the thought. Emptiness, isolation, *seclusion* ...

I shake off the ridiculous alarm and reinstate my resolve. But as I put one foot in front of the other, the notion of someone or something watching and wheezing from the ancient enclosures again prickles my skin. I creep past the sleeping Gatehouse, along the silvery path to the chapel, then I climb up the steps and peer through the panelled window. Though my hot, nervy breath clouds the glass, there's no one in the lobby area from what I can glean, so I shift across to the entrance and cautiously press down the handle. The door that's never locked reassuringly opens, so I enter and listen for movement. Satisfied that nobody is on the ground level, I tiptoe across the plush carpet, past the aged font to the open staircase at the rear.

As noiselessly as I'm able, I steal up in the darkness to a first-floor landing. Voices echo from the walls so I stop, stock still, and strain to hear over the loud thud of apprehension in my ears. The conversation's too muffled to make out, but it's coming from the right, so I turn the other way and squint through the gloom. Part of me wants to bolt out and escape whilst I can, but there's a

1

doorway and it's ajar ...

My pulse revving from intrigue and fear, I sneak across the floorboards, edge into the vaulted room and glance around. Though moonlight shines through the arched casement, it takes moments to adapt to what I'm seeing. The centre contains an adult-sized cot, for want of a better description. I stare, bemused. Is it a disabled person's bedroom? That would explain why I've never seen hide nor hair of them. No, it's too whitewashed and clinical for that and, besides, the bed is adjustable and surrounded by monitors and machines. I take in a wheeled unit with a Perspex rectangle on the top and a wall-mounted fridge beyond it. Almost mesmerised, I move to the glass door and squint at the rows of drug vials inside. The labels are handwritten and, as I strain to read them, foreboding trickles through me. What the hell? They're neatly marked with percentages of 'morphine' and 'scopolamine' and someone's initials ...

Rotating again, my gaze lands on a tray of methodically placed surgical items: suture packets, kidney bowls, scissors and a row of metal tools. I pick one up and frown. They appear to be very large spoons or tongs, but why would they be freeze-wrapped? Realisation finally cracking, I drop them. Good God, they're birthing forceps and this is a delivery suite.

My eyes slide to what I've already seen, yet not fully absorbed. Noise-cancelling earphones, a padded head restraint and blindfold, harnesses and straps for wrists, ankles and knees.

I swallow hard. Though it looks more like a ward in a lunatic asylum, this room is a secret venue for childbirth. I gape at the leather shackles again. Why the hell would any woman agree to these?

PART 1 - THE INTRUDER

Frankie and Nina

1

Frankie

Although it's only my small cabin case, Toby solicitously wheels it down the gangway to platform one for me. He stops at the barrier, takes me in his arms and kisses me like he did on our first date three years ago.

I feel the old flip of arousal, deep in my belly. It's inappropriate, for sure, with fellow passengers shouldering past, yet back in the day the need to take it further was compulsive. In the rear seat of cars, down alleyways, against trees, behind walls or in long grass wasn't uncommon and, after so many automated months of late, it's wonderful to have that rush of happy hormones back.

When he pulls away, I chuckle. 'Where did that come from?' I ask.

'A whole two days without you.' He grins his perfect, white-toothed grin. 'How will I cope?'

'I'm sure you'll find something to distract you. I thought you were off to see your dad?'

'Yeah, maybe later if I can steel myself for his usual comparisons between me and everyone else under the sun.'

I resist saying, *At least you've got one; I'd love a father to admire and impress.* 'Toby! He's proud of you, honestly. He's just rubbish at showing it,' I say instead.

'Hmm.'

I peck his lips. 'You're clever, successful, loveable, handsome,

5

incredible in bed. I could go on, but—'

'Oh, please do.'

'— but I have the eight-thirty to catch.'

'Damn.' He smooths back his fair quiff. 'Yeah, Dad's. Thought I'd pop into the office for a couple of hours first. You know, meander around and say hi to let people know I'm there?'

It's not my idea of Saturday morning fun. Not these days anyway; unlike my hubby, work is at the very bottom of my current priorities.

'Good plan. Keep me posted about who's in and any gossip.' I glance over his shoulder at the waiting Manchester train. 'I'd better hurry ...'

'Yup. Have fun with Red Nina and try not to argue. Send her my love.'

Red Nina; his name for my mum. It's pretty accurate though, as is the potential of us falling out as we inevitably do when we rub shoulders for more than twenty-four hours. Too different in personalities or way too similar; I can never decide.

'Haha. Will do.' I quickly kiss him again and set off. 'Bye and be good!'

When I'm settled in my seat, I idly listen to the announcements and go back to thoughts of Mum and our love-hate relationship. Not that I ever *hate* her, really. Not these days, anyway. The strongheaded me as a teenager might have; indeed, I escaped to university in London the moment I could, and never permanently returned home. Sometimes I catch the intense attachment in her eyes and feel a spasm of guilt, but growing up in a single-child, single-parent household wasn't easy. Sure, I had her undivided adoration, attention and praise. I also had her opinions, her influences and control, which can be horribly suffocating when you're trying to find, and be, your own person. And, unlike my hubby, I don't have a father to identify with, bounce off, look up to or emulate. Even one to resent would be nice.

I replace the old angst with a smile. My kids will have a dad and siblings; it'll be a veritable 2.4 nuclear family. Besides, I do love my mum very much. She's my absolute rock and I'm certain that this weekend, of all weekends, will not get *rocky*.

Feeling the train move, I look out of the window. Toby's still there, model-like in his houndstooth cashmere scarf and new leather jacket. Bless him. I feel a swell of affection for my 'bit of posh', as I used to put it. When we first met at work, I could see he was attractive, with a *Made in Chelsea* sort of vibe, but there was no way I'd date a guy called Tobias with a double-barrelled flaming surname. He was also charming and funny and nice so, against all the odds, I did. Six months later, he proposed.

'Wouldn't we make beautiful babies,' he said.

I rub my tummy and grin at the memory. How could I have possibly said anything other than yes?

2

Nina

It's always so lovely to have my girl home, sit either side of the sofa with a cup of Yorkshire Tea and catch up on news. I say 'girl' but, at thirty-one, she's a fully-grown woman. Though we all know that age is just a number, I don't like to advertise mine, especially as it falls within that dreadful category of 'middle-aged'. I've turned fifty-four and, on a good day, I might pass for someone in my forties on the outside; yet inside I'm still twenty-three, holding her in my arms and marvelling on how blessed I was to be given something so utterly perfect.

I look at Frankie now and study her features – her glowing skin, her startling blue gaze and that knockout smile. How did I bring her up to be such a smart, personable and lovely person, despite all the difficulties? Not to mention a feisty and independent one.

'How's Toby?' I ask her.

'He's good. Sends his love. Working too hard, of course. But if he wants to move up that notch to director, he has to make himself seen and heard twenty-four seven, suck up to the right people, take care not to offend the others and so on. It's actually a bloody nightmare trying to be all things to all men; women too.' She squints in thought. 'Being the best version of yourself all the time, or having to act it, must be exhausting.'

'I can imagine,' I reply, even though I can't. I was the first person in my family to go to university, but I didn't go far in terms of distance or career. My mum thought Greg 'held me back' from pursuing employment worthy of my academic abilities, yet what I really wanted was a nine-to-five no-pressure job, then get engaged and married and start a family. I managed three out of the four, so that isn't bad.

I go back to Frankie, absently playing with the pendant on her necklace. From years of experience with my headstrong daughter, I know better than to start sentences with a 'but'. In this instance, it might be: *But you're the same age and qualification as Toby; you're far smarter than him. Until last year, you were as ambitious as he was. Just because he's the man in the marriage, don't let him hold you back.*

Inwardly laughing at the flaming irony, I ask an open question instead. 'How's work going for you?'

'I finished the IT placement so, from Monday, I'm on the bench for a bit, thank God.'

'Oh, right.' That's certainly a surprise. Frankie usually hates being between projects and at the beck of anyone's call, so something's afoot. And now I look at her carefully, there's a pinch of exhaustion about her, a hint of lilac-tinged tiredness beneath her eyes. There's suppressed excitement too.

A surge of joy rises from my toes to my cheeks. She's pregnant, I'm sure of it. My girl is going to have a baby and I'll be a grandma. I chuckle to myself. How can that be when I'm only twenty-three years of age! But how wonderful it will be to have new life in the family, a little girl or boy to cuddle and cherish and love. It's quite honestly the greatest gift of all.

Yet an uncomfortable niggle spreads between my breastbones like heartburn. The fact that Frankie is London-based and I won't have the hands-on closeness with the child that I'd have if she lived here, close by? Or Toby and his dysfunctional family? Nope, two hours on a train isn't insurmountable and, though I can't help being a judgemental northern mother from a working-class background who thinks no one will ever be good enough for my daughter, my son-in-law has never been anything other than pleasant and polite in my company. Which leaves the past. That huge, huge blot at the very root of my psyche, a secret I've somehow managed to deeply bury and keep hidden from myself, let alone the person it affects the most.

My thoughts are splintered by Frankie's snappy tone. 'Mum!'

'Sorry, love?'

She tuts. 'This isn't how the conversation is supposed to go.'

'So, how is it—'

'Instead of you disappearing like you do, you're supposed to say: "But you hate being between projects ..." and I'd reply: "That's because I have something exciting to tell you".'

I hold my breath. 'So ...'

'I'm pregnant!'

'Oh, Frankie!' I reach out my arms. 'Congratulations! That's the best news ever.'

'You're pleased for me?'

'Of course! Why wouldn't I be?'

'Well, I know what you're like about Toby.'

She's referring – yet again – to a comment I made about the haste of their wedding. It was perfectly reasonable and said over two flaming years ago, but today is Frankie's day, so I don't take umbrage. 'I bet he's thrilled.'

Her eyes shine with tears. 'Yeah, bless him, he is.'

'Goodness, Toby a daddy! He'll be smitten. How far along are you?'

'Only nine or ten weeks, so this is just between you and me for now. And Gran, of course.' She looks at me pointedly. 'Because I know what you're like about blabbing to her.'

I want to object, but she does have a point. My mum is the one person who ekes out my sins whether I like it or not.

'But no one at the library or the running group. OK, Mum? I don't want to tell anyone until I'm twelve weeks at least.'

'Of course,' I say. 'Absolutely. It's such amazing, wonderful news. I'm so happy for you both.'

And deeply worried for my girl, my child, the baby I so desperately coveted. Always that.

3

Frankie

Breathing in the chilly February night air, I briskly walk from Mum's house towards the centre of West Didsbury. Until I come home, I forget how much I love it here; from the lines of terraced avenues named after towns in Derbyshire, to the park where I used to walk our little dog, and particularly my primary school where I was happily oblivious to not having a dad. I briefly stop outside it now and envision my group of friends – the brothers and sisters I never had – larking around in a corner of the playground.

Wondering which gender I'll be blessed with, I picture my blue-eyed children amidst them, laughing, contented, carefree. For one reason or another – not least because he was the product of his father's third out of four marriages – Toby had a tough time at his paid prep, and it didn't get a great deal better at his private academy afterwards. Which is precisely why I'm determined we'll do things differently for our kids. A state school will be the thing – a good one, of course – and though I never imagined raising a child in London, with us renting the flat in Fulham, we're completely moveable.

I continue my journey and chuckle to myself. If someone had suggested evaluating neighbourhoods on schooling rather than cafés, bars and commutability when I first dated Toby, I'd have laughed my socks off. Yet a few months into our relationship, the broody bug infected me out of nowhere, an intense, overwhelming desire to get pregnant PDQ. So when he proposed, after my initial shock, it seemed meant to be. Mum's dour face at the suggestion might have provoked me into to saying a quick yes, but our grand wedding in a marquee on the Bamford-Hogg estate was sublime and, as things turned out, conceiving wasn't as easy as I'd anticipated, so it was a bloody good job I'd followed my gut rather than waiting until I'm forty.

Absorbing the eclectic vibe of cafés, restaurants and bars – and weirdly smelling them – I tap my under-eye bags as I walk down Burton Road. My mum has always been too telepathic for comfort, so it's no surprise that she'd guessed my news, yet I know my tiredness is a telltale sign as well. It turns out that inordinate fatigue is a symptom of early pregnancy, along with sore boobs and a sudden dislike of certain food and drink. Not to mention the 'morning' sickness which comes in nauseous waves. After months of trying for this miracle, I don't mind one bit. As the books say, so long as those signs are there, so is a thriving baby.

'Francesca Whittle! Over here!'

My name snaps me back to the bustling street. Almost colliding into some guy by my side, I search out Anya's voice. She waves from a corner table beneath Folk's heated canopy.

'Oh, hi!' I call, retracing my steps. 'I overshot.'

My old school friend edges out and gives me a solid hug. 'That's because you were on another planet.' She gestures to the heaving bar beyond the open door. 'I checked and there's no room inside. It's pretty chocka out here as well, but will it do? At least it's warm.'

'Yes, absolutely.' I squeeze between the chairs and pull one out. 'So lovely to see you. Do I detect a hint of an Aussie accent?'

'Oh God, really? Though listen to you – you sound like a southerner.'

'Yeah, so Nina keeps telling me. She's clearly worried I'll lose my working-class credentials, which is ridiculous when everyone in the office thinks I sound completely Manc. And as for Toby's family ...' I chuckle. 'So there's no need for her to fret.'

'Aw, how is your lovely mum? Still living on Matlock Avenue and working at that old library in town?'

'Yup. She sends her love and asked after your parents. I bet they were really chuffed to have you home for Christmas.'

'They were, but there's only another ten days left. Time's completely flown.'

Once we've ordered drinks, Anya enthuses about her life as a teacher down under. 'I can't believe it's over two years since I last saw you,' she eventually says.

'I know, two and a half since I said, "I do".'

'Yours was one posh wedding. How the hell did they get chandeliers into a tent?'

'Beats me. I left it all to the wedding planners.'

'As for that ice sculpture of the "bride and groom" ...' She guffaws. 'Well, *their* marriage was never going to last. Is Toby up here with you?'

'Not this time. I quite like catching up with Mum on my own. You know, when we're not bickering. And it's good to visit Gran without Toby's slack jaw when he inspects their next-door neighbours' garden. A sofa has been added to the old freezer since the last time I went. But they use it for a smoke, so that's OK.'

I feel myself flush from talking too much to cover the real reason for this particular visit. Though I'm still amazed, delighted and walking on air, my secret is only apricot-sized and I don't want to tempt fate by mentioning it. 'I'm going for a pee. I'll grab some refills on the way back. Same again?'

'Perfect.'

When I return with the too-full gin glasses, I carefully inch between the benches towards Anya but, at the final hurdle, my drink splashes on a person at our neighbouring table.

'God, I'm so sorry,' I say. Bloody hell, if my spatial awareness is this bad, heaven knows what I'll be like when my pregnancy shows.

The man peers at his glistening shoulder, then looks up at me with curious eyes. 'No problem.'

'It's only tonic water, so it shouldn't stain.'

'This jacket's as old as the hills.' He smiles a self-deprecating smile. 'And it was a charity shop purchase even then, so it has probably suffered far worse than a few drops of liquid.'

It's the same dark-haired guy I almost collided with earlier. He must think I'm completely nuts. Or maybe paralytically drunk. He watches me pad the tweed fabric with a paper napkin, then he returns to his companion. 'Cheers.'

'Embarrassing!' I say, when I finally sit opposite Anya. 'Can't take me anywhere.'

'He's pretty peng too; I'm a sucker for a shadow of rugged stubble,' she replies in her usual not-quiet-enough tones. 'His date wasn't half giving you the death stare.' She squints beyond me. 'Though he prefers the much older woman if she isn't his mother, so I don't think I'll bother asking for his number.'

'Haha. First time for everything.'

'Cheeky. Anyway ...' She leans forward with raised eyebrows. 'Tonic water, eh?' She triumphantly folds her arms. 'Francesca Whittle, I bloody well knew it. You're preggers, aren't you?'

4

Nina

I can't smell the unique aroma of my workplace any more, but I know it's there, invading every fibre of my clothing so, the moment I arrive home on Thursday, I wait for Lewie to struggle through the cat flap and feed him, divest myself of all my clothing, shove it in the washing machine, then trot starkers upstairs and jump into the shower.

I chuckle at my own workday routine. The jog is a nod to keeping fit, along with the group of 'middle-aged' ladies I run or speed walk with on a Tuesday evening whilst we put the ills of the world to rights. The naked bit is to keep an eye on the old waistline, boobs and bod in general. I've never lived with a man and, quite frankly, I'd never care to, but it doesn't stop me having a sex drive. A guy with a six pack is perhaps too much to expect, yet I'm a sucker for a handsome face and a pre-beer-belly torso, so it pays to keep in good shape myself.

I lather the soap and scrub away the smell of dusty books. Though I worked school hours in various libraries around South Manchester when Frankie was younger, I've been at John Rylands for several years now. Home to rare tomes, manuscripts, maps and archives, it's a nod to my history degree and ticks that old chestnut of feeling 'fulfilled'. That and being a mother, of course.

When I dropped off Frankie for the Sunday evening train, she left me with an instruction to come up with a 'Grandma' name I can mention to my colleagues 'without hyperventilating', as she put it. Though I plan to consult the real 'Granny', I haven't had chance to pop round to Mum's. Still, she has plenty to chew on for now.

'You've been cavorting with that Colin for longer than anyone else I can recall,' she'd said on last week's visit.

'I'm not sure someone mid-menopause is allowed to cavort,' I replied. 'And even if I was, would I really do it with someone called Colin?'

In truth, my builder squeeze has become something of a permanent weekend fixture. I like him and he seems to like me, if his adoring eyes are anything to go by. Is a twelve year gap a little too big? I shrug the notion away. I once cared very much what people thought, and maybe I made the wrong call because of that, but I stopped a long time ago, thank God. And with Frankie being home, I did miss waking up next to Col's lithe body on Sunday morning and having an energetic 'workout'.

Intending to message him and say as much, I trot down to the kitchen and pour myself a large glass of red. That damned 'wrong call' needling, I avoid looking at the window ledge and go through today's mail. Refreshingly, the missives aren't all bills. One is a postcard from a mate who has my dream job of touring the libraries of the world. She always sends me a postcard which starts: *Here's this week's reason to be green with envy* ... This one happens to be from Liverpool and, though a comedown from Barcelona, Florence or Valencia, it's still an undeniably beautiful building.

Inevitably, the framed photograph above the sink draws me in. The portrait has been here forever, a fixture I look at every morning without seeing. Today I put down my drink and study it properly for the first time in thirty-three years. Do I recognise the grinning lovers any more? The sandy-haired young man with the boy-next-door good looks who's just been promoted at work? Or the darker-skinned woman who's showing off the diamond cluster he bought her with his first enhanced pay packet?

I was at my happiest that day. I had no doubt of Greg's commitment and love, but it was still touching he'd taken it upon himself to buy the ring on the quiet, then propose on one knee.

Yet what made my heart truly sing was that my dream was coming; no more jealously peering into prams or cuddling other people's newborns; I'd soon be starting my own family.

A hot flash rising, I fan my face. Though I'd like to convince myself the sweaty flush is hormonal, there's no escaping the decisions I made. A wrong or bad call, or even an omission ... I shake my head. Who am I kidding? It was nothing short of a barefaced lie.

I take a big breath and puff out the heat. Everything's fine, more than fine. Frankie is settled with a baby on the way, and I've got a saucy text to compose. I return to the post and, though I idly glance at the next envelope, a fizzle of alarm runs through me as I register the handwritten name. Greg and I never reached the altar; I never became his wife, nor adopted his name. So who on earth would be writing to 'Nina Whittle-Ward'?

5

Frankie

After a long day at work, missing the tube by a whisker, then being squashed in the next carriage like a sardine, I wearily climb up the stairs to our flat. My whole focus is on reaching the sofa and collapsing but, as the door swings open, I'm greeted by the distinctive sound of my mother-in-law's eloquent tones. When I reach the lounge, she's wending her way around, lightly stroking the ornaments, curtains and cushions with her long fingers, the 'touch test', as Toby puts it. She last came here when we moved in eight months ago, so the room was less cluttered then. Or maybe it's the woman's deep, husky tones and her Herculean personality that makes it feel tiny.

'Small and sweet,' she's saying. 'Perfect for two lovebirds but one hopes not forever. I assume you've been saving all your pennies for somewhere to buy, darling. Perhaps a little further out from the mean streets? Richmond, for example?'

Though she doesn't acknowledge me, I fix my smile and wait to see what's afoot. I like Felicia well enough in small doses, but we usually go to her place, so it feels odd that she's turned up here out of the blue. I eye up my husband. His face is plastered with that bewildered-boy look he sports around her. He surely hasn't told her our news. Sharing it with my mum is one thing, Felicia the 'foghorn' another.

I check my annoyance. No one chooses their mother. Nina can be interfering or judgemental at times, yet she didn't loudly share my adolescent worries with friends whilst I was growing up. At least not when I was present with burning cheeks. And though Toby's one of many kids paternally, he's Felicia's only child, so I get that claustrophobic pressure to please her. She builds him up to feel inordinately special, then knocks him down with a few indifferent, yet choice, words. Then there's her frequent 'woe is me; your father dumped me for a younger woman and I can't cope' yowling, which no child should have to listen to. My mum is the opposite; stiff-upper-lipped, almost to the point of secrecy, about the death of my dad. She lost her partner whilst pregnant, through no fault of her own, and just got on with being a single parent. I secretly stroke my tummy. That won't, thank God, happen to me.

Like a plaything, Felicia's now messing with Toby's fringe. 'Maybe a little trim, darling? Pierre books me in every six weeks to take care of the dead ends.'

She finally turns to me with a winning smile. I expect her to comment on my 'incongruously' blue eyes as usual, but today it's my hair.

'Your curls. So gorgeous and soft; how does that work trim-wise?' she asks.

Irritation edging back, I take a breath to make some sort of tart reply. To say that her regular comments about my appearance or the 'honey' shade of my skin aren't appropriate, that she shouldn't be doing the 'touch test' on a grown man, that Fulham won't be chosen as a setting for a Martin Scorsese drama any time soon, that she can't swan in and try to control our lives when the fancy takes her.

I don't. Instead of a hot-headed retort, I surprise myself by picturing Mum. She brought me up to be unfailingly polite, at least on the surface: *Be smart, love. Play people like that at their own passive-aggressive game. No one likes a taste of their own medicine.* Which is precisely what she did at our wedding. Without holding back her northern vowels or loud laughter, she effortlessly wowed all the nice people and pleasantly needled the others. Her unwillingness to compromise just for one day irked me at the time, yet I couldn't help smiling when she sidled up to me at some point. 'Please say you'll keep your own name,' she whispered. 'There are so many hyphens here, it's making me dizzy.'

I shake myself back to the present. Holding his hand and whispering in his ear, Felicia is guiding her son towards the kitchen, leaving only a faint whiff of her expensive perfume. It's clearly the usual 'can you lend, or preferably give me some money' dance, so my shoulders relax. However, the quandary remains, now I think of it. I heroically resisted a knee-jerk reaction to Mum's comment and kept my maiden name of Whittle after I married. What about the baby? It's no wonder Dad's surname didn't factor for me, but times have moved on too. Why should it be a foregone conclusion that our child be a Bamford-Hogg? Or even worse, a Whittle-Bamford-Hogg.

I address my stomach and smile. 'What do you say, little apricot? You could just be a Whittle. What do you think?'

And yet I know I won't do that; maybe I'm railing against my own upbringing, but that traditional nuclear family is exactly what I want.

Flopping down on the sofa, I stretch out my legs. After waiting for so long, it's hard not to get excited about the pregnancy and tell everyone from the concierge at work to the woman who does my nails or the guy who always serves me in Pret, but it's still early days, so I need to calm down. For now, eating healthily and avoiding the blue cheeses, cured meats, soft eggs and smoked fish on the banned list – which I'm hankering for already – and, of course, zero alcohol is the thing. Feigning drinking and drunken levity with the usual boozy crowd is far harder than I'd imagined, which is why I'm perfectly happy for Toby to get bladdered on his own with our office colleagues tonight.

6

Frankie

A rasp, creak or movement snaps me from deep sleep. I lift my heavy head and listen for sound. Only silence echoes up from the flat below and beyond the window looking down to the alley, so I nestle against the pillow and try to climb back into the dream.

When sleep doesn't come, I drift behind my eye mask, trying to stop my mind landing on my growing baby. Inevitably it does, so I indulge myself by replaying Anya's enthusiasm about my news and her million questions around conception. How long did it take? What positions are best? On top or beneath? Or perhaps a few Kama Sutra moves for good measure? She'd read that if you eat bananas, steak and white bread, you'd be more likely to have a boy. Which did I want? Trying to make a baby must have added a huge frisson to our sex life. Lucky me that I had such a handsome hunk, though he must have been disappointed when blow jobs became low priority ...

I gamely replied to the titivating parts; there was no point demoralising her with the real story of our trying and failing to conceive for well over a year, the sheer longing for it to happen, the stunning disappointment every time a period appeared. And, of course, the need for poor Toby to perform the moment an ovulation tester strip told us I was fertile. In truth, I didn't want to share what had felt like his failure and, besides, everything has come good.

Knowing I'll be knackered in the morning if I don't get back off, I focus on slow breathing from my diaphragm. My ears prick again. There's activity from somewhere in the flat, hushed but definitely there. Toby's home already and creeping around, bless him, which is nothing short of a miracle. He usually blunders in, guffawing to himself as he bumps across the kitchen, opening cupboards and drawers, slotting bread in the toaster and slugging down water straight from the tap.

I shuffle my legs then stop, straining to listen over the sudden clatter of my heart. What the hell ... Goosebumps stab my arms. There it is again. A noise from the lounge, much closer this time. Toby? Is it Toby? No. No sink nor toilet vibrations, no rattling footsteps, no *ordinary* sounds.

Alarm jangling through me, I inch off my eye mask and hold my breath. Oh, my God, oh, my God. The quiet scrape of the handle, the near silent swish of the door ... Rustling, shuffling, motion. Christ, someone's actually in the room. It isn't Toby; the smell isn't right. Something malevolent is in here. Watching, hovering, wheezing.

I tense my whole being for two seconds, three, five seconds and ten. When quietness falls again, I cautiously lift my shoulders and peer into the gloom. What the fuck is wrong with me? No one is there. No looming figure or ghostly apparition. Along with my heightened tastebuds and nostrils, an overactive imagination is clearly another flaming symptom of pregnancy.

As relief eases through me, I nervously chuckle. I can't. My mouth is shockingly, abruptly stifled. So stunned, I simply freeze. What's happening? What the hell is happening? My lips are clamped by ... A hand. A gloved hand. From ... Oh, Christ, from under the bed. The weight of the whole body immediately follows, then the solid pin of their legs so I can't move an inch, let alone escape.

I squeeze my eyes shut and reason with myself. A burglar. This person is a burglar. He's here to rob stuff that really doesn't matter. I just have to stay calm and let him take what he wants. A beat of time passes then another and another. Yes, everything will be fine if I obey and don't panic.

My heart jolting from my chest, I cower afresh. My cheek. He's lightly pressing something against my skin. Something rigid and cold and, oh, Christ, metallic ...

Acid sears my veins. It's a knife. Why does a thief need a fucking knife?

Forcing my eyelids open, I attempt to absorb what I'm seeing. A balaclava, a black handle and, yes, the silver glint of a blade. As if he's been waiting for me to heed it, the intruder slowly slides it to my neck and presses the curved point against the hollow of my throat.

Dread quakes my very being. The man's glistening gaze; the discernible pleasure he's taking from my terror. He isn't a burglar. He isn't here to harm me, cut or kill me. He's here to—

Unable to even shape the terrifying word in my mind, I strive to communicate a silent plea to my captor. Yet when he tugs at the duvet, a petrified gasp splutters out. Both paralysed and shaking, I prepare myself and my baby for the worst.

Evidently relishing the moment, he pauses. Then he yanks my arm from the covers and taps my wrist.

It takes a huge effort to adjust. 'My watch?' I try to say.

He lowers his grip to allow me to speak. 'My watch?' I repeat, my voice strangled and faltering with fear and tentative hope. 'It's over there on charge. An Apple watch. Have it. Please. And anything else.'

He points to Toby's side of the bed.

'He'll be wearing it ...'

On reflection, I know he won't. Someone tried to nab his Rolex when we visited Barcelona last year and he's only worn it to dinners or family events since. It was a twenty-first gift from his father that he treasures. I don't fucking care. In fact, I feel bloody delirious I have something to offer. My body is violently trembling now; I need to get this man off me and out of my home.

'Second drawer at the back,' I croak. 'Everything's there, including a Rolex. Take what you want, then please go.'

7

Frankie

I eventually sit up and madly grope for my mobile. I don't know how long I've stayed frozen beneath the duvet, waiting for the intruder to rifle through our belongings. I strain my ears for a sound or a sign that he's definitely gone, but it's now almost two o'clock.

I input 999 with clumsy fingers, unstick my thick tongue and ask the operator for the police. I explain who I am and haltingly describe what has happened yet, even as I'm giving my address, feelings of sheer violation and intrusion shudder through my body in a crashing wave of nausea, so I hurl from the bed, reaching the bathroom just in time to vomit into the toilet bowl.

Dizzy and breathless, I continue to convulse for several minutes until only bile trickles out. When I finally pull myself upright, I peer at my surroundings through blurry, bloodshot eyes. Yellow stripy towels, matching bath mat. Shampoo, conditioner and body wash. Toby's skincare products neatly arranged on the shelf above the sink. Normality; regular life.

'It's fine,' I whisper. 'He's gone. It was only a burglary. Everything's OK.'

Yet I'm relieved I'm in a room with a lock; I'm honestly too scared to venture out.

Vacant minutes pass. I feel so queasy and insubstantial, it's a huge effort to focus but I know I have to try. The police said they were on their way. Someone needs to let them in.

Toby. Call Toby.

Panic hitting me again, I thrash around the floor. My phone. Where's my bloody phone? I find it half hidden beneath a vomit-scented flannel and fumble to call my husband. It rings out until voicemail kicks in. I try again. And again, and again.

'Where the hell are you, Toby?' I say to the four walls. 'Why aren't you picking up?'

Tears finally seep from my eyes. I've never felt so fearful, so frail, so small and alone. What now? What should I do now?

I nod in acknowledgement. Even through our disagreements, tetchy arguments and standoffs, my rock is always there. Constant, solid, safe.

Mum. I'll call my mum.

8

Nina

I know I'm strutting around my kitchen with my chin jutting out, but I'm angry; angry with Toby, angry with the police, angry with the world. And bloody furious with the burglar who thought it was OK to invade my daughter's home, her bedroom, her privacy, her safe space, for some gold trinkets, adornments which are actually pieces of metal, and wholly worthless in comparison with what my girl went through.

After she called 999, I was the second person she spoke to last night. Toby not hearing – or maybe ignoring – his phone on a riotous evening out might have been understandable had his wife not been pregnant. As things stood, he should have looked at his bloody mobile from time to time, even checked in to speak to her before bed. So Frankie called me, apologising between sobs for worrying me when there was nothing I could do to physically help.

Admittedly she was right, and I was hopping with impotent frustration, but at least I was able to stay on the line, talking about something and nothing until her husband and the police turned up around the same time in the early hours.

'I can hear voices. I think Toby's here,' she said to me. 'How do I know, Mum? How will I ever know again?'

I had to keep the need to weep in check. 'It's fine, love. Call his name. I'll wait here until you're sure it's him.'

Anxiety stuck in my chest, I held on at my end, hearing

snippets of conversation: 'Where have you been, Toby? Why didn't you answer your phone?'

I couldn't make out his shocked, slurry timbre or the muffled dialogue after, and I drifted off, then Frankie's shrill tones brought me back with a jerk: 'No, I'm not staying here, Toby. No way!'

The call was cut off after that. An hour or so later I had a text chat with Frankie:

The police have finished taking a statement. I'm coming home in the car.

Are you sure about driving yourself? You've had a dreadful shock. How about getting a taxi? I'll pay.

With some stranger? No way.

I'll come and get you.

Thanks but I need to leave now. I'm not staying here a moment longer.

Please take care. Stop at a services if you're not up to it. I can always drive and meet you there.

I didn't like to ask if Toby was in tow, but when Frankie's VW rolled up at eight o'clock this morning, he was in the passenger seat, looking somewhat green. I sent him up to the spare room to sleep and he's been there ever since – hiding, probably. Frankie went for a nap in my bed for a couple of hours, then she came downstairs and settled on the sofa five minutes ago.

'A nice cuppa?' I asked her, which is why I'm here in the kitchen letting off steam along with the kettle.

When I've settled my features into something resembling calm, I take our drinks through to the lounge, put the tray on the coffee table and sit next to her.

'Oh, love,' I hold out my arms. 'How are you feeling?'

'I don't know. Empty, tired, weary.'

'I'm not surprised after the night you've had.'

She grimaces. 'And guilty.'

'How so?'

'The ... the bastard took Toby's Rolex and some other bits.'

I try to maintain an equanimous expression. Toby's flaming watch was the one thing she kept mentioning about her ordeal on the phone. 'I know, you said, but they are *replaceable* bits ...'

'Apparently not. The cufflinks and timepiece were family heirlooms.'

I breathe through my annoyance. It seems the bloody hoity-toity's precious *things* are more important than people. 'Well, I can see that's disappointing for him. It isn't the end of the world, though. Your safety is what's paramount.'

I rub her back. Last night she was unable to give a coherent account of what had happened, but I can tell from her shrunken stance that it was horribly frightening.

She fingers the gold chain around her neck. 'I didn't think about this until afterwards. I guess the pendant must have slipped to one side and was hidden from view. In fairness to Toby, I'd have been really upset to lose it, hence the guilt.'

Guilt. I rise above the association between that very word and her necklace and focus on her sunny smile when I gave it to her on her thirteenth birthday instead. A delicate sapphire wasn't the type of thing I expected a feisty teenager to like, but she put it on that day and has pretty much worn it ever since.

'How about some breakfast? I have ...' I almost offer a boiled or poached egg, then quickly remember runny yolk is on her no-no pregnancy food list. 'I can go out and buy croissants or other pastries if you fancy, otherwise there's muesli and toast.'

She grabs my hand. 'No. Don't go anywhere. Not yet.' Taking a deep, shuddery breath, she gazes at me through hollow eyes. 'He had a knife, Mum.' Her voice cracks with emotion. 'The point was curved and he put it here ...' She pats the base of her throat. 'And his gaze was ... God, I don't know, but I honestly thought he'd come to rape me.'

9

Frankie

I jerk awake and try to drag in some air. I can't. My nose and mouth are blocked by a ... oh God, a hand, a gloved hand, pressing down on my lips and pinching my nostrils. Pinpricks stab my skin. My heart batters my chest. My lungs ache with the need to exhale.

'Look at me.'

'No!'

'Look at this. Now.'

I do as I'm told, and the knife is above me, glinting, glistening, the curved tip slowly descending to my neck. And those eyes behind the balaclava, creased by a smirk.

'So soft. How easy it would be to cut you.'

'No. Don't. Please don't. I beg you. Take what you like. Anything. Please.'

'You think I'm here to rob you?'

'Yes, that's why you're here.' Terror bubbles inside me. 'That's why you're here!'

'Wrong.' The mass of his body bores down. 'I'm here to—'

'No!'

I jolt upright and pant out my hot, heavy breath for several long moments. Finally daring to look around, I take in the matching pine wardrobe and drawers, the heart-shaped pink rug, the basket full of teddies and the higgledy-piggledy bookcase.

Relief oozes from every pore of my body. I suck in some oxygen, focus on my respiration and talk to myself like an infant:

Everything's fine, Frankie. You're in your old bedroom at home. You're safe. You're OK. Just breathe. In and out, slowly, in and out.

Tears sting my eyes. I'm not fine; I'm not OK. Despite thoroughly searching beneath the bed before retiring, I've had these terrors every evening since Toby returned to London. I groped my way to Mum's room and spent the rest of the night with her on Sunday, but I'm not a child any more. I hate showing my weakness; I have to grow up and get a grip on this horror.

As I shuffle back beneath the duvet, the knife flashes into my psyche again. The nightmare changes a little each time, yet that blade remains the main focus, the detail of which seems to get increasingly clearer. And just now there was also a voice, wasn't there?

As if it might give me a clue about the real intruder, I strain to remember what it sounded like. Nope, it's gone, and anyway the actual burglar didn't speak. Why didn't he? It hasn't occurred to me before, but it does seem odd.

I rock my head to the empty pillow next to me. Will sleep improve when I have Toby's solid presence by my side again? I honestly don't know. At the weekend he offered to remain in Manchester for a few days, but I chivvied him back to London. Apart from his various meetings in the City, I know he needs to be seen in the office, attend all the socials and drinks and so on, whereas I can do my job from anywhere, at least until the next placement.

I nod. Working from here is what I'll continue to do until ... Until what? God, I don't know what the future holds. I am sure of one thing, though. I do *not* want to return to the flat. Ever.

I'm absolutely certain about that.

10

Frankie

'Earth to Frankie?'

I look up from my laptop. Mum's dressed in a scarf and coat, clearly ready to leave for her working day.

'Oh, is it that time already?' I rub my eyes. I didn't manage to get back to sleep, so I eventually got up, had a shower and a cuppa, then began ploughing my way through a backlog of emails.

'Everything OK?' she asks. 'You were up early.'

'Yeah.'

'I bet next door could hear the bashing and banging. "Frankie's back then", they'll be saying this morning.'

I know it's not her fault and that she's only trying to lighten the atmosphere, but I can't help snapping. 'Well, I guess that's what happens when you jolt awake at four after a terrifying nightmare.'

'Oh, love, not again. You should have come in and—'

'I'm thirty-one, Mum, not a kid. And I'm actually OK. It's over, so things can't get any worse.'

'Well, like it or not, you'll always be my baby and I worry about you.' She cocks her head, her chestnut eyes shining with concern. 'It's early days; your subconscious will be processing the trauma. Would you like me to stay at home this morning? I could call in and swap—'

'No, I'm fine.' Being an only child can be bloody suffocating at times. For the millionth time, I wish I had a sibling. 'Thanks for the offer, though.' I force a smile. 'Have you remembered your butty for your lunch?'

'It's a Friday half day, so you can make it for when I get back.' She playfully winks. 'I'll deduct it from your rent.'

Dull angst hits my chest. 'I'm only staying for now. You know, whilst I work out what to do.'

'Oh, love, I'm only joking about the rent.' Her face has fallen. 'I'd keep you at home forever if I could have my way.'

Which is precisely the problem between Mum and me. Part of me wants to stay cocooned in her fierce, protective love forever, part of me needs to get away. When I finally left for London, I was able to spread my wings, make my own decisions and be me rather than a moulded mini-Nina. The freedom was sublime, yet I missed her terribly too.

I push away this peculiar blend of emotions she always invokes and take a steadying breath. 'I'm sorry for being so precious. It's just that ...' That I do not – that I *will not* – return to the flat. Ever. It feels like a mantra to help me cope. 'I'm basically hungry.'

On reflection, it's actually true. I've normally grazed on a banana or ginger biscuit to ease the morning biliousness by now.

I smile a wonky smile. 'Or maybe I should say hangry; I haven't had any breakfast.'

'Those avocados looked ripe, and I bought in a selection of pastries on the way home yesterday.'

'Yeah, I saw those. Bad mother! I'll end up getting fat.'

'I doubt that. Still, if there's any time in life to have that excuse ...' She chuckles. 'You know, growing your own "bun in the oven" as Gran would say.'

I don't reply. A sense of dread is slowly spreading like poison through my chest.

'What is it, love? What's wrong?'

I try not to panic. It's fine; I've simply been preoccupied with the burglary and my troubled sleep. And yet, now I think about it, I haven't been sick or even felt nauseous for days. The aroma of coffee or cheese hasn't turned my stomach. That overwhelming tiredness hasn't hit late afternoon. I pat my boobs. They were sensitive to the point of soreness two weeks ago. They feel normal now.

My pulse thuds in my ears. Oh, my God. Oh, my God; what the hell does this mean?

11

Frankie

Absently staring at the artwork on the whitewashed walls, I try to steady my palpitating heart. There's an endless supply of free drinks, biscuits and fruit at this glossy BUPA hospital, but I couldn't eat or swallow anything if I tried. Me and Mum have been waiting here for forty long minutes to see the sonographer, yet I still feel winded and shaky and rushed.

This cannot be happening to me. It took over a year to make my baby. I can't possibly be losing it or have already lost it. Can I? Terrifyingly, on some level, I know that I have. I took my eye off the ball; for the last seven days I've put myself and my own needs before his or hers.

Mum has been great, arguing her hind legs off with the truculent manager at our local GP surgery – who still turned me away for no longer being registered – but I can't look at her. Like a mirror, my stark fear is reflected on her face. She must know it too, as she addresses her occasional comments to her folded hands.

'Thank goodness you remembered about your insurance,' she's now saying. 'Otherwise, we'd still be in that ridiculous queue at A&E just to speak to a receptionist.'

I have no power of speech, so I nod. After the palaver of finding a parking space at Wythenshawe hospital and standing for a good half hour, my logical mind finally snapped in.

'God, why didn't I think of it before now,' I muttered.

'Think of what?' Mum asked.

'I have private health cover. I wonder if it includes having a ...'

I couldn't say the word. I still can't shape it on my lips.

'We don't know that's happened for sure, love,' Mum replied. 'You haven't had any bleeding, so ...'

I didn't reply. *But we do*, seemed to echo up from deep inside me.

'Are you sure you don't want to call Toby?' she now asks.

'No, not yet. Not until I'm certain.'

So I guess I do have hope after all. I can't analyse why I still have that glimmer right now; all I can do is stare at the clinician's door, torn between the urgent need for the truth and bolting. It opens. Fuck, it's opening. A rosy-cheeked woman in her forties appears with a clipboard.

'Francesca Whittle?'

My legs insubstantial, I get to my feet. 'That's me.'

I turn to Mum and her demeanour is so bleak that, for a moment of sheer panic, I'm convinced she'll make me do this alone. But she stands and grasps my hand. 'You're strong; you can do this,' she says.

Her tone high and lilting, the sonographer checks my details and the date of my last period on her chart, then she asks me to lower my joggers and lie down on the examination couch. 'So I'm going to have a look to see how the baby is doing. OK?'

I nod.

'I'll apply a blob of jelly to your tummy, then I'll gently press the probe around your abdomen and see what's going on. Are you ready? I'm sorry if the jelly is a wee bit cold.'

If it's cold, I don't feel it. How can I when I'm frozen, my body trembling with a will of its own. She doesn't turn the monitor to an angle I can see, so I look at her, searching her face for any glimpse of good news. She spends several seconds peering intently at the screen and, though her blank expression doesn't falter, I know from her tiny frown and her silence that it's bad.

'What's wrong?' I say, my voice cracked with emotion. 'Tell me.'

She sits back and drags her gaze to me. For seconds I convince myself that the strange pull around her mouth is a smile, but as she opens it to speak, I realise she has a repaired upper lip.

'The baby is smaller than I'd expect at twelve weeks' gestation and ...' As though summoning the resolve to spit the words out, she pauses and fingers a shiny capital 'C' pendant at the base of her throat. 'I'm afraid I can't find a heartbeat.'

The blow is stunning, sickening. No heartbeat; no heartbeat. I understand what that means. I still grope for something to hold on to. 'Why does smaller matter? It might be a small baby.'

Her eyes sliding away, she wipes my stomach with tissue. 'I'll write up my findings and the obstetrician will explain everything in detail—'

'Explain what?' I tug up my bottoms and, though Mum puts a hand on my shoulder, I find myself shouting. 'Just tell me, for God's sake. Has my baby died?'

She blinks and nods. 'I'm afraid so. Your consultant may recommend another scan in a few days, but the results suggest the baby has died in the womb. I'm so sorry.'

Died. That one immutable, irrefutable word. The remaining embers of hope drain from me. 'So what now?' I ask, climbing from the couch with leaden limbs.

'I'll give you a moment with your mum then, if you return to the waiting area, Doctor Gauss will be with you very soon.' Her aqua eyes loaded with sympathy, she rubs the top of my arm. 'I'm so sorry for your loss, Francesca. Sometimes things aren't meant to be. Their destiny comes from a higher power, if you like. I wish you all the very best.'

12

Nina

I'm still reeling from the devastating news – as well as the technician's astonishing religious claptrap, which is surely not allowed – when a clipped voice fires in from above us. 'Ms Francesca Whittle?'

We both look up at a tall woman around my age. She holds out a briskly efficient hand to Frankie. 'I'm Doctor P Gauss, your appointed consultant.' She gestures to a corridor. 'I'm around the corner, so if you'd like to follow me.'

Frankie stands and wobbles. I've never seen her so drained, so absent, so lost. 'Is it OK if my mum accompanies me?'

Like I might not pass muster, the doctor appraises me through pale eyes. 'Of course,' she says after a beat. 'Of course. Do come through.'

When we reach her room, she invites us to sit, immediately takes a deep breath and addresses Frankie. I'm guessing she's the type of emotionless medic who keeps to the point and I'm right. Yet that's a good thing; though Frankie's clearly numb and in shock, it's precisely what I need to stop me from howling with grief on her behalf.

'I've studied the results of the scan and you've had what we term a "missed miscarriage",' the obstetrician launches in. 'The next steps are to wait for a natural expulsion, or undergo a dilation and curettage procedure – known as D&C – during which the tissue from the uterus is cleared. Because your body hasn't initiated the miscarriage at this stage, there are more risks, such as increased blood loss, if you choose the former. The latter is a straightforward operation performed under a light anaesthetic and some women choose to defer it for a few days. However, I'm available to do it myself personally later this—'

'Today?' Frankie animates and finally speaks. 'The D&C, please. I want to get rid of it now.'

I take a sharp breath. I know it's not my choice, and that I'll be accused of interference as usual, but this all seems ridiculously hurried, even knee-jerk. And how has Frankie's pregnancy gone from 'baby' to 'it' in a matter of minutes?

'Surely a second opinion or another scan to—' I begin.

Doctor Gauss cuts me off as if I'm not here. 'As you wish.' She gestures to the telephone. 'I can action it straight away. Any more questions?'

'Frankie?' I try to read her glazed expression. I understand I've never been through this particular trauma, but I feel the need to press pause. 'Shouldn't you speak to Toby first?'

'What for? To ask his bloody permission?' she snaps. 'You heard what they've both said. The ... the baby has died. What difference does it make?' She lowers her head and puffs in and out for several moments. She finally looks at me through hollow eyes. 'Toby will be up tomorrow anyway; it's better to tell him in person rather than worry him.' She reaches out a trembling hand. 'I've had enough, Mum. I need to put this behind me. This is my way of coping. OK?'

This pushing down of her grief scares me far more than crying or hysteria would. I swallow back my own tears. 'OK, love. If that's what you want.'

'It is, Mum. Honestly.' Reverting to the doctor, she takes a deep shuddery breath. 'I have one query. Why did the pregnancy fail?'

Doctor Gauss taps her lips with pressed palms. 'Early miscarriage is a lot more common than people realise. Before twelve weeks, it's likely to be chromosomal abnormalities which are random in nature and can occur without notice.' She finally gives a sympathetic smile. 'It is important to note that, outside of extreme behaviours such as excessive drug or alcohol use, the loss of a pregnancy is nothing the mother could have caused. It's sadly one of those things. No one is to blame.'

'OK, thanks,' Frankie replies.

Yet I can tell from her clenched jaw exactly what she's thinking: *someone is to blame. It can't possibly be coincidental. It's the burglar's fault. The man with that black-handled knife.*

13

Frankie

Contemplating how the other half live, I glance around the handsome wood-panelled walls of *Drs Baden and Gauss* consulting rooms on St John Street in central Manchester and wait for the receptionist to finish her phone call. Ten days have now passed since the D&C procedure, so I'm here for my post-operative consultation with Doctor Gauss.

Reminded by Mum's sucked in cheeks when we first arrived in the BUPA hospital's reception, I was already aware how lucky I was to have health insurance and the benefit of private treatment, but I've since joined an online community where people share their missed miscarriage stories, mostly under the care of the NHS. Losing a baby is a dreadful, dark time in any woman's life, yet I was shocked to discover that several were put on units with mothers who were nursing their newborns, that some had to wait for hours in gaping patient gowns down foul-smelling corridors, and that others were on a conveyor belt of one-in one-out terminations without an iota of TLC. On the contrary, I was led to a spotless single ward with an en suite – fluffy robe, TV remote control and glossy magazine included – whilst I waited to be taken to theatre like royalty.

I feel quite guilty about it, yet my more 'comfortable' experience has its downsides, too. It felt – and still feels – a surreal, bizarrely hotel-like way to lose a child. Though Mum later greeted me with a face puffy from tears, guided me to the car, clipped on my seatbelt and took extra care with the road bumps like I was an invalid, that dreamlike state continued. Even the blood-smeared sanitary towel didn't bring reality home. That finally came the following morning when I drove to Stockport station and broke the news to Toby.

'What is it?' he asked, the moment his eyes locked onto mine. Then before I could speak, 'Christ, you're not leaving me, are you?'

'No! Why on earth would you say that?'

'Then what is it, Frankie? What's happened?'

And it was a bitter-sweet moment because I'd forgotten why I'd married him for a while. It was a stark reminder of his love for me. And, of course, mine for him.

'I've ... we've lost the baby.'

'What? What do you mean?'

'I've had a miscarriage. I'm so sorry, Toby.'

'Oh, my God! So you ...' His face was white with worry. 'When? When did this happen?'

'It was yesterday. In hospital.'

'In a hospital? Like, you gave birth? All alone?' Tears sprang to his eyes. 'Why didn't you call me? I'd have—'

I cut him off with an emotional kiss. 'Mum was with me. Let's get in the car and I'll explain.'

Same as I had, he wanted to know why, so I gave him the generic 'who knows' explanation I was given by Doctor Gauss.

'Is that it?' he asked, clearly shocked and bewildered. 'We lose our baby and everyone just shrugs?'

'Investigations with a first miscarriage aren't the norm, especially under NHS care, but ...' I smiled thinly. 'We're lucky, believe it or not. Seems our health insurance covers a follow-up scan and a chat with the consultant.'

Which is why I'm here this morning. Toby offered to take time off work and come with me, but I declined his sweet gesture. I know I'm internalising my devastation, yet I also have a sense that he's taking this loss as another failure on his part, so it's easier all around to gloss over the depth of my heartache. And my frothing anger. The burglary nightmare has receded, and yet, ironically, I wake in the early hours and pick over the events of that night anyway. There's no rhyme nor reason for it – other than their slim build and the fact they didn't speak – but I have a nagging sensation the intruder was female.

'Good morning. How can I help?' The chirpy voice of the woman at the desk breaks my thoughts.

'Hi. Francesca Whittle for Doctor Gauss, please.'

With a shudder, I notice she's wearing the same gold pendant as the sonographer last week. Indeed, she looks so like the technician, they could be twins. Though when I peer at her more closely, it's probably their noticeable cleft palate scars.

Clearly reading my thoughts, she gestures to a Perspex stand. 'The Hundred Club. Help yourself.'

'Oh, right.' Embarrassed to have been caught ogling, I study that same pronounced serif script capital C. This time it's a logo at the top of a glossy pamphlet. I pull one out. 'So ...'

'The Latin symbol for a hundred? Hence the name of the charity.' She looks at it warmly. 'It's an amazing cause for disabled children if you're interested in supporting us.'

In all honestly, the groomed and grinning white kids on the front – let alone the tall, charismatic-type of older guy standing behind them – look more like an advert for toothpaste.

'Congenital disorders, such as cystic fibrosis and heart conditions,' the receptionist adds.

Duly chastened, I nod. 'Of course. It sounds a wonderful—'

I'm saved by the sound of the door, so I quickly retreat, take a seat and watch a fair-haired woman approach the desk.

'Doctor Baden at noon. I'm Minta Atkinson. You might have me down as Araminta?' she says, slightly struggling with the 'r' in her name.

The receptionist consults her computer. 'Found you, Araminta. Perfect. I'm afraid he's running a little late, so do help yourself to water.'

I can't help staring at the doll-like neat features of my fellow 'client'. Presumably she's here for similar reasons to me, but she looks too petite to carry a baby. She selects a bottle of San Pellegrino, sits two seats away, then makes me jump from my skin when she addresses me.

'Hiya. I think I saw you at the ultrasound department at the Spire. You were with your mum.'

A hot flush spreads across my cheeks. I was blind to my surroundings that day, and that debilitating twenty-four hours isn't something I want to discuss with anyone, let alone a stranger, albeit one with a friendly, guileless face. 'Oh, did you?'

She bites her lip. 'Oh gosh, I see.' She looks at her tiny hands, then takes a quick breath. 'I'm so sorry. And for being, well, so stupidly tactless. I do understand, though.' Her pretty eyes glisten. 'I thought maybe third time lucky.'

I'm so used to my reticent mother, it takes a moment to adjust to someone so open. 'You mean ...?'

'Yes, three miscarriages.'

'That's awful.' The notion of going through this more than once thumps me in the chest. 'Have they got to the bottom of why? I mean, three times is a lot.'

'It is.'

'God, that was really rude of me. Sorry. And for your dreadful losses too.'

'It's fine. After the first I also wanted an explanation, something to work with, you know? So it's a relief to get an answer, especially when the finger seems to be pointed at the female every time.'

I'm a little shocked at her willingness to share something so personal. I'm still all ears. 'So, it's the ...'

'The male.' She nods. 'Poor quality sperm. Something to do with DNA damage.'

'Really?'

'Yes, it can cause both infertility and miscarriage, and it's actually more common than people realise.'

'Wow. I didn't realise that was a thing.'

'I know, right?' She smiles a sunny smile. 'But with Doctor Baden's help, we'll definitely get there by hook or by crook and

43

have the fairytale ending he's promised.'

Both humbled and lightened by her plucky positivity, I wipe away an escaped tear. 'I love your upbeat thinking.'

'I'm a great believer in manifesting. You're in great hands, so you'll be lucky too.' She tilts her head and seems to peer into my very soul. 'I'm certain of it.'

14

Nina

I sit at a corner table in The Metropolitan and watch Col approach with a tray and a grin.

'So what do you think?' he asks.

His question could be any number of things, ranging from himself to the meal we've just eaten, to the fact I'm out with him in public. The first reply would be 'bloody damned attractive', the second, 'not a patch on your cooking', and the third ... Well, I'm not sure about the answer as I haven't been to a pub with a man for years and I'm still adjusting. It's certainly a whole different vibe from staying in, but I wanted to give Frankie and Toby some space at home.

'The jury's out,' I say. 'It's good to know you scrub up so nicely, though.'

'Pleased to hear it. I already knew you did, but seeing you in your glad rags is most ... alluring.'

I chuckle. 'Glad rags and alluring, eh? Which century are you from?'

'I thought we weren't going to talk about age.' He pecks my lips. 'Mind you, your stats would be a whole lot better at the parkrun if you'd given your real one when you signed up.'

We ran at Fletcher Moss this morning and it was sweet of him to go at my pace. It was even sweeter when I pulled off my top layer and he held out his hand to take it from me, turned it the right way, then tied it around his own waist. The notion makes me squirm with something that feels a little like ... blimey, surely not love?

'Well, they say you're as old as you feel,' I reply, shocked at my own train of thought. After Greg, I made a vow never to give my heart to anyone and, so far, I've stuck to it.

'Very true.' Col grins. 'So let's talk about when I can remove said glad rags ...'

Col and his wife are separated, but still live together with their twelve-year-old daughter, so popping to his place is a non-starter, and I'm certainly not going down the route of a quickie in the back seat of a car like I did for all those years with Greg.

'I'm afraid that will have to wait for now.'

'The anticipation will make it all the more exciting.' He slugs back his beer. 'How's everything going with Frankie? Is she OK?'

I sip my wine and think about that. My poor girl has had an appalling double whammy and I know she's convinced the burglary and the miscarriage are linked, but I'm not sure that's a healthy way to look at it. Though she's not saying it in those particular terms, I get the impression she thinks it's something to do with Toby's family, not least because the intruder didn't steal her necklace and seemed to know about the valuable heirlooms. I'm not at all keen on that entitled bloody lot, yet it's a notion which seems wholly bizarre to me, and my worry is that she's deeply mulling and fixating, as only my daughter can.

'She's putting on a brave face for Toby,' I reply. 'She's also adamant that she won't return to the flat.'

'So, what's the plan?'

'She's started looking at somewhere to buy.'

'In London?'

'No, around here.'

Col strokes his perfect square chin. 'And how will that go down with Toby?'

'No idea. They're probably discussing it this very moment.' I raise my eyebrows. 'But when Frankie gets a bee in her bonnet ... Well, let's watch this space.'

15

Frankie

I eye up my husband across Mum's kitchen table. He's picking at his food, even though tonight's Indian takeout was his choice.

My stomach turns as I absorb his faraway expression. I know he's mega stressed at work, but I can't help feeling he's been distant since the break in ... I shake the notion away. Though a little jarring when I'm a perfectly capable woman, his treating me like a china doll has been sweet. Which must mean I'm only projecting. Something feels off about the burglary the more I think about it. Why didn't the robber speak, and pretty much only took Toby's valuables? And, when I mentally zoom in on the knife, I can see an archaic engraving on the blade which doesn't fit with an opportunist thief. The terrifying episode happened only hours after Toby turned down Felicia's request for a sizeable sum of money. It's probably some form of psychological response or just my wild imagination, yet I'm now convinced a faint aroma of perfume had pervaded the air.

I drop my gaze and top up our wine glasses. I'm aware these things are the thoughts of a crazy person, and I wouldn't dream of burdening Toby, but it does make the desire to increase the distance between myself and the Bamford-Hogg clan all the more imperative. The challenge is to get Toby on side. On our walkabout today, I subtly pointed out the highlights of Burton Road, the attractive Victorian houses in West Didsbury and the beautiful countryside surrounding the River Mersey. In the same breath, I lightly suggested a move up north would be affordable, interesting and fun. Annoyingly it appears to have fallen on deaf ears.

As if Toby's read my very thoughts, he reaches for my hand. 'The flat isn't the same without you. Maybe it's time?'

'Time for what?'

'To come home, of course. How about we drive back tomorrow? I really miss you.'

'*Home?*' My plans for low-key persuasion all gone, I pull my arm back. 'Someone broke in. I was traumatised at knifepoint, Toby. It's the last place I'd call home.'

'I know, and that must have been horrendous, but ...'

'But what, exactly?'

His cheeks pink. 'Well, at some point I guess you need to face it and move on.'

I can't believe he's being so insensitive. 'If it was that simple, rest assured, I would.' I'm torn between yelling and crying. 'We lost our baby, Toby. Or have you forgotten?'

'Of course I haven't. I'm devastated too, and that's all the more reason to settle down, get back on track and try again.' He lowers his head to meet my eyes. 'Look, I completely understand your reluctance, but we're meant to be a couple, Frankie. Once the lease comes to an end, we can find another place.'

'So you honestly expect me to live there for another four months?'

'It's a contract. We can't get out of it. Moving somewhere else would mean we're paying rent twice.'

Sheer pique taking over, I fold my arms. 'Fine. You stay there and I'll continue living here.'

'You and Nina will drive each other nuts.' He takes a big breath. 'But that apart ... We agreed to stay in London and move south of the river. We've saved up with that plan in mind.'

'I've saved up. And we didn't plan, Toby. Your mother—'

'So that makes it OK to drag me up north? On what level is that fair? My family are in London, my friends are there, our jobs are.'

So he was listening on our afternoon walk. I try for a more cajoling tone. 'Not necessarily. We could both transfer to the Manchester office.'

'Manchester?'

'Yes. It's definitely doable.'

'Doable? What does that mean?'

'That we can, basically. In fact, I've made enquiries.'

'What?' Apparently, the deepest possible betrayal. He sits back, his expression aghast. 'I can't believe you did that.'

'It's no big deal, Toby. It was a generic question to HR. I didn't put you forward or even mention your name.'

His flush spreads to his neck. 'You did this when you know I'm trying for director?'

'It was just a casual query.'

'By someone who happens to be married to me. HR are the biggest gossips. It'll be all around the office.'

'Now you're being ridiculous.'

'Am I? Well, thanks for that.' He drags back his chair and strides away, then pauses at the door and turns. 'You know how important this promotion is to me, Frankie. It's why I'm working all hours, including a meeting tomorrow afternoon.' His sudden tears are replaced by a stubborn scowl. 'So if a lift to the station isn't a totally *ridiculous* thing to ask of you, I'm catching the ten past ten in the morning.'

16

Frankie

Attempting to shake off my annoyance, I clear up the dishes, then pad to the lounge, stare out of the window and consider whether Toby has a point. Am I being unfair or unreasonable? Should I be facing the burglary and moving on?

As though hit by a hammer, I abruptly bend double. Out of nowhere, my heart is battering the walls of my chest so violently that I struggle to breathe. I fall to my knees and try to suck in some air. This smothering sensation feels terrifyingly familiar ... I squeeze my eyes shut to fend them off, but the memories flash in like stills from a film. A disembodied gloved hand, the glint of metal, the gleam of eyes; the pinched face of the sonographer, her hissing the words 'loss' and 'higher power'.

Puffing in and out, I reason to myself: this isn't real; it's a form of post-traumatic stress; it'll pass. Yet the fact that it's back is overwhelming, alarming. If even the suggestion of returning to the flat causes *this*, how will I cope with the real thing? I'm not going back; I'm not ready to. If Toby can't see that, it's his loss, not mine.

Once my palpitations have settled, I glance around for something to distract me. What better than one of Mum's well-thumbed collection of classics she insisted I read despite my belligerent objections. Of course, she was annoyingly right when she said that I'd love them and feel a huge sense of achievement once I'd finished; none more so than Middlemarch. I pull it out now, curl up on the sofa and open it up. An envelope falls out – presumably to mark a chapter – but when I casually look at the front, it's addressed to 'Nina Whittle-Ward'. Mum was engaged to my dad, so it's not so very odd, yet I'm intrigued who'd be writing to her.

Feeling a touch guilty, I slide out the single sheet of paper and briefly read it.

'That's mine.'

I jolt around to Mum at the door. Her cheeks are flushed. From annoyance or a few drinks, I can't tell. 'Oh, hi. I didn't hear you come in.'

'Clearly.'

Her sharp tone shows it's the former. She holds out her palm. 'I can't recall opening your mail.'

I shrug to cover my embarrassment. 'If I had something to hide, I wouldn't leave it in plain sight.'

'A book which belongs to me isn't ...' She shakes her head. 'How was your night? Has Toby gone up already?'

'Yeah.' With a frown I return to my discovery. 'Why is it a secret anyway?'

'It isn't. Not at all.'

'OK. Then why didn't you tell me about it? It's as much my business as yours.'

Evidently stumped for a reply, she stares, her gaze swamped with what I can only describe as panic. 'I've had a glass or two too many, so let's talk in the morning.'

I read the short letter again. 'This guy, Billy Malloy, says he's Dad's birth brother.'

'Yes, I know.'

'Which makes him my uncle. You've always said I have no family other than you, Gran and Baba. This says that I have.'

'It also says that Greg was adopted, Frankie. That's news to me, so ...'

'Fair enough. But why stash it away rather than telling me about it?'

She sighs. 'Back burner, that's all. I fully intended to mention it at some point. After the last couple of weeks, I didn't want to make things any worse.'

I come back to reality with a thud. The anxiety attack just now, Toby's intransigence, let alone the rest. 'How could my life get any worse?'

'It couldn't, but ...' Mum perches next to me. 'An alleged sibling who happens to live abroad. Who says it's genuine? Fraudsters and scammers are everywhere, aren't they? If you'd received this by email, you'd have immediately deleted it.'

'Hmm, maybe.'

'So I wasn't concealing it so much as giving it time to brew. Talking of which, shall I make us one to take up?'

'It's fine, I'll do it.'

I shuffle towards the kitchen.

'Frankie?'

I turn. 'Yes?'

'All good?'

'Sure,' I reply.

I'm not. The flash of alarm in her eyes ... What the hell was *that* all about?

17

Frankie

Rather than mull on Mum's peculiar response to Uncle Billy's letter – or on how pissed off I was with Toby – I grabbed my laptop, got comfy beneath the sofa throw and began a trawl of properties newly listed in the South Manchester area. I stopped at a familiar-looking old church. It took a moment to place it. I soon twigged I'd seen it on Mum's doormat, accompanied by another flyer for cosmetic surgery. I remembered thinking, with a droll smile, that the ancient building had clearly had a facelift, and a spectacular one at that.

Drawn by the coincidence, I spent a good fifteen minutes reading about the development and, by the time I slipped into bed next to Toby, I was giddy with excitement. The three-bedroom town house for sale ticked every box: the old-but-refurbished aesthetic, fronted by the gorgeous grade II listed chapel and other buildings, the stunning landscaped gardens, the contemporary high-end fixtures and fittings, the secure off-road parking and the price. And the icing on the cake was the original high railings and sturdy iron gates, now electronic and accessed solely by the residents. In short, a fort; strong, safe and impenetrable to bloody burglars.

I planned to share my enthusiasm with Toby at breakfast but, when I arrived in the kitchen, he was dressed, po-faced and looking meaningfully at the clock. So I asked my mum to come with me to the estate agent's instead, which is why she's now peering in the window.

'So which one am I looking at?' She snorts with amusement. 'They're all fairly close to mine. Have you had a blow to your head?'

'Haha. Near but not too near.' I look as well. 'I can't see it. Maybe it's on display inside. Or perhaps they haven't printed off a brochure yet. Come on, Mother, let's go in and make an appointment to view it.'

She pauses and slowly inhales. 'You know I'm your number one fan, however ... Are you sure you don't want to wait until next weekend when Toby's around?'

I think about that for all of two seconds. I woke up feeling positive for the first time in weeks; I want to look forwards, not back.

'We're here now. And if it doesn't satisfy my expectations, I'm not wasting his time. Besides, it might go if we don't get in quickly.' I chuckle. 'It was on a flyer in your junk mail the other day, and it veritably winked at me. So it's clearly serendipity, a spiritual sign from Mount Olympus that I must follow.'

'Well, in that case ... One can't possibly disobey the gods. You lead the way.'

There's a queue for both suited guys at their desks, so my mind drifts as we wait to be served. Is it OK to do this without Toby? The thought of yesterday's panic attack brings on a breathy shudder. So yes, actually. When it comes to this particular decision about our future, I'm entitled to have the final vote. And he'll come round to my way of thinking if I play my cards right. Won't he?

'Frankie?' Mum's voice brings me back. 'It's your turn.'

I get the younger agent who looks tired and demoralised. 'Hi, how can I help?'

'Pavilion Gardens. One of the townhouses is for sale?' I make a wish for things to finally go my way. 'It was listed on Rightmove, so hopefully it's still—'

'Pavilion Gardens? It is indeed. Number three.' He sits a little straighter. 'It's only the second one to go on the market since the original owners moved in, so it's likely to go fast.' He types on his keyboard and turns the screen, and I'm hit afresh by that glorious image of the chapel. 'The Grade II listed buildings have been converted into residential properties, and they're set within the original walls, railings and gates. So if you like a historic setting ...'

Worried that somehow this opportunity will slip through my fingers, I cut to the chase. 'It's fine; I've read about it online. Basically I'm a first-time buyer with a pretty decent deposit and I'd like to have a viewing. Today would be good.'

It's clearly the right thing to say as his eyes light up. 'Excellent. Let me make some enquiries. So you are ...?'

Once he has my details, he grabs a handset, swivels around on his chair and speaks to someone in a low voice for a minute or two.

He comes back with a grin. 'How about two o'clock this afternoon?'

'Sounds serendipitous,' Mum whispers from the corner of her mouth.

'I think we can squeeze it in,' I say, as though we're seeing loads. 'Will you take us round or ...'

'The vendor is happy to do it herself.' He looks at his notes. 'A Mrs Logan.'

'Great.'

'And I expect the Peppercorns will be there.'

'The Peppercorns?'

'Yup. I'm fairly new here, so I don't know the ins and outs, but they're like guardians, if you like, and they're paid a ground rent.' He quickly lifts his hands. 'Don't worry, it's nominal. By all accounts, they're lovely people.' He leans forward confidentially. 'Between you and me, they recently suffered a family tragedy, and I think they like to keep busy.'

18

Nina

Rather than traipse back home, me and Frankie nip into Dish and Spoon for refreshments.

'Well, he screamed estate agent,' I comment.

'The gelled quiff and fake tan? Not to mention the obvious hangover.'

'And the clothing. I didn't know trousers came that tight.'

'You shouldn't be looking, Mother. He pulled his finger out, though.'

'Didn't he just. I think the words "decent deposit" might have been a factor.'

'Yeah, so long as I can persuade Toby to chip in. And if not ...' She lifts a shoulder. 'Well, let's see what happens.'

I sip my cappuccino thoughtfully. I'm delighted that Frankie wants to move back, yet I can't help feeling a little concerned at her skittishness. There's no doubt she has her leadership qualities of single-mindedness and determination, but is this decision more knee-jerk than reasoned? My stomaching clenching with anxiety, I picture that damned left-field letter from 'Billy'. Decisions made from the heart aren't always the right ones. They can spectacularly unravel out of nowhere.

The scrape of her chair brings me back. 'I just need a pee, then shall we go?' she asks.

I look at my watch. 'It's not for another twenty-five minutes.'

'Ten minutes to stroll there and a mooch around to get our

bearings?'

Goodness, Francesca Whittle means business. Which hopefully means she'll forget about her discovery last night. I throw back my coffee. 'Righto. Let's go.'

*

Though the March afternoon is sharply cold, the sun cracks a smile as we take a right turn.

'Ah, that's where Thyme Out is. Debs from running has recommended it a few times,' I comment as we pass.

'Good to know for when I move here. Breakfast almost on my doorstep!'

I chuckle. '"When"? You haven't even looked at—' A strong sense of déjà vu strikes me and I halt. 'Golly, I didn't realise this is where you meant. The building was around here. It was an annex, sixties Portakabin style as I recall, so it must have been demolished.'

Frankie narrows her eyes. 'Is this a guessing game or are you going to tell me what you're talking about?'

'The antenatal clinic.' Those days should be imprinted on my memory, yet they're vague.

'You mean from when you were pregnant with me?'

'Of course; who else.'

I try to think back, and though I can picture the waiting room and the cubicles on the inside, I honestly can't remember much about the surroundings. I was so tightly coiled with what the future might hold, I must have been blind to them.

'So this wasn't just a hospital, but *my* hospital? I was actually born here?'

'Yup. My perfect, perfect little girl.' I catch her flinch. 'Gosh, sorry, love. I didn't mean to be tactless.'

'It's fine, you weren't.' We continue to amble past the old railings. 'Tell me more.'

If she means the birth itself, I can't. I focus on what I know about the history of the site instead. 'The infirmary was a

57

"pavilion plan" design, so very much state-of-the art for those days. Hence the new name of the development, I guess. Apparently Florence Nightingale gave it the seal of approval.' I pull a wry face. 'Sadly it had gone downhill by the time I came and closed its doors a couple of years after.'

'So where were the maternity wards?'

I point to a red brick structure peeking out at the rear. 'In there. My room had a faded yellow curtain, as thin as a handkerchief and too short, so any chance of sleep was zilch. The whole set-up was grotty; I never noticed how beautiful it was on the outside. And, of course, when you have a baby, you only have eyes for ...' Realising I've done it again, my voice trails away.

'For God's sake, stop checking yourself! Onwards and upwards, OK? I've a good feeling about this place.'

'OK. Got it.'

Frankie moves on and frowns. 'So you were given a single suite rather than a ward with other women? Even though it was the NHS?'

'A *suite* is pushing it, but yes.' I feel hot, so I loosen my scarf. 'It must have been simple luck; the right place at the right time.'

'Ah, luck ...' She stops at the wrought-iron gates and lightly strokes the black painted slats. 'Just look at these. Solid, safe.' She peers inside the somewhat polished and preened and too perfect complex. 'I love it already. It feels ...'

I recognise the scene from ancient plans and scratchy photographs in dusty tomes at work. 'Serendipitous?'

'It does, it really does.'

Though I feel a shiver, she beams. It's the first genuine smile I've seen for weeks.

'It's exactly what I need, Mum.'

'Is it me, or is it unbelievably quiet? You could hear a penny drop.' I nod to the central feature; a pale stone chapel with huge arched windows and an ornate roof structure. 'Maybe the residents are in there for compulsory Sunday worship. You'd better not let on you prefer the Greek gods.'

'Ha.' Frankie looks up to the imposing bell tower. 'Gorgeous, though, isn't it? I think the former nave is a central foyer and communal space for the residents. There's also a private penthouse flat above it.' She peers at an intercom keypad. 'We're only ten or so minutes early, so let's give it a try.'

'Maybe we should ...' I start, but she's already pressed the buzzer for number three.

It's immediately answered. 'Hello?'

'Mrs Logan? It's Francesca Whittle here for my viewing. I'm a little early, but I wondered if I could have a look around the gardens before we—'

'It's fine to come in now. In fact, that suits me better. I'm on the right-hand side. See you in a moment.'

Frankie grins. 'Keen or what?'

'You or her?' The barriers creak and judder before slowly parting and, despite feeling that sense of unease again, I flash a smile. 'Newfangled with old-fangled, eh? Best of both worlds, like you and me, kiddo,' I say.

19

Frankie

Whether it's the weak sunshine or a sense of relief, honeyed warmth seeps through me as the gates clang behind us. Breathing in the crisp air, I take a moment to inspect the two mansion-style properties which flank the entrance. Though clearly the original Victorian buildings, they've been scrubbed up too, like twins suited and shaved in readiness for an elegant dinner party.

'I wonder if these have been divided into flats or whether they're single homes?' It's so silent, I find myself whispering. 'They're flaming massive if they are.'

'How the other half live, eh?' Mum says, somewhat inevitably. She peeps in the bay window. 'Very posh. My guess is they've kept this as a whole unit.' She snorts. 'Or as a museum, from the looks of it. I'll have to see if I can gain entry and pinch a few things for the library.'

Thank God she steps away and lowers her voice as we make our way along a privet-lined walkway. 'You wouldn't believe it was once a workhouse.'

'I thought you said—'

'Before that. It first opened in the mid-eighteen-hundreds,' she says.

'Remember it well, do you?'

'Very droll.'

Her expression thoughtful, she peers up at the far building where I was born.

'Go on, then,' I prompt. 'Give me the lowdown.'

She gives a little jump. 'About ...?'

'This workhouse malarkey.'

'Right. Well, the original design was cruciform. You know, in the form of the Latin cross like most medieval Gothic churches? The chapel was in the south wing and the dining halls, segregated dormitories and so on were in the north, east and west.'

'Interesting.'

'The architects' "bird's-eye view" plan is in the library, along with a whole raft of other reading matter from records to personal accounts, mostly from visitors and the warders. You should take a look.'

'Maybe I will.'

She gestures back to the big house. 'Workhouses generally had a medical officer, so I expect Doctor something or other lived in one, and maybe the master or governor resided on the other side of the ...' Her lips twitch. 'The sallyport.'

'Which is?'

'A prison entrance.'

'Hilarious.'

'So it was very nice for some. You know, unlike the rat-infested and grimy accommodation of the poor folk.' She tuts. 'They were called "inmates", can you believe. Men, women, children, the infirm and the able-bodied were housed separately, kept apart from their families and pretty much fed gruel.' She glances over her shoulder again. 'In there, in fact, now I think of it. Conditions were cramped with beds squashed together, little light and hardly any space to move. They were expected to work for their keep, and unfortunately that included forced child labour, long hours, malnutrition, beatings and neglect.'

'Bloody hell, I wish I hadn't asked.'

Mum elbows me and chuckles. 'Be warned. Strict rules warned against drunkenness and swearing, and inmates were not allowed to leave the premises without permission from the wardens.'

'Noted.'

'But in fairness, there were some honest, charitable guardians who were altruistic benefactors and genuinely wanted to help.'

'Let's hope the current ones are from that line.' Glad she's got off her high horse, I motion to the immaculate lawn at the centre of the quadrangle. 'Done by hand scissors, do you think?' I rotate to a row of terraced houses and jolt in surprise. Rubbing her arms as though she's cold, a slim woman is at the second door. 'Shit, that must be our vendor. Let's hope she hasn't been listening to us.'

Mum turns too. 'Hmm. Identical front gardens and matching plants to boot.'

'Behave.' I wave. 'Hello. Mrs Logan?'

She nods, so I head down a path clearly shared with number one. 'Nice rhododendron bushes,' I comment, for something to say. 'I bet they'll look lovely when they flower.'

'Yes. Everything is communal, run by a management company. A leasehold thing, you know? So gardeners appear and do the necessary.' Her sentences sound like questions and she seems a little nervy. 'Which was perfect for me and Ben. No need for spades, secateurs or a lawnmower. Or indeed, weeding.'

'Suits me too. Remember your accident with the strimmer?' I ask Mum.

'We had a dog at the time and I didn't spot his poop in the long grass. You can imagine what happened when the rotating blades caught it.' She rolls her eyes. 'Children don't forget anything, do they?'

'Oh, we weren't blessed.' Mrs Logan leads us in and motions to the staircase. 'Upstairs first? I'll leave you to it, shall I? I'll be down here if you have any questions.'

'Great, thanks.' I take a step then come back. 'Actually, here's one to begin with. Have you found somewhere yourself? The agent said there wasn't a chain and that I could move in fairly quickly. If we go ahead, of course.'

'Oh really?' She seems thrown. 'Well yes, I have a sister who has plenty of space. Heritage Grove in Didsbury village? Another housing estate with gates, as it happens, but she's on the outside, so it's not quite so, so—'

'Afternoon! Welcome, welcome.' A dapper silver-fox type has appeared at the threshold. 'All right if I pop in, Julia?'

'Yes, of course. In fact, it's perfect timing.' Mrs Logan drifts away. 'I'll be outside.'

I take in the man's cravat, his affable expression and his sparkling blue eyes. 'I gather you're Mr Peppercorn?' I say.

'I am.' He holds out his hand and shakes mine with a dry, firm grip. 'Though I'd rather Fabian. Ursula and I live at The Gatehouse, so I'm only here to answer any technical questions, so to speak.' He stands back. 'Do help yourselves and give me a shout if you need anything.'

'Thank you, we will.'

'Do we know him from somewhere?' Mum asks when we're out of his earshot.

'No and no flirting. I know what you're like with handsome men.'

'He's probably sixty, so far too old for me,' she quips in reply.

We tour the front bedroom, a small guest room and the pristine bathroom. 'Everything's like new and really good quality,' I hiss in Mum's ear. 'Maybe I'm comparing it to London prices, but it seems like a bloody bargain.'

She stops at a wedding portrait on the landing wall. 'I wonder what happened to Ben? Another woman?'

'Yeah, perhaps. She seems a bit sad.'

When we reach the room at the back, Mum takes in the wallpaper and pulls a face. 'No actual cot, but it's somewhat nursery-like, wouldn't you say? Odd, when she said they "weren't blessed". Wishful thinking, maybe?'

Or a miscarriage, inevitably pops into my head. Willing Mum to stop the tart commentary, I check myself to see how I'm feeling about my own situation. Right now there's simply a sense of hope. And yes, that powerful serendipity. I don't want her rolling her eyes again, so I move to the window and look down at the enclosed garden below. 'The main road is just beyond here but you wouldn't know it was there. The railings and privet make it cosy and private.'

Mum joins me. 'Good for a sneaky ciggie, by the looks of it.' She frowns. 'Poor Julia. She looks so lost. Something's definitely happened to her, don't you think?'

'I know what you mean, but ... well, I know I'm being somewhat brutal.' I can't stop myself from grinning. 'Her loss might just be my gain.'

20

Nina

We weave our way around the downstairs of the townhouse. It's probably about the same size as mine, but there the similarity ends. From the Chinese rug, the chintz drapes, leather sofas and set of coffee tables in the lounge, to the polished table and plush chairs in the dining room, everything looks like it has been beamed down from the showroom of Arighi Bianchi.

Frankie's eyes light up more with every kitchen cupboard she opens.

'Wow, a Ninja Multi-Cooker,' she says. 'I wonder if that comes with the house.'

'And one of those is?' I ask.

'Really? It basically does everything. Pressure cooks, air fries, grills, bakes, proves, sautés, steams, slow cooks—'

'Ah, middle class domesticity. I'll look forward to you sending Toby round to mine with a basket of warm baps come a Sunday morning.'

She gives me a look. 'Stop taking the piss and be happy for me, will you.'

'I am happy for you, but—'

'Look, I really like it here, Mum. It feels safe, it has all that fascinating history and character yet with the mod cons of a new build. A win–win.'

It's so nice to see her glow again, and I don't want to burst her bubble, but it still feels a little hasty. I go for pragmatic. 'How about Toby? Will he see it like that?'

'He'd bloody better.' She sighs. 'Thing is, Mum … it took us ages to conceive and I honestly feel somewhere like this will help for the next time we try.' She smiles a wonky smile. 'You know, less stress, less booze and late nights; a healthier all round lifestyle.'

I take a breath to say something about Toby's work ambitions, but Fabian clears his throat at the door. 'Sorry to interrupt, ladies. How about a quick tour of the grounds whilst I'm willing and able?'

'Yes, that'd be great, thanks. Come on, Mum.'

Inhaling the fragrant air, I try to shake off whatever is bothering me. I'm not even sure what it is. The flawless, claustrophobic vibe? That creeping sense of déjà vu? I glance up at the red brick building. Or the insidious creeping in of the past?

Fabian gives a summary of the professional residents. 'I understand you and your husband are in project management?' he asks Frankie.

'Yes. We're London based for now, but looking to move back up north.'

'Any kids?' Though I notice her frown, Fabian continues to amiably speak. 'I ask because we have a crèche of sorts here.' He motions to the chapel. 'Very much an informal set-up just for our community; finding childcare for working parents can be a struggle. Ah, here she is.'

A tall woman with erratic hair and a huge beam bounds towards us like a puppy. 'Hello, hello. Sorry, I got caught up chatting to Jerome. It's so lovely to have him home.' Her whole demeanour screams an excess of energy. 'We're having roast beef, roast potatoes, Yorkshire puds and the works, a veritable feast for the prodigal—'

'Ursula, this is Francesca and her mother. Here to view number three.'

Frankie all but curtsies, so I have to stifle a snigger. 'Hello, pleased to meet you,' she says. 'I'm Frankie and this is Nina.'

'I was telling them about the daycare you provide, dear.'

'Hardly that. However, yes, I help out with the toddlers in a rather nice space we've kitted out like a soft play area. With books and toys, age appropriate, of course. And it's rather lovely because the older children join in and entertain the younger ones during the holidays. It really is quite joyful to behold. One big happy family. The chapel door is always open and welcoming. Or unlocked, should I say! Wouldn't do for our little ones to get a chill.' Ursula grasps Frankie's hand. 'So yes, when you're blessed, you'll know where to come. It will be an absolute pleasure to have you.'

21

Frankie

'I'm off. See you later,' Mum calls up the stairs.

'Have fun,' I call back. 'Send everyone my love.'

'Will do.'

I wait for the door to slam, then relax my knotty shoulders. Finally! Mum's gone for a curry with her running group, so I have the house to myself at last. I can have a long soak in the bath without her coming in for her deodorant or a pee; I can order a flaming takeout without her sucked-in, judgemental cheeks; I don't have to worry about saying something which doesn't quite fit with her politics. Or have her concerned eyes inspecting me when she thinks I'm not looking.

I catch my moody frown in the mirror. Oh God, what a harridan. It's not Mum's fault that she's getting on my nerves – and this is her place, after all – but living with her is not how I expected my early thirties to be. I envisioned a family home and a newborn, even a toddler and another baby on the way by now. I didn't anticipate bloody burglars and miscarriages and a sulky flaming husband.

I make my way to the sofa, plonk down and fold my arms. My eyes slide to the bookshelf and the mystery it's harbouring, yet other concerns are more imperative right now. Toby hasn't been in touch since he stomped off for the train on Sunday morning. Three whole days! Why should I have to call him first?

I inwardly groan. If I want to ultimately get my own way, both baby- and house-wise, I have to 'play it smart'. Mum's wise words – and she's annoyingly right.

Fixing a smile, I scoop up my mobile and call my husband. He answers, thank God.

'Frankie!' There's a note of relief in his voice – a good start.

'How's things?'

'Better for hearing from you. I've really missed you.'

I feel a stab of affection. 'I've missed you too. Are you on the tube?'

'Yeah. Just on my way home. Work's been a shit-show today.'

'Oh no! So what's—'

'Andrew Maher's been headhunted now. Which leaves only me at my level who hasn't been.'

'Yeah, sorry, I heard about Andy. But he's going to a start-up in the middle of nowhere, so it could easily go pear-shaped. Your time will come soon, Toby, I'm sure of it.'

'Will it?'

'It honestly will. I understand it's not easy, but patience is the thing.'

I have the good grace to blush at my own hypocrisy. 'You know how you're desperately missing me?' I ask.

I hear his smile. 'Yeah ...?'

'Well, I've found a perfect place for a Manchester base. It's somewhere affordable, so that'll allow us to keep the flat for now.' He audibly inhales, so I quickly continue. 'Hear me out first, Toby. It's a gated development with a historic past, so the aesthetic is to die for. They have gardeners to keep all the common parts tidy, so you won't need to pluck even one weed, it's a stone's throw from all the cafés and bars on Burton Road, it has three bedrooms so we can have people to stay and it's like new inside. I'll send you a link. Look it up.'

Clearly reading the particulars, he goes quiet for several moments. 'Yeah, I can see the house is nice, but we're only thirty-one. The estate looks like a commune for old people.'

'It isn't. Honestly, Toby. The guy who gave the tour said the residents are all young professionals. He and his wife are the oldest ones there.'

'Bloody hell, Frankie. You went to view it without me?'

Shit. 'Just a quick look around because it's likely to sell if we don't get there first.' Mentally crossing my fingers, I tense. 'Which is why I made another appointment for Friday.'

'Friday? I'm—'

'Working. I know, but you could do it remotely like me. I thought it could be a trial run. Friday and the weekend in Manchester, the rest of the week in London, if that's what you want.'

'What I *want* is to do what we agreed. Buy somewhere south of the—'

'It has a crèche and helpful people, Toby. All I'm asking you to do is to take a look. Please? Just a quick peek, for me?'

'Look, our stop's coming up.'

'Then say yes! I'll make it worth your while ...'

'Is that a promise?'

'Absolutely!'

He laughs. 'Then I guess it has to be a yes.'

22

Nina

Attempting to block out Frankie and Toby's conversation echoing through from the lounge, I bang pots and pans as I wash up in the kitchen. Short of wearing noise muffling headphones, there's not a lot I can do about it in such a small house. He's clearly not got the promotion he'd hoped for.

'As if it wasn't excruciating enough,' he's saying, 'they expected me to hang around, sport a smile and listen to their sodding feedback.'

'Oh God, poor you.'

He apes a woman's voice. '"It was a close-run thing, Tobias, but your competitors had the edge because they'd done more micromanaging than you." There was only one other competitor! The one who's done it to me since school.'

'Marcus?'

'Yes, bloody Marcus. Then there were my client/user handling capabilities. Apparently, they could be a "little stronger". Oh, and I need to push for more POC activities. How can I be the point of contact when they don't make me one?'

'I know. It's so frustrating for you.'

'Does bloody Marcus Penny micromanage, or any of those other things?'

'I doubt it.'

'Precisely. So what with the headhunting, it ended up being a race for two and I couldn't even win that. Dad'll have a field day.

As for Mum ... well, I suppose it depends what mood she's in. She'll either cold shoulder me for weeks or smother me with love.'

'Then don't tell either of them.'

'He knows I was in the running so ...'

'And Felicia?'

'She popped round last night.'

'And you blabbed that it was on the cards?'

'She's my mother, Frankie.'

'True, but there are some things you don't even share with—'

Not caring to hear the rest, I move to the back door, open up and stare out at the black night. Though spring is underway, there's still a determined nip in the air once the sun disappears. I shake away the shiver and replace the disquiet in my chest with pragmatism. The majority of children don't tell their parents everything. I was the exception to the rule with my mum, and even then it was only because I desperately needed someone to share the burden after Greg died. And I do better than most with Frankie from a mutual liking and trust. At least, I hope so.

My lips twitch despite poor Toby's despair. As my daughter succinctly put it the other day, his lost promotion might just be her gain. It isn't a nice way to think about things, but it's only akin to making something good happen out of something bad. Better a winner by default than have no winner at all. And Frankie does very much want her new house and new beginning. After the trauma she's suffered, she deserves it.

A snapshot jumps into my mind, one I haven't pictured for many a year. It's of me admiring my reflection in Mum's long wardrobe mirror. The wedding gown still needed a dry-clean, but the fit was perfect and my eyes glowed with sheer elation. At that moment I was so in love and so utterly innocent, I had no idea that life could turn on a sixpence.

I blink the image away and feel my stomach flip. Frankie may keep some things from me; how I wish it wasn't the other way too.

23

Frankie

Praying that Toby will like the townhouse as much as I do, I hold his hand tightly and fill him in about the workhouse-cum-hospital backdrop as we approach Pavilion Gardens. The bygone aspects are actually a bonus as a history degree is the one thing him and Mum have in common.

I glance at the deep frown marring his handsome face. Maybe he should have taught the subject – not in a challenging state school like mine, where it wasn't uncommon for a fight to break out in the classroom – but somewhere fee-paying where, at least in theory, the kids are more invested to learn. Still, I know better than to suggest a degree-related change of career when I read biology at uni with a view to pursuing something medically-related. And anyway, Toby's whole *raison d'être* is to 'be valued and respected' at our professional services firm – 'one of the largest in the UK and part of a global network spanning 150 countries and territories' as the website says. And be 'paid a shitload' as he puts it. Indeed, it has been a challenge to keep him off that very subject and 'Marcus fucking Penny' all morning.

I now gesture to the rooftop I'm already picturing as mine. 'That's the one for sale, number three,' I say quietly in case Mrs Logan is smoking in her garden again. 'Not that you can see much with the railings and hedge. And that's good, yeah? You can sunbathe in your speedos and no one will be any the wiser.'

Toby doesn't reply. He isn't for chivvying today. I understand he's disappointed about the promotion news, yet at some stage he needs to get a grip, just like I did about the miscarriage, on the outside, at least. More recently my nightmares have morphed into baby ones – glimpsing a heartbeat on that monitor, her being stolen by the burglar, fighting for her with some unknown force in a graphic tug-of-war battle – but I don't inflict them on him.

'Come on, Toby. Please try for a smile. Look at these gates and those old lamps on the pillars. Aren't they beautiful?'

'Yeah, I guess. So, how do we get in?'

There's still fifteen minutes until our appointment and I don't want to appear overly keen. 'It isn't yet eleven. I need to get a few bits and bobs from the Co-op. Are you coming? You can select something you fancy for lunch.'

'You go.' He pulls out his mobile. 'I'll wait here.'

I stare at my husband for a second or two. Quite frankly, I'd like to take him by the shoulders and shake this childish behaviour out of him, but there's a messy-haired bloke talking on his phone a stone's throw away from us. He has a khaki medical bag slung across one shoulder – a veterinarian's by the sound of it – and he's calming a pet owner with his mellifluous tones. I snigger to myself. If Mum was here, she'd make a quip about borrowing him to do the same with flaming Toby.

Apparently reading my very thoughts, the stranger catches my eye and briefly smiles before turning away to continue his conversation.

'OK,' I say to Toby. 'I'll be no more than ten minutes. Anything you need whilst I'm there?'

He miraculously lifts his head and considers the question. 'A blueberry muffin might help.'

*

The bakery shelf is empty, so I choose a selection of chocolate bars, swipe them through the self-service till and hurry back. To my surprise, Toby isn't sullenly reading the sport's news on his phone but amiably chatting to the vet guy about it.

I wait for them to finish their conversation about tomorrow's local derby. 'All ready, Toby?'

'Yup.' He smiles at his new friend. 'Nice to meet you. Let's see if you're right.'

I wait until the portal has clanked behind us. 'Right about what, and who is he?'

'Arteta's line up for the cup match tonight. And he's a neighbour who's recently moved in, apparently.'

I'm pleased he's found someone around our age; intrigued too. 'Ooh really, which house?'

'No idea. He knows his football, though.'

'That's all right then.' As though I already live here, I slot my arm through his and reiterate the potted history Fabian gave me as we stride towards the quadrangle. I stop at the top of our path and admire the nineteenth century orange brickwork. 'She's called Julia Logan, by the way. And she seems a nervous type, so be gentle.'

'As if—'

The door swings open. 'Welcome, welcome! Come on through.'

It's Ursula, looking marginally less dishevelled than she did the last time, yet wearing an apron caked with flour nonetheless. Almost expecting her to present a tray of hot scones from the oven, I follow her and the aroma of baking to the kitchen.

She collects her handbag. 'I only popped over to let you in.' Her pale eyes rest on Toby. 'You look peckish, young man. Knock on when you've finished here. They should be ready by then.'

'As in ...?'

She pats his shoulder. 'A selection of homemade muffins and, though I say so myself, they're rather tasty.'

The woman obviously has telepathy. Toby's face lights up. 'Will do. Which number are you—'

'The Gatehouse.' She chuckles. 'We've been here since year dot, so we have a name as opposed to a digit.'

'That's so kind of you,' I reply. 'So, which of the two houses is that?'

Her genial beam falls. 'We're on the right. The Lodge on the left was Stefan's.' She sniffs. 'But all is well. We have our Jerome back.'

Her grief is so palpable, I struggle to shape a reply. I'm saved by Fabian's large presence in the doorway. 'Morning, morning. Here to relieve my good wife.' He kisses her cheek. 'Sorry, darling, everything's running somewhat late today, I'm afraid.' He's dressed as stylishly as last week, but he's clearly been rushing and has what appears to be a latex glove stuffed in his top pocket.

'Lovely to see you again, Francesca.' He holds out his hand to Toby. 'And you must be the man of the house. Welcome. Welcome both.'

I try not to bristle, Mum-like. 'Thank you. Is Mrs Logan here, or should we help ourselves?'

'Julia's gone to her sister's to ...' He taps his chin. 'How should one put it? Yes, let's say she's sadly suffering from matters of the heart.'

24

Frankie

'Sorry about him seeking you out last night,' I say to Mum when Toby leaves the table for a pee. 'He wants the promotion so much, you know? I honestly don't get that deep need to impress his father – and the rest of the clan who don't seem to lift a finger – but ... well, I guess I need to be fair. He probably didn't understand the whole broody thing, yet he went with it for me.'

'What else are mothers-in-law good for if not to have a little whinge? And he's all right, is our Toby.' There's that mischievous glint in her eyes. 'It's not his fault he was cursed with a triple barrelled surname and those haughty inbreds he has to count as his family.'

'Mum ...'

'Sorry, I can't resist. He seems to have cheered up now, though.'

'Yup, that's what temptation does to my hubby.'

'Temptation ...?'

'Cake made by Ursula's fair hands.'

'As in jolly hockey sticks Ursula from Pavilion Gardens?'

I give her a look, but she does have a point. 'Seems he's fallen in love. "I'd happily swap her with Felicia any day of the week", he said on the way back.'

'Goodness, praise indeed.' Mum leans forward. 'Go on, then. I know you're dying to tell me. How did it go?'

'Apart from Toby hanging out with his new flame in The

Gatehouse and leaving me with Fabian who insisted on showing me how every gadget works, from the underfloor heating to the electronic blinds, even though we haven't made an offer?'

'So is the famous Ninja robot included?'

'It was still there, so let's hope so.'

'Why? Had some of the contents gone?'

'Yup, Julia's personal stuff. You know, photos and nick-nacks.'

She frowns. 'She's left already? Isn't that a bit strange?'

I ignore her usual suspicion or cynicism or whatever it is. 'No, Mum, not at all. Her sister lives in Didsbury village, so she's moved in with her.'

'OK ...'

I don't know why I have to justify it, but I do. '"Matters of the heart", Fabian said.'

'Ben the love rat?'

'I didn't ask for flaming specifics!'

'Men! Poor bloody woman.'

'Yeah, I know. But it also means there's now vacant possession. Fabian mentioned the possibility of informally leasing it for a short period whilst the conveyancing goes through. You know, because it's still fully furnished and it would help Julia out.' I laugh. 'Don't look so stressed, Mum. We're still paying for the flat, so it's not something we'd take up.'

'So has Toby said yes?'

'I think I've just about convinced him it isn't a retirement village, so that's a start.'

'Only a start?'

'He wants to check the terms of the lease to see if they allow dogs.'

Mum rolls her eyes. 'Uh oh. I can't see them permitting an animal to pee on those immaculate borders.'

I bite back a snappy retort. 'However ...'

His hair newly groomed, Toby returns to the room and settles in his place. 'However, what?'

'I was telling Mum about your new friend.'

'Ha. Which one?'

'The vet guy, whatever his name is.'

'It's Jerome.' Toby's changed designer shirts. 'He lives on the other side of the gates. The Lodge.'

'Really? You never said anything! So he must be the—'

'Yeah, the son. He was at his mum's when I was there.'

I sit back and fold my arms. 'Bloody hell, Toby. Anything else you'd like to share with the class?'

'Yeah.' He wafts his phone. 'The cup match is on television tonight, so we're going to watch it over a pint in the Met.' He pulls back his chair. 'So sorry, ladies, it's time to love you and leave you.'

'Charming,' Mum says when the front door clicks to. 'Why do men do that? They swing from spilling out their guts to the very opposite.'

I'm actually a bit miffed about Toby's date – and his smug secrecy – as he usually tells me everything. And why wasn't the flaming 'lady' of the house invited? I move the conversation on before Mum says the very same. 'Is that what Colin does?' I say.

'Sorry?'

'Colin.' It's my turn to smirk. 'Your "fancy man", as Gran put it, when we visited at lunchtime. She says he's been around for a while. Might I have the honour of meeting this one?'

'I wouldn't want to break a precedent, so let's call that a no.'

I wonder whether to open this particular can of worms. Her love life has always been a taboo subject, somehow. Still, I am intrigued why she never gave me the chance of a stepdad and those longed for siblings. 'Why the criterion to start with, though?' I ask. 'I'm sure one or two must have been keepers.'

She shrugs. 'Let's face it, most blokes are a waste of space. And who wants more upset, loss and grief? Once bitten and all that. Besides, I had you to consider. You might have got attached to someone you saw as a father figure. Suppose it all went pear-shaped at my end and I wanted to get rid? Or vice versa. That'd have broken your heart too, so I wasn't going to risk it.'

'On the other hand, you might have found someone you really

adored and had more kids.'

She pulls a face. 'More nightmares like you? Give me a break! And I bet you'd have been a horrible big sister. Not sharing your make-up, your million crop tops, your Kylie perfume, your Blue CDs.'

On the contrary, I'd have loved someone to play with and dilute the intensity of her love at times, but it's another unmentionable. 'Was I a nightmare, though? I mean the giving birth bit?' I ask instead.

She sweeps a pile of crumbs into her palm. 'I honestly can't recall much about it, so I guess you must have been a dream rather than a nightmare. So thank you, my perfect daughter.' Then, with a wonky smile, 'And your dad – I'm sorry you never got to know him. Better the amazing one you had in absentia rather than a disappointing substitute, if you know what I mean.'

If he was so 'amazing', I wonder why she so rarely mentions him. With that very thought in mind, I waft her away. 'OK, got it. Off you go.'

'Anywhere in particular?'

'Get thee to the bathroom whilst the house is man free! See, dearest mother, you're not the only one around here who's telepathic.'

'Hmm, so long as you can't read my every thought ...'

Once she's gone, I listen out for running water, then creep into the lounge. The letter from Billy Malloy is still really bugging me. Mum's reaction last week was decidedly odd. And despite her explanation, why hide it?

Half expecting the envelope to have disappeared, I slip Middlemarch from the shelf, extract the letter and read it again. Is he really my dad's brother, and therefore my uncle? Or is he a hustler of some sort?

I pull over my laptop and open a new message. There's no harm in trying to find out.

25

Nina

After a hectic day on my feet in the library, I'd like to go home to an empty house and do the old shedding-clothes-and-having-a-thorough-shower routine. Housing a lodger – or two, when Toby is around – has put paid to that, but I'm pleased that Frankie turned down the leasing suggestion and is staying with me for now.

Inhaling the balmy April Fool's Day air, I wait at Castlefield-Deansgate station for the next tram to arrive. It has been a good week so far, particularly at work. Me and a colleague have been donning gloves and carefully unearthing books and other treasures donated by the widow of a collector, a job I enjoy as there are always surprises of one sort or another. Quite often we find a rare artefact or a first edition, and more than once we've discovered pornographic literature, along with accompanying sex toys.

'Thank God for widows,' we say, raising a cuppa to Enriqueta Rylands, or even speaking to her in person by addressing her statue in the main hall.

The following quips inevitably ensue:

Me: *One thing's for sure; I'll never be one.*

Dorothy: *A widow? I can't wait! One thing's for sure; when the day comes, I won't be giving any of his money away.*

I absolutely never intend to get married, yet Frankie's query about Col has prayed on my mind. We've barely met in person over the past few weeks, but we've weirdly spent more time chatting on the phone or by FaceTime. So by seeing him less, I feel I know him more. And I do enjoy his company very much. He makes me squirm with pleasure and laugh out loud, sometimes at the same time. I said as much to Sue, our intrepid running-group leader.

'Sounds like he's a keeper,' she said.

'Oh God, wrong answer,' I replied.

'Well, I'd normally say, "if it ain't broke, don't fix it", but something tells me you want to get out your tool kit and meddle anyway.'

I sigh. Do I? Is that true?

Pushing those thoughts away, I concentrate on finding a spot in the carriage where I won't get squashed or stuck beneath a sweaty armpit, or so close to some old guy that I can count his nostril hair. Why Thursdays are so bad, heaven knows, but Frankie offered to cook tea tonight, so that's something to look forward to.

The notion of nice food brings on thoughts of Col again. His cooking skills on top of the squirming and laughter! How could I have forgotten? I make a metal note to mention them to Sue at next week's session, then turn my thoughts to another man in the mix. Toby. He's back in London and not making any concessions on the working front – yet – but he gave Frankie the go ahead to make an offer on 3 Pavilion Gardens, which was duly accepted, and now the conveyancing is underway. Moving cities is a huge, life-changing decision and I have the strong impression that her 'serendipity' notions are the driver, but my saying it out loud would result in an argument. And who am I to object because of some sixth-sense discomfort? I, more than anyone, understand her urgent desire to start a family and her consultant has given her the all clear to try again.

The dull disquiet that seems to constantly line my belly goes up a notch. I sigh it away. I'm starting to feel Frankie's loss already, that's all. Which is ridiculous when she'll be living just a few minutes down the road.

Practically popping out of the stuffy tram carriage, I climb up the steps to the street, bypass Tesco Metro, then stop and turn back. Though Frankie is trying for a healthy lifestyle, she hasn't totally given up alcohol, so I buy a bottle of Prosecco for the two of us to raise a glass to the good times over dinner.

Finally at my front door, I open it up with a grin of anticipation. My smile immediately falls at the sight of her suitcase at the bottom of the stairs. Disappointment for us both spreads in my chest. She was allocated a new work placement last week, which she'd hoped to do remotely, rather than live in a hotel for three months. Noting the lack of cooking aromas in the air, my heart sinks even further; her departure to Lincolnshire must be imminent.

I glance into the lounge. 'There you are! Looks like you're Lincoln bound after all,' I say. I take in her folded arms and her peculiar expression. 'Or London? Is everything OK? Is it Toby? Is he—?'

'No, everything is not OK,' she snaps. '"OK" doesn't even begin to cover it.'

For seconds I wonder if this is an April Fool's joke. But her sapphire-blue eyes laser through me, telling me otherwise. She's furious; angrier that I've ever seen her before. 'Has the purchase fallen—'

'Who is Kim?'

'Kim? I have no idea. Why, has she gazumped your offer or ...?'

'Let's try the name Lindsay instead, then. Does that sound more familiar?'

Like a winding, sickening thump to the belly, I realise what and who she means. I should have burned that bloody envelope the moment I saw it.

'I sent Billy Malloy an email, then we had an exchange of messages,' she continues in a staccato tone. 'My uncle Billy. You know, the man whose letter you fucking hid.'

'I see.'

'My dead father's brother. My uncle Billy by *blood*.'

Anxiety consumes me; my tongue sticks to the roof of my mouth. This is the very moment I have dreaded since the day she was born.

'Go on, then, Mother. Explain.'

I grope for a way out of this conversation. 'As I already said ...' I clear the clot from my throat. 'Until it arrived, I didn't know Greg had a brother. Honestly. That's why I was wary. There are a million scams out there. It could still be a hoax, someone after money. How do you know it isn't—'

'Stop, Mum, just stop.' She jabs a finger at me. 'You *know* because of Lindsay and Kim. I saw it in your face the moment I mentioned Lindsay's name.'

I have no idea how to reply, so I sit down and wait for the nightmare to unravel. Did I know my decision – my lie – would catch up with me one day? For so long it felt like mine alone to make, but I can see from Frankie's burning glare that I was wrong. The question is how honest I can be. I've buried the past so deeply, I'm not sure I can—

'All those years I longed for more family, instead of being a cosseted, smothered only child.'

Panic overwhelms my rational mind. I can't think straight. And Frankie is firing her rage at me.

'I have a sister, Mum; I have a sister you fucking kept secret from me! Why would you do that? Are you even listening?'

All I can do is study my shaking hands.

'She was brought up in Stockport, for Christ's sake. That's, what, three miles away? Close enough to know properly, hang out with, have fun with, confide in, go to clubs with.'

I finally speak, my voice small as the words fall out. 'I thought they were in Norwich.'

'Norwich, Stockport, what the fuck does it matter? It's still in the UK, still close enough to do all those things.'

'You had all that with your pals.'

'But it's not the same, is it? Whatever they say about choosing your friends, it matters, blood matters.'

Blood matters, it does. There's no escaping that. All I can

focus on is the thud of my heart, loud in my ears.

'For the past thirty-one years I could have had a relationship with my sister. You deprived me of that.'

'Half-sister,' slithers out.

'Still a bloody relative, Mum. Someone other than you constantly there and suffocating me.'

Her sneer pierces my very being. It feels so very unfair. I was simply a compliant, loving girlfriend who wanted babies, a family. It wasn't me who set the ball rolling. It was Greg and his—

Frankie marches to the door. 'Failing to tell me is unforgivable.'

My own anger finally surfacing, I stand and follow her. 'What was *unforgivable* was my boyfriend – no, not only my boyfriend, but my fiancé – cheating on me. Something I was stupidly, stupidly blind to.' Tears burn my eyes, just as they did the day I found out Lindsay was pregnant. Tears of disbelief and the deepest grief. 'It was devastating. It felt like she'd stolen my baby.'

Frankie shakes her head and grasps the handle of her suitcase. Realisation dawns that she's leaving. Searching for *something* to make her stay, I hold out my arms. 'But against all the odds – like serendipity as you'd say – a little miracle was already baking inside. You. An incredible blessing I'm still thankful for every single day.'

She flinches away. 'None of that changes the fact that you lied to me. Whether Stockport or fucking Norfolk, you were fully aware I had a brother or sister you'd never told me about, not even when I was old enough to make a choice whether or not to have them in my life. You knew perfectly well how much having a sibling meant to me. Me, this person you're supposed to love and want the very best for. I can't bear to look at you.'

Frustration makes me snappy. 'So instead of being pragmatic and working things through, you're going to run away and go back to the flat?'

She lifts her chin. 'Don't speak to me as though I'm a child. I've spent all day being *pragmatic*, as you put it. The short-term lease at Pavilion Gardens has been agreed and I already have the keys. I'm moving in tonight.' She turns before leaving and looks at me with those authoritative, determined, almost scary blue eyes. 'Don't bother getting in touch or trying to call round. You won't be welcome.'

PART 2 - PAVILION GARDENS

Frankie

26

Pulsing with sheer anger about my astonishing discovery, I negotiate the bustling Burton Road with shallow breath and gritted teeth. When I pull up outside the gates and squint at the immaculate scene beyond them, I thank God there's already a sense of reassuring calm. I hop out of the car and input the code Fabian gave me into the keypad. He mentioned I'll get an 'open sesame' fob to control it remotely at some point as Julia's old one has gone AWOL for now.

As I wait for my new life to yawn ajar, I will my thrashing heart to quell. I understand the heavy feeling in my chest is shock, the rug being pulled from beneath my feet out of nowhere, but bloody hell. How could my mother have betrayed me like this? She kept the truth about my sister from me my whole life. Some part of me hoped she'd plead ignorance yet, by her own admission, she knew about Lindsay's pregnancy, Greg's other baby. It hurts, it really does. No wonder she's always been so circumspect, even secretive, about my dad.

And, of course, Gran will have known too. Which simply wounds me even more.

Absorbing my surroundings afresh, I slowly drive towards the parking area. The handsome buildings and grounds appear as clean and fresh as I remember, both innocent and welcoming somehow. I duly park in the allotted space for number three and give myself a few moments to respire. Good God; how life can sickeningly pivot in an instant. One minute I was attending a work Teams meeting, the next I noticed a long email from Billy Malloy had popped up on my phone. Though I started to idly scan it, some parts horribly snagged:

I was thrilled to discover I had a brother, Greg, only then to find out he died over thirty years ago. When I dug a little further to see if he'd had any children, I was delighted to discover I had not one but two nieces. When I saw that you and Kim were born a few months apart, I realised it might be a delicate situation, which is why I thought it best to contact both mothers first. I'm eternally grateful to Nina that she had the kindness to put you and I in touch. I'm hoping that Lindsay will be as courteous, as I'd love to correspond – and perhaps even meet – both you and Kim, as my wife and I weren't able to have our own kids ...

God knows how I managed to get through the long work conference. Even the gist of the email made me feel physically ill. When it was finally over, I read Billy's words again and again, reeling more each time. Two nieces. Born a few months apart. The fact I have a half-sister called Kim is something I need to absorb and can think about later. What consumes me right now is my mother's astonishing omission or lies.

A rattle or a creak jerks me back to the present. Fully expecting someone or something pernicious nearby, I hunch my shoulders and freeze. After a second or two, I tentatively inch my head around. At ground level I'm greeted by the neat rows of maze-like privet, the pristine lawn and budding trees and, when I look up, the arched clerestory windows of the chapel all appear to be covered with blinds. Relief flutters through me. There is no human being with malevolent intent; indeed there's no one in the vicinity at all.

Recognising the snap of panic as another instance of post-traumatic stress, I rub the goosebumps from my arms. 'This is why you're here, Frankie,' I say out loud. 'You'll be safe and shielded behind those gates.'

I take another moment to drain the remaining tension from my body. Nobody will come here to threaten me with a knife. On the contrary, the cloak of *something* gathering around my shoulders feels warm and protective. The evening sun is casting soft shadows. It's sturdy and secure here. All is well. I'm in this new-but-old cocoon, away from the various shit-shows surrounding me.

I allow myself a last heavy sigh before climbing out. I didn't think they'd include my own mother, for fuck's sake, yet there's no point in dwelling on that. I'm here now; my fresh adventure is starting; I'll do my damnedest to enjoy every moment of it.

Seeming to protest, my luggage yanks at my arm as I heft it out of the boot. I had to steal a few items such as bedding and towels from Mum but, hey, that's small fry compared to a lifetime of deceit. Certain my decision to leave is absolutely the right one, I wheel my case around the weed-free paving, stop outside number three and insert my key. I give a little emotional sniff; Toby should be here at this auspicious moment. Still, we can have the grand stepping-over-the-threshold when our names are on the title deeds. For now, I'm single and strong.

'Oh, hi!'

My hand to my chest, I jolt around to my right. A shiny-haired woman cups her mouth in a gesture of apology.

'I'm so sorry to make you jump,' she says.

'No worries at all. It's just so silent here.'

'I know. Sometimes I can hear my own footsteps on the paths, but you get used to it.' She gestures to the quadrangle. 'I guess it's so much space and so few residents compared with the norm. We lived in a flat in central Manchester before, so it took a while to get used to the lack of banging, shouting, music and so on. We loved the vibe back then, but life moves on.' She rubs her pregnant belly. 'Priorities change. Scott thought we were getting old before our time and he's a convert now. He loves being a dad.'

'Oh, so you already have—'

'Yes, a little boy, Noah. In fact, I was just on my way to collect him from the crèche.'

'The one here?'

'Yes, it's brilliant to drop him off with Ursula for an hour now and then.' She rolls her eyes. 'You know, so I can have a nap, a shower or even make dinner.'

'Oh right.'

She chuckles. 'You clearly haven't been blessed yet.'

'Is it that obvious?'

'It was the perplexed look when I mentioned the shower.' She rubs her bump. 'I'll be lucky to get a toilet break, let alone a sandwich when this one comes.'

Not sure if she's joking, I narrow my eyes. 'Really?'

'Sort of. It's so worth it, though, and all the mums here help each other out. I'm Pippa, by the way.'

'Nice to meet you. I'm Frankie.'

'I'd better get off. Ursula is brilliant in every way, but she's a stickler for timekeeping.' Pippa tilts her head. 'Fancy coming to take a look? See what it's like for when your time comes?'

I can't help but grin at the exhilarating thought. I push the shopping and suitcase into my hallway. 'Absolutely. Wild horses couldn't stop me.'

27

Both nervous and excited, I accompany my new friend towards the hub of our residence. The pathway is flanked by more manicured bushes and the grass in between appears – and smells – newly mown. Finally looking ahead, I can't help gasping with pleasure at the chapel's facade, as the sunset has lit its neat stone cladding, Palladian windows and crow-stepped gables with orange licks of fire.

'Beautiful, isn't it? I never tire of looking at it. First thing in the morning and last thing at night,' Pippa says.

I look at her quizzically.

She gestures behind us. 'From my bedroom window. Same as you when you wake up tomorrow. It's Grade II listed and the roof terrace has panoramic views of ... well, half of South Manchester.'

'The particulars showed there's a penthouse flat at the top.'

'Oh really?' She slips her arm into mine. 'Come on, we don't want to be late!'

We make our way up the steps and into the carpeted foyer, complete with the state-of-the-art sofas and tables I saw online. I stop at what I'd assumed were large antique brass vases.

'Are these ...?'

'Yes, church fonts from back in the day.' She smiles. 'But no longer filled with holy water, so not a danger to anyone.'

'From when this was a working church, so to speak?'

'I guess so. Ask Fabian, he's the expert on pretty much everything. Him and Ursula have lived here forever.'

'In The Gatehouse?'

'Yes.'

'Ah, interesting.' I think back to what the estate agent briefly touched on. Something about a family tragedy. Then there was Ursula's comment about The Lodge being 'Stefan's'. Yet Toby said Jerome lives there now. 'They have Jerome, but presumably they also had—'

'Jerome?' Pippa's eyes widen. 'He's back?'

'Well, yes. My hubby saw him at his mum's and they went for a pint the other day.'

'At Ursula's? Really?'

'Yes. Why is that surprising?'

She lowers her voice. 'She's always called him the prodigal son, so I got the impression he was *persona non grata*. No idea why, though.'

'How strange.' And yet Ursula was making him a Sunday roast when I visited with Mum. I've been here all of two minutes and I'm already intrigued. 'So what happened to the other—'

But Pippa's opening an arched doorway with a finger to her lips. I follow her into the heart of the building, a spacious area with a vaulted beamed ceiling. Though I can distinctly picture it lined with dark wooden pews for the *inmates* to practice their worship, today it's the airy cushioned play area Fabian described. Bringing a gust of energy with her, Ursula bounds towards us. In contrast to the neatly arranged teddies and tidy surfaces, her hair and clothing look particularly chaotic.

She scrapes back her granite-coloured locks with a tortoiseshell hairband. 'That's better, I can see you now! Hello, Pippa – perfect timing, thank you – and welcome to the family, Francesca!'

Holding out her fleshy arms, she gathers me against her ample chest. When she finally releases me, she takes my hand and squeezes it tightly. I'm not normally sentimental, yet it brings on a burn behind my eyes. Because it's a motherly gesture, I suppose, though, in contrast to Mum's soft palms, Ursula's are as large as a man's and decidedly raspy.

As if reading my mind, she looks down at them. 'Too much detergent, I expect. Cleaning, scrubbing, disinfecting; assisting

Fabian, looking after our little ones. And baking, of course. Not that I would have it any other way. I like to keep busy.' She beams. 'How lovely you've come to visit our crèche. Have you settled in at number three?'

'Other than leaving my belongings in the hallway, I haven't stepped in yet.'

'But you've met Pippa. Excellent. Let me introduce you to today's cohort.'

She moves to one side, allowing me a view of the rest of the room. Bright from the long picture windows and lined with bookcases and toys, the far side is clearly for toddlers and older children. Though the three women are busy with satchels and lunch boxes, they turn when Ursula claps.

'Everyone meet our new recruit, Francesca.' She introduces mother and child in turn, giving names I know I'll instantly forget. 'Then today's helper ...' she finishes, spinning around as if she's lost her. 'Ah, of course! She's in our small kitchen, on washing-up duties.'

'Hi everybody,' I say, giving a small wave. 'Lovely to meet you all. Feel free to call me Frankie. I'm at number three. Or at least I will be when I've unpacked.'

Pleased they all seem as smiley, warm and friendly as Ursula, I have a few words with each mum as she leaves. Bringing up the rear, Pippa rubs her tummy. 'So nice to have a new neighbour. Prosecco and Nozeco at mine before this one makes an appearance, yes?'

'That would be great. Thank you for being so welcoming.'

'Not at all.' She addresses someone over my shoulder. 'Are you up for a glass of Nozeco at mine with nibbles?'

'Absolutely. Sounds really fun.'

Trying to place the slight lisp, I turn. 'Oh, hi ...' It's the petite woman I met in Doctor Gauss' waiting room. She has an unusual name ... It pings. That's right; Minta, she said, short for Araminta.

Her face flushes with delight. 'Wow, hi to you too! I knew someone was moving into number three. I had no idea it was you.' She rushes forward and gives me a tight hug. 'I'm so pleased to meet you again.'

'I'd better get off. See you later,' Pippa says. She glances from Minta to me. 'I'm assuming you two already know each other. You look like old friends.'

'Not exactly,' Minta replies. 'But I know we will be.'

Excitement flowering in my belly, I inwardly nod. I can't quite say why, but I'm sure of it too.

28

We saunter down the pathway together.

'So, which house is yours?' I ask Minta at the bottom.

'Guess. It's my lucky number.'

Remembering her sunny positivity, I laugh. 'Don't tell me, it's seven.'

'Correct, two doors down from you. So we're going the same way. Not that you'd get lost with only nine homes each side of the gates.'

'So that building ...' I waft a hand at the old workhouse dormitories and my place of birth. 'It's not part of Pavilion Gardens?'

'No, it's now offices, apparently, with a different entrance to ours. We have a total of eighteen here, which is perfect, don't you think? Small enough for people to feel like family, help each other out, borrow sugar and so on. Big enough not to be in each other's pockets. No one wants that.'

'Agreed. Then again, I don't think I've ever actually spoken to our London neighbours, so just conversing with you is progress.' I take a quick breath and gesture to number three. 'Do you fancy coming in for a tea or coffee? If you're not busy with other things such as making dinner, of course.'

'No to caffeine at this time, but yes to ...' She chuckles. '*Conversing* and juice if you have it. Or water's fine.'

'Great, come in.' Ridiculously relieved she hasn't turned me down, I open up and motion to my stuff. 'I'll just grab a few bits and bobs for our drinks.'

'Okey-dokey. Shall I head through?'

'Yeah, sure.'

All fingers and thumbs, I unzip my suitcase and pull out the items I purloined from Mum's. When I reach the kitchen, Minta's emptying the bag of groceries. 'Chilled in the fridge, dry stuff in this one, if that's OK.'

'That's great, thanks.' I would have used the cupboard on the left, but it's nice to have a friend who isn't afraid to get stuck in.

Minta seems to follow my train of thought. 'That one's already full.'

'Oh, really?'

'Yup, look.'

'Oh, right.' I count Julia's neat rows of crockery and glassware. 'Six of everything. The full monty.'

'It's the same in the cutlery and saucepan drawers.'

I shrug away my surprise. 'I guess this is what "fully furnished" means.' I show Minta my swag, including two tumblers and mugs. 'I needn't have stolen these from my mother's after all.' I nervously chuckle. The thought of a stranger's belongings being in situ is a little disconcerting. 'Mind you, if it comes to Julia's towels and sheets, I think I'd rather use my own.'

'Oh God, I agree.'

It feels unseemly to rush upstairs and check, so I pour the fresh orange and we sit at the table. 'Did you know Julia well?' I ask. I've no idea why I framed it in the past tense. 'Sorry, do you know Julia well?'

'Not really. Everyone here is fairly friendly, but she kept herself to herself. Living on the same row, you'd think she might have introduced herself to us when we moved in, even knocked on the door with a bottle of vino, but hey, you're here now and I'm so pleased.'

'What about the husband?'

'Ben?' She considers the question. 'He was more chatty. However, to be honest, sometimes it felt a bit ...'

'What?'

'Well, a bit invasive, I guess. You know, cornering me and asking questions that were a little too personal.'

Though I don't want to pry – or indeed be invasive myself – I presume from her deep blush that the bloody letch propositioned her. And it would make sense of Fabian's 'matters of the heart' comment if Ben was a womaniser.

'Men, eh ...?' I begin, yet there's something about the way Minta rests a hand on her stomach. Remembering Pippa's meaningful look when she mentioned the alcohol-free fizz, I take in the dark smudges beneath her eyes.

She reads my mind again. 'Yes, I am.'

'Pregnant?'

'Yes!'

As though she's been a friend forever, I feel a swell of joy. 'Oh, my God, that's wonderful! Congratulations!' Then remembering she's had three miscarriages compared to my horrendous one, 'How are you feeling about it? Thrilled but nervous, I imagine.'

'I'm OK, actually. I feel really upbeat this time.' Her eyes are bright. 'As well as a new consultant I have one hundred and fifty per cent faith in, I've been manifesting this time around. Have you tried it?'

'No. At least not deliberately.' I frown in thought. 'I think you mentioned it when we met in Doctor Gauss' rooms.'

'Did I?' She chuckles. 'Well, there you go. See how it works!'

God, I so want the same. 'So it's like making wishes or saying prayers?'

'Not really. It's more mentally visualising it. Changing your mindset and believing you already have it. So, for example, I can see myself here in a few months, chatting to you around this very table and feeding my newborn baby.' She pauses and closes her eyes. When she opens them again, she gestures to the seat opposite and beams. 'Perfect! You're sitting right there, with a huge pregnant tummy!'

29

The sunshine streaming in through the crack in the blinds, I stretch and yawn. I haven't glided so slowly and contentedly into consciousness for as long as I can remember. There were no nightmares last night, just blissful, black sleep. Even now as I take in my bearings and remember where I am – including the offensive, wounding why – there's a wonderful sensation of serenity I haven't felt for months. No 'will I conceive this time?' anxious thoughts that seemed to clutter my mind constantly, which moved on to, 'will I keep this baby?' when I did.

Feeling a little guilty that my loss – and the sharp grief I kept under wraps – has diluted, I pause for a moment or two. In all honesty, I believed I would see that pregnancy through to full term. That turned out to be false hope, whereas the current feeling in my chest – whatever it is – is buoyant and energising.

I swing out my legs and smile at the efficacy of positive thinking. God knows how after all those weeks of gloom, it feels like Minta gave me a huge dose of happiness in just half an hour last night. She's so lovely and this house is ideal. When I finally came upstairs and tentatively opened the landing closet and the bedroom wardrobes, they were empty, thank God. It actually makes sense; Julia moved in with her sister, so she took clothes and toiletries and other personal effects, but didn't need the crockery. Or indeed household gadgets. I chuckle at the notion of my very own Ninja Multi-Cooker; all around, it's a veritable win–win.

Remembering what Pippa said about the view from my window, I draw back the curtains and study the clock tower, once greyish, dull and dusty and now transformed to this picture of beauty. Certain that anything and everything is possible, I smooth a hand over my tummy, close my eyes and envisage the wonderfully curved bump that Minta described. When I open them again, I give a reality-check snort. I'm not going to get pregnant without my hubby around and, more to the point, without having sex. That didn't feel right beneath Mum's roof – another bonus of being here – but I'll collect Toby from Stockport station at seven this evening, and my mission to conceive can begin with gusto. I'm pretty sure it's the perfect timing in my monthly cycle, so it feels like ... well, serendipity.

I hum to myself, pad to the bathroom and peer in the mirror above the sink. It's so nice to admire what I see, especially the vitality glowing through my skin, but when I catch the ovulation kit on the shelf, my smile falls. If I'm honest, really honest, intercourse with Toby had become a means to an end, robotic almost, in the months before we conceived. If one of those testing sticks had said yes, he was expected to perform, effectively giving a donation of sperm which had nothing to do with fun or sexual desire. Which is actually very sad; our compulsive physical attraction is what brought us together against the odds. We couldn't get enough of each other back then; I couldn't get enough. Then that urgency went up a notch at the notion of making both love and a baby.

I go back to my reflection. This time I see my naked husband beside me, and my nose burns at the recollection. That morning three years ago, I'd woken up to his intent, loving gaze.

'Oh, hi,' I'd said, a little disorientated from the unfamiliar surroundings of his father's house.

'I've been watching you sleep.'

'Very romantic. I hope I wasn't dribbling.'

'And I've decided something.'

'Oh yeah?'

'You make me feel special, complete. I want you to be my wife.' I'd expected him to declare his love, but a proposal after only six months was a shock. 'Marry me, Frankie.'

Though gobsmacked, my need for a wee was genuine, so I'd been able to escape to the en suite and breathe. When I returned to the bedroom, I still had no idea what to say. Then Toby tugged me to the full-length mirror and gestured to our bare bodies.

'Just look at us, Frankie. Wouldn't we make beautiful babies?'

He must have seen the delight and excitement which thundered through my very being, as he beamed. 'Say yes. I know you want to say yes!'

The old craving for sex now stirs in the pit of my belly. Pleasurable, heady; I'd almost forgotten. My lips curving gain, I make a silent vow. New home, new beginnings; I'll *make love* with my gorgeous man until we conceive our baby, which I absolutely know we will.

Pleased with my resolve, I turn on the shower and check the water temperature. Something makes me snap around. A vibrating sensation, almost like someone touching me ... No one is there, so I stand still and listen, then finally make out a buzzing sound. Spooky panic over! It's only the intercom.

Quickly donning my robe, I fly down the stairs. Wishing Toby was here for this surreal 'first' moment, I speak into the microphone.

'Hello?'

'A floral delivery for number three.'

'Great. One moment and I'll let you in.'

When I've pressed the button to open the gates, I unlock the front door and look out. Shielding my eyes from the same shaft of light which woke me this morning, I take in the spotless eight a.m. scene. To one side of the car park, a thirtyish bearded man is climbing into a gleaming car, to the other a daddy is pushing his toddler in a buggy. And there's Jerome, walking a handsome German shepherd on a lead. As he waves and smiles, I feel another warm spread of contentment. There are young guys here, and dogs are allowed. Another win–win for when Toby arrives.

Certain the bouquet will be from him, I thank the flower man and take the stunning display of lilies to the kitchen table. With a grin, I extract the tiny card from the envelope.

I read the message once, then again with a frown. *Sorry for your loss.*

30

Keeping my annoyance in check, I pull up my VW next to a brand-new grey Jaguar in the Pavilion car park. I'd carefully applied lipstick and was all eager smiles whilst I waited on the railway station cobbles for Toby to appear, but he heaved our big suitcase into the boot, climbed into the passenger seat and instead of offering a kiss or a greeting – or even a flaming 'thank you' for the lift – he just slumped and said, 'I hate that bloody journey. The train's never on time and it's always rammed.'

The drive here only took twenty minutes. Instead of chatting, he muttered something about a boozy late night and closed his eyes. Admittedly I'm not ready to talk about the fallout with Mum, yet he didn't show an iota of curiosity about why I'd suddenly decided that moving out of Matlock Avenue and temporarily renting here was the best for us after all. Then there's this morning's flower delivery. I'd planned to discuss it with him straight away, but he clearly wasn't in the mood for conversation, let alone speculation.

Taking a steadying breath, I search for positive energy and turn to him. 'Home at last! The gardens look gorgeous in the evening sunlight, don't they?'

'Sure.'

'Come on, then. I've already prepped dinner, so we can have a G&T, a sit down and catch-up to start an evening of sheer relaxation. How does that appeal?'

He dismounts and stretches. 'Yeah, sounds good.'

I slip my hand through his elbow. 'So what are your first impressions now you're an elite member of a gated community?'

He nods to the F-Pace SUV. 'If I get one of those, I'm in,' he replies. 'Though I'd go for the F-Type Coupe, given a choice.'

A flaming coupe is hardly child-friendly. I bite back the retort and try for humour instead. 'You'd better put a tenner on the lottery this week, then.'

'Or get the lucky break I deserve.'

I inhale to say something duly supportive, but his miserable features are transformed by a beam. 'Hey!' Breaking away from me, he strides over the central lawn. 'Hey, man,' he calls. 'Jerome!'

Jerome rotates and lifts his hand. 'Hi, how's things?'

Not wanting to miss out, I leave the suitcase behind and risk the wrath of Fabian by following my husband's footsteps.

'All good,' he's saying when I catch up. 'Just back for the weekend.' He drapes an arm around my shoulders and grins. 'And giving my poor wife grief about the game-of-sardines trek up from London.' He kisses my forehead. 'Sorry, I'm over it now.'

'Glad to hear it.'

Jerome turns to me. 'Hi, Frankie. How are you?'

'Well, thanks.'

'I spotted you first thing. Time was ticking, so sorry I didn't come over and say hello.'

It's the first time we've spoken. His voice is rich like his dad's, but there's something sweetly shy about him too. Then again, I was wearing that skimpy robe when I opened up this morning, so perhaps he's embarrassed. 'No worries at all. I didn't know you had a dog.'

'Ah. You weren't supposed to see Ossie.'

'Ossie?' Toby asks.

'Oswald.' He rakes a hand through his almost black hair. 'He's a rescue, so the name wasn't my choice. He comes with me into work, so he isn't really here, if you know what I mean.'

'Got it. My lips are sealed on the condition I can come over and give him a cuddle.'

'He'll appreciate that.' Jerome comes back to me. 'How's everything going so far?'

Those lilies flash in. His demeanour is so cordial, I consider saying something. That would be odd, though; despite feeling the contrary, I don't know him from Adam. 'All good, thanks. I really like it here already.'

'Great. Anything you need, just shout.' He smiles wryly. 'Not that my knowledge is a patch on my father's. Has he been round with helpful pointers?'

'Not yet. But he gave me a tour of the gadgets the last time I was here.'

'Then hopefully you're safe from another lecture.' He glances back to The Gatehouse. 'Or maybe he's been working today.'

'Oh, so he hasn't ...' I feel myself blush. 'Sorry, I have no idea why I thought he'd retired.'

'He's getting there. Part-time for now.' He looks at his watch. 'Dinner's calling and I'm not a rebellious teenager any more, so I'd better not be late.'

'Cooked by your mum, I'm guessing?' Toby says. 'If her baking is anything to go by, you're a fortunate man to have food on tap.'

Jerome grimaces. 'I'm not sure "fortunate" is the word. I'll see you—'

'How about a pint afterwards?' Toby looks at me. 'If that's OK with you?'

Knowing he means another bloody 'lad's only' drink, I inhale to reply.

Jerome speaks first. 'Yeah, sounds like a plan.' I thought his eyes were brown, but they're navy blue and they're kind. 'Shall I knock on for you both when I've been given dispensation to leave the dining quarters? Probably around nine-ish or so?'

'Perfect.' Toby pats his shoulder. 'See you then.' He watches his new bestie walk away. 'Great bloke,' he says when he's vanished from sight. 'Nice of him to invite you too.'

'It is.' I tug him away before our heels make dents in the grass. 'Don't worry, I won't spoil your thunder by accepting.'

Forcing down my indignation, I focus on the positives: Toby was on a high after his last outing with Jerome; unlike his other pals, the guy seems to have the knack of boosting his confidence and making him feel good about himself. Plus, any incentives for a permanent transfer to Manchester can only be a good thing. Not starting on my *making love* vows is a touch disappointing, but we have all weekend to get cosy.

As we approach our new home, I eye up my neighbours' doors and I nod. That's actually an excellent idea; if Toby is out with his mate, it's a perfect opportunity to develop my own budding friendships.

31

Stirring to a brand-new Saturday, I flip my head to the other pillow. It was still empty at one a.m., then at two, but Toby's there now, lightly snoring.

'Please join us,' Jerome said when I answered the door at nine last night. 'Otherwise I'll feel like a schoolboy knocking on and asking my mate out to play on the swings.'

'Well, now you mention it ...' I replied with a chuckle. 'But it's fine. I'm going to don leg warmers, then rally the girls and see who's up for roller skating.'

He glanced over his shoulder. 'Tell you what, with those paths it's a bloody good idea. I think you should put in a request to the committee for a dedicated speed track.'

'Is there a committee?'

'The elders who will be obeyed? In all probability. I don't ask on the basis that if I don't know what's going on or what the rules are, then I can't breach them.'

Looking freshly scrubbed in comparison to Jerome's messy hair and dark stubble, Toby appeared then. 'Onward, comrade,' he said. 'Where you lead, I shall follow.'

I now inwardly guffaw. He wasn't wrong. Wherever it was, Toby didn't get home until the early hours. When the two of them set off, despite my bravado, I did feel a little left out, and thoughts of Mum prodded. I could picture her at home with cheeks sucked in, arms folded and thinking, if not actually saying, *Sometimes you're too hot-headed, Frankie. Don't let that be your downfall. Always stay cool and play it smart.*

Worrying she was right, I paced around. Thank God the lily

display brought me back to my senses. When I'd first read the word 'sorry' on the greeting card, I'd immediately assumed they were from her – a flaming apology, at last. They weren't and not even a text has arrived, so my anger was reinstated: my mother, of all people, had kept a huge secret from me; she'd effectively lied to me my whole life and she hadn't had the decency to get in touch and say sorry, let alone beg my forgiveness. It was the impetus I needed. I shook myself down, and though I was apprehensive about tapping on doors at that time, I did, returning home ten minutes later with a mission.

A house party. I smile at the thought. Albeit small, me and Toby will host our first neighbourly gathering tonight.

I slip from the bed, pad to the bathroom and squeeze toothpaste onto my brush. It feels so surreal that Julia Logan did this every morning not so long ago. 'Invasive' Ben, too. Though he departed at some stage, leaving his poor wife struggling with 'matters of the heart'.

The words on the greeting card flash into my psyche again. I didn't end up telling Toby about them and he didn't ask where the flowers had come from, despite the glorious array taking over the kitchen table.

I cock my head at my own reflection. Should I have chased after the delivery guy and handed them back? Phoned the florists and explained the mix-up? I shrug a shoulder. Nope; they could have been meant for me. They might be belated miscarriage flowers from Gran; it's not an entirely speculative thought.

I look away from my flushed cheeks. Or is it a justification for benefiting from someone else's misfortune again ...

Casting off the uncomfortable thought, I pick up the ovulation testing kit. I fully intend to initiate sex the way I used to; stretch out the lovemaking, kiss and tease and build the sheer tension until we both explode, but there's no harm in checking my fertility out. Why I read the instruction leaflet every time, I don't know; I must be word-perfect by now.

When I return to the bedroom, Toby opens an eye. 'Please tell me we have some paracetamol.'

'That bad?'

'Yup.'

I perch on the mattress. 'Where were you all night?'

'The pub until closing. Then I stopped off to meet Ossie and had a couple of brandies there.'

'Brandy makes you ill.'

'I know.'

He still drank it, though ... I replace the tad of negativity with a smile, briefly close my eyes and visualise my baby in a cot beneath the back bedroom window.

I peck Toby's lips. 'So two things, then I'll get you some water and pills.'

'OK ...'

'Firstly, we're going to have a soirée this evening.'

'A soirée?'

'Drinks and nibbles with Pippa and Minta and their hubbies. Feel free to invite Jerome and his partner if he has one.'

'Don't think so. Seems to prefer animals.'

'Sadly inviting Ossie might be a step too far.'

'Ha.'

'Both women are pregnant, so it isn't going to be a piss-up, OK?'

'Fine by me.' He covers his eyes. 'I'll be on orange squash for at least a week.'

'Good, because I need you to be on your best performance.'

He smiles faintly. 'I think you can rely on me to win over the neighbours.'

'They aren't the ones you need to charm.' I show him the smiley face on the ovulation tester. 'Peak fertility day! Think you'll be up to it by tonight? Start trying again for a new Bamford-Hogg?'

Rather than the jokey response I expect, he seems to stare right through me. With a spasm of alarm, I steady myself for *something* – his being pissed off with my usual intercourse demands, or it not being the right time to start a family workwise. Or, God forbid, him having another woman stashed away in London.

Thank God he shakes himself back and grins. 'Yup, absolutely. Try and stop me.'

32

I step out of my front door and inhale the fresh April atmosphere.

'Is it me or does the air smell cleaner here?'

Toby laughs. 'It's you.'

'It's always sunny too. Have you noticed that?'

'Can't say that I have.' He gives me a peck. 'I think someone is smitten. So are we on foot or are we driving?'

I look at my hessian bag and consider the question. I had great plans to stroll to Burton Road and support the local greengrocers, butchers and delicatessen. On reflection, I could bump into Mum. As I take a breath to reply, the click clack of high heels on the path makes me turn. A blonde-haired, stylish older woman is striding towards us. Probably in her seventies, but wearing extremely well, she flashes Toby a warm grin.

'Morning! I think today's going to be a glorious day, don't you?'

He looks like a rabbit caught in the headlights. 'Yes, totally.'

Apparently waiting for him to embellish, she continues to gaze at him. She has forceful Felicia vibes, so I take pity on him.

'I'm not sure my husband appreciates the niceties of the weather.'

Her eyes slide to me and, though she continues to smile, there's a frostiness about them. 'Well, do enjoy it.' She slots on a huge pair of sunglasses. 'I fully intend to.'

'I take it you know her,' I say, when she's out of sight.

'"Know" is a strong word. She popped into Jerome's last night. A cousin or something.' His brow creases. 'Anyway, why do you say that?'

'She's clearly *smitten*, as you put it.'

'Really?'

'Yup.' I tap my nose. 'Her pearly beam for you, the withering look for me.' I nudge him and chuckle. 'You're drop-dead gorgeous, so who can blame her.'

'I'll take that.' He dangles the car keys. 'Come on then; we've party food to buy.'

As we motor past the zillion Southern Cemetery headstones either side of Nell Lane, I absorb the beauty of the world. Pink and yellow blossom is bursting from the trees and bedding plants blanket the newer graves. New life is springing from the old! It feels symbolic; tonight we're celebrating just that by having a gathering and possible conception to boot. That sense of hope spreading again, I take in my handsome husband, fully recovered from his hangover if his huge breakfast was anything to go by. I so want him to feel as contented as me.

'You will have that car,' I say with a smile.

He glances at me. 'What car?'

'The Jaguar F-Pace, of course.' He flushes, so I quickly continue. 'Because you'll get that promotion. I'm certain of it.'

'You are?'

'Yup, I'm manifesting you at the wheel right now. You might have to wait a little while, but the *anticipation* will make the pleasure all the more intense.' I raise my eyebrows meaningfully. 'Like our post party date tonight.'

He grins. 'Now you're talking. By the way, we saw Nina in the Met last night.'

'In the pub?' I try not to jolt at the mention of Mum's name. Save to say that she was getting on my nerves, I still haven't explained about the falling out. Quite honestly, I want to move forward, not pick at the whole depressing thing. 'Really? Did you speak to her?'

'No. She was all tarted up and with some muscle-bound bloke, so I thought it best to give them a wide berth.'

'Tarted up? Bloody hell, Toby.'

'Sorry.' He smooths his hair. 'That's what Jerome said.'

'What? That my mother looked like a—'

'No! He suggested "attractive" might be a better choice of word type-of-thing. But in a nice way, you know? Not giving me a flaming lecture for making a quip. In fact I'll nip over to The Lodge and invite him to our soirée when we get back.'

I play with my necklace and inwardly grimace. My flaming mother is so upset by our rift that she's done herself up and gone out on a date. Glad my decision to leave and not look back is the right one, I focus on those positives. Toby's happiness, mine, our future, a baby. 'Your man crush is still going strong then?'

'My man crush?' His cheeks pinking again, he laughs. 'Well, if I was that way inclined, he'd be the first on my hit list.'

'A hit list! Bloody hell, was I on one?'

'Yup.' He stops at the traffic lights and softly kisses my lips. 'And I only go for ten out of tens.'

Though desire shoots in my belly, I find myself picturing the furnished back bedroom. The navy St Ives convertible cot-to-toddler bed I just happened to see on the internet would be a perfect fit. I return my hubby's broad beam. 'Very glad to hear it.'

33

Feeling a little like a seventies housewife, I sashay around my lounge and offer another selection of cold crudités on the rather nice platter I found in a dining room cupboard. Effectively being the waitress tonight is perfect, as I can say a few words to each of our guests rather than get embroiled in a long-winded discussion with someone I've only just met. Mum always fires in with some sardonic political or social commentary, so people know exactly where she stands, but I've learned from experience that it pays to be more circumspect and find out who your audience is first.

Thrilled that everyone is chatting, I glance around. I knew Pippa's husband would be the guy who was pushing little Noah around the quadrangle in a buggy, and it turns out I'd also seen Minta's other half too, as he's the bearded guy who owns the new Jaguar. Toby naturally gravitated towards him, and they've been discussing its performance ever since, so it's a good job Jerome arrived and evened the male numbers. Though in fairness, he's amiably making as much effort to chat to Minta and Pippa as he is to Scott.

I return to the kitchen and top up my own glass. I definitely don't want to get bladdered tonight of all nights, but my hands are trembling and my heart is fluttering, so a little more Dutch courage is in order. I throw back the Prosecco and hiss 'for fuck's sake, Frankie! What's wrong with you?' out loud for good measure. And it's true; I'm not usually nervous in social settings. I guess they've generally been work-based in the past, where I'm either already on good terms with the client or I don't give two hoots whether they warm to me or not. Whereas here I do care very much what people think.

Though my lips twitch at my own ridiculousness, I can't help it. This is my fresh start, my new life, and it feels hugely important to be a fully-fledged and integrated member of the community, someone whom everyone likes. I peer through the door at Toby. His shoulders squared off, hips facing forward and hands down at the sides, he looks supremely confident, even dominant. Bloody hell, are we turning into stay-at-home wife and macho head honcho stereotypes?

Not sure if that's an entirely disagreeable notion, I don oven mitts, pull out a tray of piping hot vol-au-vents and smile at the retro-nod. When I was eyeing up all the goodies behind Barbakan Delicatessen's glass counters, I fretted about what to buy for two pregnant woman and their hubbies, who might not actually be the meat eaters they appear to be. I needn't have worried as Minta appeared with these mid-afternoon.

'Ta da! Abigail's Party or what?' she said, whisking off a tea towel to reveal her offering.

'Well, now that you mention it ... Thanks so much! They look really tasty.'

'A pleasure. And check out the fillings – chicken, creamy mushroom, cranberry and avocado. I would have made my all-time fave of prawns and brie but, hey ho, some things are worth forgoing for now. Right, what else can I do to assist the hostess?'

I could have kissed her; Toby had popped over to Jerome's for 'five minutes' to invite him and hadn't returned, and it was nice to have someone to ... well, calm me, I guess. I expected Toby to come back bleary-eyed but, in fairness, he'd only imbibed coffee.

'Sorry, just chatting and time flew,' he said when he noticed the kitchen clock.

I have no idea what the two men discussed for nearly three hours, though I wouldn't be surprised if a plate of home baking had found its way from The Gatehouse to The Lodge. I want to be miffed about the lure of both muffins and Jerome, but he seems like a genuine, nice guy.

'Anything I can do to help?'

I jolt around to the subject of my thoughts.

'Sorry, I didn't mean to startle you. They smell delicious. Mum will be worried she has competition. You know, with her temptress ways.' He pulls a wry face and pats his flat belly. 'I learned long ago to resist.'

'I can't take the credit for these, I'm afraid. Minta brought them over earlier.' A notion occurs. 'Heck, I never thought. Should I have invited your parents?'

'God, no.' Then lifting his shoulders apologetically, 'Though knowing them, they might be "passing" and duck in to say hello anyway.'

'Good. I hope they do.' I feel myself blushing. 'I really should have asked them. It's just that ...'

'I know. School mistress and master? They have that effect on everyone.' A shadow seems to pass through his navy gaze. 'Even me at the ripe age of thirty-three. Don't worry, they very much like you.'

34

Feeling Toby climb from the bed, I swim to the surface of consciousness.

He kisses my forehead. 'Go back to sleep. I'm on washing-up duties. I'll bring you up a cuppa when I've finished.'

The offer of napping feels too delicious to resist. I'm warm and snug and the fantasy I was having was, quite frankly, erotic. 'OK. Thanks.' As I turn, the sheet feels a little damp beneath me. I lift my chin. 'Toby?'

'Yeah?' he calls from the landing.

My head feels as if it's stuffed with candy floss. It's not painful so much as spongy, insubstantial. 'Last night ... Did we?'

He returns with a grin. 'We sure did.' His smile falls. 'You don't remember?'

Feeling bad about his sweetly crestfallen expression, I try to focus. The memory is alcohol-fudged hazy, but the sense of it tingles my skin. Warm, sensual, arousing, like the dream. 'No, I do. I'm just a bit hung—'

'You insisted!'

'Oh God, did I?'

'Yes, most provocatively and worth the wait that you promised.' Though hurt flashes through his eyes, he strives for humour. 'Don't tell me you can't remember my superlative performance?'

'Actually, I do ...' Recall seeps in. Not the usual quickie after he's had a few drinks. A slower, unhurried affair, bless him. One which brought on a shuddering climax. A little embarrassed, I laugh. 'Yes, now you mention it ...'

'See? I'm not only a pretty face. And I read that the female orgasm can assist conception.'

'Why thank you, kind sir. Very gallant of you!'

'Honestly, the pleasure was all mine. See you in twenty minutes.'

Inhaling the smell of his new aftershave, I snuggle back beneath the covers and contemplate my first Manchester party. It was a small yet perfect affair. Though my recall of the evening is somewhat sketchy towards the end, everyone got on and, more importantly, they laughed, especially at Toby's eloquent stories about the exploits of the Bamford-Hogg clan. In truth, he embellishes them a little each time, but it was so nice to see him take centre stage and bask in an appreciative audience.

I gently rub my tummy. Fingers crossed, it was an all-around successful event. If I hadn't been out like a light, I would have stealthily lifted my pelvis and given the sperm a better chance to find its soulmate. Yet maybe I was right about passion and pleasure rather than the mechanics of conception. They say to go with the moment, which, aided and abetted by too much Prosecco, I clearly did!

When sleep doesn't come, I climb into my dressing gown and amble down the stairs. Toby's crouched in front of the dishwasher. 'Perfect timing,' he says over his shoulder. 'Loaded with OCD precision, but I can't work out how to programme the bloody thing.'

'You should have stayed for Fabian's tutorial instead of seeking out cake.' I rotate and peer at the muffins I must have subliminally seen on the counter. 'Talking of which, have I missed Ursula this morning?'

'No, she "dropped in" with Fabian last night.'

I groan. 'Oh God, did they?'

He guffaws. 'How much did you drink?'

'Haha. I'll let you have the higher moral ground just this once. Actually, I do remember hearing their voices.' I picture Jerome's wry smile and his 'school mistress and master' comment. 'Perhaps I was hiding in the kitchen. Please tell me I wasn't blind drunk and embarrassing myself.'

'Not at all. You were merry and having a dance with Minta, but that's all.'

I cover my face. 'I'd be mortified if I made a fool of myself.'

'Frankie.' He stands and gathers me in his arms. 'You didn't. Not one bit.' He pulls away and peers at me. 'Hey, what's up?'

I sniff away the threatening tears and think about it. Apart from the falling out with my mum, everything is pretty damned good. 'Nothing.'

'Precisely! Nothing.' He gives me a soft kiss. 'I just know it, Frankie. We deserve some luck, and I feel it in my bones that everything will go our way. In the meantime, we're off for a walk.'

'As in you and me?'

'Yup.'

'Tobias Bamford-Hogg is going for a walk? Anywhere in particular?'

'No idea. Apparently, it's a thing around here. Attendance isn't compulsory, but whoever happens to be free at eleven o'clock on a Sunday goes for a child-friendly stroll somewhere up the road. Are you up for it? You know, with you being the hangover culprit today ...'

'Cheeky.' I shake my head to test it. 'All clear, so I am.'

'Then you'd better tell me how to work this damned thing, then get dressed. I don't think a sultry robe is allowed.'

35

'Ready to go?'

I look up from my book to my husband. His fair hair is back to the usual groomed quiff and his leather jacket is draped over one arm, his overnight bag in the other.

'What's the time?' I glance at my watch. 'Your train isn't until six. We'll be too early.'

He kisses my forehead. 'Better three hours too soon than a minute too late.'

I chuckle. 'Who is this transformed man who's quoting Shakespeare?'

'The Merry Wives of Windsor, as I recall.'

'Wow.'

'Shows I can still surprise you.' He tugs me upright. 'I like to keep you on your ...' He reaches for my loafers and sweetly slips them over my socks. '... feet.'

'Now I'm ready for the ball, let's make tracks.' I scoop up my mobile. 'Do you think I'll need a—'

'Coat?' He opens the front door and peers out. 'Nope. The sun shines on the righteous, remember.'

I follow him out and take his proffered palm. 'Ha. Who said that then?'

'Matthew. As in the Bible. Though that isn't a direct quote.'

'Impressive again.'

We stroll towards the car park. 'The benefits – or perhaps the drawbacks – of a private school education.'

'Ah.' I climb into the car and study his handsome profile. He's being charming and funny, yet I sense a sadness behind his chirpiness. After such a brilliant few days, I feel it too. Perhaps our mutual soulfulness is a good thing; it shows we still care; it demonstrates that a part-time marriage can work. And maybe, over the next few weekends, he'll come around to the idea of transferring to the Manchester office. He's made friends here now and, though I wouldn't dream of saying it, a big fish in a smaller pond might work better for his promotion prospects.

'Shall I take the scenic route seeing as we've got plenty of time?' I ask, as the gates shudder behind us.

'Go for it,' he says. He waves as we pass the tall privet at the back of our house. 'Bye, number three.'

'You mean "Au Revoir, But Not Goodbye". Who said or sang that?'

He cocks an eyebrow. 'As erudite as I am ...'

As we wait for a gap between cyclists on Burton Road, I point out a police placard. 'God, it looks as though there was an accident here on Friday night. At midnight, it says. I wonder what happened.'

Toby squints at the writing. '"Can you help" and a phone number. That sounds like the culprits scarpered.'

My stomach lunges. I haven't thought about the burglary for days. 'A stabbing or mugging, do you think?'

'Nah. That's a road traffic sign. Someone crossing the street and getting clipped is my guess. Let's hope the poor sod wasn't too badly injured. Just grazes rather than broken bones.'

A shiver runs down my spine. 'Or a fatality. It doesn't bear thinking about.' I reach for his hand. When Toby starts drinking, he has a tendency not to stop. 'Maybe it was someone the worse for wear at that time of night. Promise me you'll always take care?'

He reacts with a squeeze. 'Listen, after my virtually-no-booze Saturday, I'm a transformed person.'

I laugh. 'I'll believe that when I next see it ...'

We arrive at Stockport station with twenty minutes to spare. 'I told you we'd be too early!'

He pecks my lips. 'Gives us time to chat. You know, to each other rather than the polite parley with our fellow inmates around that huge lake.'

'Inmates, eh?'

'Yup, Fabian gave me the lowdown about the workhouse days. Complete with maps, photos and memorabilia.'

'At The Gatehouse?'

'Yes.'

Mum's comment about the front room being like a museum flashes in. I bat it away and change the subject. 'The walk was OK, though, wasn't it?'

The Sunday outing turned out to be at Chorlton Water Park. Though not that far away, the families with children went by car, which was everyone bar us. It was nice to saunter along the riverbank, linking arms and taking in the rays. Then when we arrived, we completed the 'royal flush', as Toby put it, by meeting the final couple on our row.

'Yeah, it was.' He guffaws. 'Those mating ducks, however ...'

'I know. The kids all pointing and the parents tugging them away.'

'"If they're only playing, why can't I watch, Mummy?"'

I chuckle. 'When the time comes, I'll leave that explanation to Daddy.'

He frowns and I know he's thinking about his own father's gruff explanation about 'a man's needs' when he dumped Felicia for a new model.

'So how are the old legs doing after the unexpected exertion?' I ask.

'The old legs?' Toby stretches them. 'Glad they'll be resting behind a desk all week.'

'Come on, I know you enjoyed it really. Though even I admit hanging around the playground for an hour was a little too long.'

'Thank God there was an ice cream van is all I'm saying.'

I nudge him playfully. 'You were just sulking because your bestie wasn't there.'

'True.' Then, with a thoughtful frown, 'But he's nice, the sort of bloke you could call if you had an emergency, don't you think?'

'I guess so ...' I sit back. There's something about the way he said it. 'Are you OK?'

'Yeah. No. Oh, I don't know. It's just the thought of you being there with friendly people and me alone in a London flat.' He shrugs and smiles sadly. 'I guess I'm missing you already.'

I consider pushing my transfer-to-the-Manchester-office case. I sense he's getting there all by himself, so instead I give him a soft kiss to remember me by. 'Love you.'

'Do you?'

'Yes, of course!'

He wraps me tightly in his arms. 'Christ, Frankie, I love you so much too.'

36

On Monday evening I unzip the suitcase of my belongings Toby lugged back from London and spend several enjoyable hours removing Julia's cushions, throws and generic wall art, stashing them in a cupboard and replacing them with my own. My quirky stuff doesn't match her conservative tastes, but they add a splash of colour, and curling beneath my own throw or sipping from my favourite mug makes it feel even more like home. On Tuesday I move onto my novels and other nick-nacks and, by the time I leave for Lincoln on Wednesday morning, my moving in feels complete.

When I return to Pavilion Gardens on Thursday, I still have a spring in my step. Toby and I have spent half an hour chatting on FaceTime before bed each night and I feel in my bones we're on track. He'll be up for the weekend tomorrow and I've already sketched out an agenda of activities I know he'll enjoy, a final push to get him over the winning line. The only dent in my happiness is a phone call I received from a partner at work; he'd received such brilliant feedback from my last project that it was time for me to consider my 'next steps'. I have undoubted leadership qualities, he said, if I were to apply for the role of director, he'd be right behind me.

Shelving that thorny conundrum for now, I amble up the path and delve into my handbag for keys. I open up with a smile, but the moment I step into the lounge, my senses lurch to attention like a slap. Goosebumps pricking my skin, I slowly glance around. Have my deep-red and forest-green cushions been moved? God, I don't know; I *scattered* them as per their description. And what about the order of my books? Did I subconsciously file the A to D alphabetically? Yeah, maybe. I sniff the air. Is there really a faint smell of scent?

Felicia's 'touch test' flashes in behind my eyes. I blink it away. The burglary and my miscarriage are in the past. I won't let the trauma infect my new life. I clock Julia's plug-in air freshener and snort at my silly moment of panic. Yup, Francesca Whittle needs to get a grip. Still, it'd be nice to see Toby's reassuring smile.

I make a hot drink, settle down on the sofa and FaceTime him.

'Hey,' I say when he answers. I squint at the backdrop. 'Is that the Cock Tavern?'

'Yeah. Thought I'd stop for a snifter.'

His eyes are bleary. My guess is a couple of large whiskeys even though it's only seven. 'On your own?'

'Yup. I'm just finishing up, then I'll grab a takeout.'

His demeanour seems weary, jaded. 'Are you OK?'

'I was going to call you later.'

'Why? What's going on?'

He sighs. 'Got my new placement, starting on Monday.'

'Oh right. They told you today?'

His gaze slides away. 'Couple of days ago, actually.'

A couple of days ago? A bad feeling lodges in my chest like a stone. 'Why didn't you tell me?'

'I've been trying to get out of it.'

'But you haven't.'

'Yeah.'

'OK, so what is it?'

'It's no biggie ...'

'Then tell me!'

'It's actually a secondment.' He smooths back his hair. 'I pretty much have no choice if I want to make director the next time around.'

'A secondment? For how long?'

'A month, but it could be longer. The bloke I'm replacing has had an operation or something.'

My shoulders relax. 'That's manageable. So what's the

problem?'

'I'm flying out tomorrow.'

So much for my weekend plans. 'So abroad, then? Lucky for some.'

'Thing is, it's too far away to come back to the UK until the end.'

I'd imagined somewhere in Europe. My stomach turns. 'Where is it, Toby?'

'Of all bloody places ...' He pulls a rueful face. 'It's Hong Kong.'

37

Including the overnight stay in Lincoln each Wednesday, the next few weeks pass in a hectic blur of work, catching up with pals on the phone or by FaceTime to let them know my change of address, and hanging out with Pippa and Minta. By the time May Day comes around, I'm badly feeling the loss of my hubby. Mum too, though I'm trying very hard not to think about that. I'm her only child and she hasn't even managed a simple 'how are you settling in?' text. I understand I forcefully – and perhaps unkindly – told her not to get in touch and that this is, in all likelihood, another stubborn standoff by us both, but *I* didn't do anything that warrants an apology. Several times before sleep I've drafted messages which have ranged from conciliatory to jokey, to outright bloody angry. I've had the good sense not to actually send them, and at least they've been a therapy of sorts. That and talking to Minta, who's here now, peachy, pretty and sipping juice at the kitchen table. She's an impressively attentive listener, quite opinionated too.

'I appreciate I wasn't there, but at the end of the day, she's the parent and you are the child. The approach should come from her. I can't believe she kept the truth from you for so many years. I'd be fuming. It makes you question if she ever would have said anything. You know, had it not been for the letter from Uncle Billy. Do you think you'll get in touch with him again? Or track down Kim?'

'I honestly don't know. Despite everything, I feel I should discuss it with Mum first.'

'I sort of get that but ...' Minta pulls her duck face. 'I'm sorry, what she did is really not on.' She rubs her growing belly. 'It's our duty to do what's best for the child, even if it's hard, you know? Sacrifice is one of the ... well, one of the conditions of parenthood, if you like.'

I feel my heart sink. It isn't really what I want to hear. Without Toby around, there's no one to give me a proper, solid hug. Mum is great at them. My gran too. Which is another reason to be irate. The two women come as a team; there's no way Sylvia wouldn't have known the truth about Greg's other child. My grandad and his bumbling ways, maybe not, but definitely Gran. She hasn't been in touch either, so that says it all. I've effectively lost her too.

'What's Toby's take?' Minta asks, interrupting my thoughts.

'Sorry?'

'What's his take on the mum-sister thing?'

I pause at that. I never got around to telling him and, though we have brief chats by FaceTime most evenings, it doesn't feel appropriate to raise my problems when he's looking hassled and bedraggled in Hong Kong. I've tried to be upbeat by saying this quasi-director role is a huge vote of confidence, that Hong Kong is one of *the* places in the world to visit, that most people would give their right arm for an opportunity to work there, me included.

His initial response was, 'Yeah, you're right, you really are. I should look at this as a stepping stone to the dream job.' But his positivity has waned, especially as the initial month has been extended to two. I chivvy him when we speak, teasing him about the reams of clothes he'll have bought from the 'paradise for shopaholics' and encouraging him to visit Disneyland, Ocean Park, Victoria Peak, Tian Tan Buddha and so on. He simply complains: there are no other Brits around his age; a luxurious hotel is fun to start with, but it soon gets repetitive with the same old surroundings, same old food, same old films. He's even bored of the porn channel now. Sure, he's done all the tours and taken a million photographs yet, at the end of the day, London is the only city worth its salt in the long-term.

I had to fix a smile at that particular comment; I'd hoped – even thought – his weekend here had converted him, or at least shown him that a transfer to Manchester had its compensations in terms of friendships and community. And bringing up a child.

I stop myself at that notion. When Toby left for Hong Kong, I shelved all hopes of pregnancy for now. It's still a touch disheartening that he hasn't even alluded to our 'conception' night, though. Sure an outright 'have you had your period?' might be too much, but maybe something about his 'superlative performance' as a nod to it would be nice.

The sound of the letterbox snaps me back to the present and saves me from having to address Minta's question.

'I wonder if it'll be anything other than flaming ...' I begin automatically. I quickly change tack. I know how wearing negativity can be from my conversations with Toby and I don't want to inflict that on a friend. I smile. 'However ... I'm manifesting a voucher from Bents for a free cream cake and coffee.'

'Ooh, I'm in if there is one.'

I return with the post. 'OK, ready for the big revelation?' I flick through it and stop at a white sleeve, clearly containing a greetings missive of some sort. I raise my eyebrows. 'A German stamp and addressed to Julia ...' I motion to the pile of other mail for 'Mrs Logan' on the hall table. 'They look like junk but this is handwritten. A condolence card, do you think?'

Minta's eyes widen. 'Gosh, that's a leap. I'd have gone for birthday, anniversary, even happy divorce day, which I'd say is the most probable in Julia's case ...'

I'm surprised at my blurted assumption too. But that damned bouquet of lilies still bugs me. 'Do you think so?'

'That's my guess. She kept herself to herself as far as the mums were concerned. Yet when it came to the little ones, she was all smiles. Pippa once said the intense way she looked at baby Noah freaked her out.' She finishes her drink. 'I'm popping to the shops for some fruit. I can drop off the envelope at The Gatehouse as I pass, if you like. Fabian'll know where to redirect it.'

'Yeah, good idea. Thanks.'

She peers at me and chuckles. 'Honestly, Frankie! I can see the cogs of your mind whirring. You've missed your vocation; you should have been an author of mysteries.'

'Haha. It's never too late! The brother died, didn't he?'

'Julia had a brother?'

'No! Not that I know of, anyway.' Why I'm making these connections, I have no idea. 'I meant Jerome's brother. Stefan, I think he was called.'

'Ah, I see what you mean. I sort of forget Jerome is Fabian and Ursula's son too.'

'Why?'

She shrugs. 'Chalk and cheese, I'd say. Jerome's a newbie like you and Toby, so you probably know more about him than I do.' There's a mischievous glint in her eyes. 'Maybe we should persuade him to join us on our walk this Sunday. If you find out anything scandalous, be sure to share.'

38

I open my eyes to a new morning and yawn. I no longer flip my head to the other pillow before remembering my husband is four thousand miles away on another continent. And, in truth, it's actually nice to have a whole bed to myself in this surprising May heat; I can roll over or stretch out my legs to find a cool spot and not be woken by Toby's usual early-hours pee.

That notion breaks a dream, or is it a memory? I sit up and look at the curtains. Yes, there were sounds in the night; nothing that would be worthy of comment at my old flat, but noticeable here because of the usual dense quietness. Low voices and the thud of a door. I strained to listen for more then, propelled by sheer nosiness, I actually got up and peered through the window. The quadrangle, the lawn, the yew hedging and the shadowy trees were starkly silent and still. The only remarkable thing was a light in the upstairs of the chapel before it was extinguished by blackout blinds. Someone must live in the penthouse flat after all; or perhaps a new resident has moved in.

I chuckle at my choice of the word 'remarkable'. Footsteps and illumination are hardly that, so perhaps I am becoming institutionalised, all agog with intrigue over nothing, like a pensioner looking for adventure in a retirement home.

However ... I fall back against the mattress and frown thoughtfully. My inquisitiveness last night was unbridled, instinctive. It made me jump from the bed to investigate the noises without a second's thought. Not so long ago I'd have frozen, consumed with fear and unable to do anything other than listen to the rapid thud of my heart, which means the old Frankie is making a comeback. The scars of my trauma are healing; perhaps they have even healed. And I have Pavilion Gardens to thank for that.

I focus on today. It's Sunday, which means ... My lips twitch again. A walk to the water park with the rest of my OAP cohorts. There's nothing wrong with that, though. It's exercise, fresh air and chatter with people I can firmly now call my friends. And my solo trek there along the riverside will be an opportunity to clear my mind and contemplate whether to break the ice by popping round to Gran's or even visiting my mum.

Glad of the plan to shape my day, I fling back the duvet and pad to the bathroom. How I get through so much toilet paper, I have no idea. I crouch down to the cupboard beneath the sink to pull out a new roll, then rock back in surprise. The pregnancy testing kit packet I'd hidden at the very back has somehow inched its way to the front. I find myself holding my breath. Oh God, is this a subliminal sign it's time to use it?

No. I blink it away; I'm not ready to think about that.

39

'Hey, Frankie. Hold up.'

Wearing aviator style shades, Jerome slips through the gates an iota of a second before they clang together.

'Oh, hi.'

Hoping the flip of pleasure doesn't show, I take him in. His dark stubble is more beard-like than usual, his hair shorter, more styled.

He drags his fingers through it. 'I know. Dreadful. Too much talk about footie in The Village Barber yesterday. Next thing I knew ... well, this. I've washed it just now but I can still feel some "product" or other he slapped on at the end.'

I can't help laughing at the tufts he's created.

'What?' he asks with half a smile.

'Nothing. It looks nice.' I feel myself flushing. 'How are you? I've not seen you for a while.'

'Yeah, busy. So, Minta collared me earlier about a walk? She said it was optional in a "it's compulsory" type of manner.'

'About sums it up!'

'Is that where you're off to?' He gestures towards the parkway. 'This way, I believe?'

'Yes, though ...' I nod ahead. 'I was planning to take a more circuitous route along the Mersey for a bit of exercise. You know, more a stride than a stroll.'

'Fancy a bit of company for your stride? Only if that's OK. You might want to listen to a podcast or fancy some thinking time on your own.'

'I was, as it happens. I suspect distraction is preferable to navel gazing, though.'

'Distraction? A tall order. Nevertheless, I'll try my best.' His lips twitch. 'So long as it doesn't involve a song and dance routine.'

'What? No *Macarena*?'

'Afraid not. Only on birthdays.' He pulls a worried face. 'Please don't tell me it's your birthday.'

I tap my nose. 'Not today, but offer noted.'

The sun on our shoulders, we make small talk as we wend our way down to Barlow Moor Road, then weave past the huge houses on Darley Avenue.

At the bottom of the slope, he stops at the railings, rakes back his sunglasses and takes in the view of the river below. 'The water's beautiful on a sunny day. I'd forgotten. We used to come down here and muck about. Well, I'd muck about and Stefan would fish because that's the reason we came armed with all the kit and caboodle.' He points in the direction of Northenden. 'Further down there by the bridge, though. Once we'd spotted the grey heron we felt compelled to search it out. Or at least I did. You know, for good luck.'

'The one that hangs around the weir?'

'You know it?' He smiles faintly. 'I might have been known to climb down the bank and paddle alongside it. Mum wasn't impressed when I returned home caked in mud.'

My interest is piqued. 'I assume Stefan was your brother?'

'Yup.' Though he replaces his shades, I catch the grief in his eyes. He motions upstream. 'This way, I'm assuming?'

'Yes.'

We don't speak for a while and I'm on the cusp of apologising for my lack of tact when he turns and chuckles. 'I'm not sure this terrain is striding material.'

So relieved I haven't offended him, I find myself gabbling. 'You're probably right. When I still lived at Mum's, I used to come down here for a run. One time I was impressively gazelle-like until I tripped on a stone, fell somewhat ungainly and cut my head. Only I didn't realise it – or that it had bled – until I got home and looked in the mirror. By then I'd been in and out of every shop on Burton Road. God knows what they thought. It wasn't a pretty sight.'

'That I don't believe.'

'No, really.' I demonstrate with a finger over my cheek bone. 'The blood was all down here.'

'I meant the not looking pretty bit.'

'Ah.' Feeling an inappropriate spurt of delight, I grope for something to say. 'You should have brought Ossie with you today. I'm sure he'd have deftly avoided the pitfalls.'

He shakes his head. 'Poor old Oswald. I must put down at least one animal a week, and though it's the right thing to do every time, it doesn't get any easier.'

'God, I'm so sorry.' I bite my lip at another faux pas. 'I had no idea.'

'It's fine, why would you? His time had come and I guess it makes things ... less challenging.'

'Oh?'

'No more lectures from Mum about following the rules like everyone else.'

'Is that why you're the prodigal son?'

Bloody hell, what's wrong with me today? Thank God he snorts and answers easily. 'You've heard that one? Yeah, figuratively, at least. But it was easy for me to avoid the family legacy as they had Stefan, their son and heir, the poor sod.'

'The family legacy?' It seems a strange thing to say.

'Yeah. Not that I was a complete rebel. I only went as far as Fallowfield and I still studied medicine, albeit veterinary.'

'So ...' I frown. 'So Stefan and your dad are ... or were doctors?'

'Yes, from a long family line of the same.'

I take a breath to shape another question, but he stops and looks up to the sky. 'Stefan ... escaped.' He reverts to me and smiles grimly. 'So now the whole inheritance is mine.'

I itch to ask more about the brothers as we amble. What happened to Stefan; how did he die? Is Jerome really only interested in animals, as Toby put it, or does he have a love interest? A girl or even a guy? He's a good-looking bloke and surely a catch ... I sense I've pushed my curiosity as far as I can and our silence is amiable, so I inhale the balmy air and enjoy watching the families of ducks, the sparkling ripples and the shades-of-green view.

When we reach the park, Jerome stops on the hillock, removes his aviators and takes in the vista. 'Yup, I remember the lake now.' He points to a clump of trees by the water. 'That was the best spot for collecting frogspawn in old pickled onion jars. We'd picnic up there on the grass, then buy an ice cream from the van and spend half an hour on the slide and the swings.' He ruffles his hair. 'We had fun. Play-fighting, chatting; laughing raucously over nothing as you do when you're a kid.'

'That sounds so nice.'

'Yeah, blissful childhood.'

He seems so nostalgic and sorrowful, it's all I can do not to reach out my arms and give him a hug.

He turns back to me. 'You didn't – or don't – have any siblings?'

'No. Well, not really.' I pull a rueful face. 'It's a long story.'

He lifts his dark eyebrows. 'Seeing as we're oversharing today, maybe it's an item to discuss on our return journey.'

Realising that I might well do that, I gaze at him for a second or two. Perhaps it's because he's used to dealing with sick animals; there's a reflective calmness or a kindness about him. As well as his gently sardonic humour. No wonder Toby likes him. I'd love to study him properly and work out all the layers. That would definitely be odd, so I tear my eyes away. 'You might regret that offer.'

'Not at all. I'll look forward to it.'

'OK, then it's a date.'

Cringing at my own choice of words again, I try to think of a way to downplay it. I'm saved by the sound of Minta's voice. 'Frankie! We're over here.'

I spin around to search her out, finally spotting her waving from the huddle of children throwing bread to the swans.

'OK, coming!' I call back.

When I rotate to my walking companion, he's gone.

40

Chatting to a different family each loop, I saunter along the dusty path which circles the mere and try to convince myself I'm not looking out for Jerome. By the time the kids have run out of energy and finished their iced lolly treats, I've reconciled myself to the fact that he's scarpered. So much for me coughing up my guts about my situation to the flaming kind and thoughtful man!

Berating myself for my disappointment, I say goodbye to Minta. 'Right, I'm getting off. I'll see you back ...'

Sensing someone watching me, I glance over my shoulder. Frustratingly, it isn't Jerome but a distinguished, silver-haired man in conversation with the couple who live opposite me. Apparently unconcerned he's been caught staring at me, he smiles broadly, regally nods his head, then returns to his group.

He looks so very familiar, yet I struggle to place him. 'Who's that?' I ask Minta.

Her face fills with delight. 'Oh wow! I haven't actually met him in person. He's really lovely online and speaks so passionately. You know, on the website.'

'On a website?'

'Yes, he founded the ...' She taps her forehead. 'My woolly mind! The Cognati children's charity. What's it called?'

Knowing exactly what she means, I inwardly roll my eyes at the fizzle of recognition which fired through me. Though he looks a little older, he's not some old matinee film star, but the guy surrounded by the toothpaste kids on the Latin-'C'-meaning-a-hundred pamphlet. Clever, really. 'The Hundred Club?'

'That's it!' Her smile fading, she bites her lip and looks down to her rounded tummy. 'It's an amazing cause, and those kids couldn't ask for better care, yet it's definitely a worry, don't you think? You know, having a child with a congenital disability?'

Her sudden loss of positivity surprises me. I inhale to say that it's hopefully unlikely when she swivels away and gestures to her car. 'You're welcome to travel home with us.'

The sight of her gleaming Jag brings on a wave of sadness at Toby's absence. 'No, it's fine, thanks. Exercise and all that.'

'Then I'll walk with you.'

'Are you sure? I wouldn't want—'

'You won't!' She slips her arm into mine. 'None of the miscarriages were caused by anything physical. We only drove to help out with Noah and, as you can see, Dominic is on the job.' Her eyes crinkle. 'In fact, a bit of practice with a toddler without me interfering can only be a good thing.'

'Oh right, so ...' I watch Dominic belt the little boy into his car seat. Finally I twig why. 'Pippa and Scott have gone to the hospital?'

'Basically, yes!'

'Oh, my God. That's awesome. Presumably her water's broke or she started contractions?'

'She's gone in to be ... well, induced, I guess.' Minta beams. 'So the new baby should be with us soon.'

'That's so exciting!' Though I'm delighted for Pippa, I shiver. Mum feigned not remembering my birth, but Felicia didn't hold back her horribly graphic accounts of Toby's. 'A bit scary too, if I'm honest.'

'How so?'

'Well, the prize at the end is worth it, obviously, but there's a long way to go until then.' I pull an awkward face. 'You know, the agony of going through labour for hours if not days, let alone pushing a seven-pound human being out. Then stitches and so on ...'

'Ah, I get you.'

'Though Pippa's done it before, so I guess she knows what to expect.' I laugh unsteadily. 'Is that a good or a bad thing? Whereas you and me – well, is ignorance bliss?'

'They say that women wouldn't have another if they remembered the unpleasant parts. And anyway, I'm all for manifesting the perfect newborn in my arms and blocking out the rest.' She propels me away. 'And going for whatever drugs are on offer!'

Her calmness makes me feel like a drama queen. Still, it isn't something I need to worry about. It probably won't be for a long, long time. 'Good plan.'

'How about you?' She gives me a sidelong glance. 'Any news your end?'

Her look is so peculiar that a notion hits. Pregnancy testing kits can't move by themselves. Did Minta have a nosey in the packet to see if either strip had been used? I shake the idea away. She wouldn't be asking if she had. More likely it got dislodged when one of us was replacing a toilet roll.

'Nothing to report,' I reply. 'When there is, you'll be the first person to know.'

'Wonderful.' She chuckles. 'It might be an idea to tell the daddy first, so I'll very happily be the second.'

As if in reply, my mobile beeps in my pocket. Fully expecting it to be Toby from some kind of telepathy, I pull it out and peer at the screen. The message is from Jerome:

Sorry for deserting you earlier. An emergency came up. Another time?

41

After three full-on days in the clients' stylish offices and two evenings in a diametrically opposite hotel in Lincoln, I pull up at the gates and wearily climb from my VW to input the code late on Wednesday. Reminding myself to ask Fabian for the replacement remote fob, I park in my space and peer at the dark windows of Pippa's house. Surely she's given birth by now? Minta promised to keep me posted and nothing has come through ...

My stomach clenches with concern for my friend. I'm totally demoralised about my own situation, but the thought of carrying a baby through to full term and then to lose it is simply unbearable.

I rest my forehead on the steering wheel and give a silent scream. Quite frankly, I'd like to pummel it with my fists. After sitting in a meeting and being virtually shouted at by some middle-aged, overweight and sexist mansplainer for something *I* hadn't done, I felt a horrible dripping sensation in my undies this morning. I wanted to rush out to the ladies' to check whether it was blood, but I wasn't going to give him, or my male colleagues who were letting me take the flack, the satisfaction of seeing my distress. So I lifted my chin and got on with defending my team, all the more effectively because I couldn't give a shit if I got sacked on the spot: albeit subliminally, I'd let sodding hope in; I wasn't pregnant after all, and with my husband holed up in Hong Kong, I wouldn't be any time soon.

A tap on the windscreen brings me back to the present. Blushing at my clearly odd behaviour, I cautiously look up. It's Jerome rather than either of his parents, thank God, yet it's still not great to get caught.

I open the door and decide just to say it. 'Sorry, I was having a moment.'

He rubs his bristly chin. 'No pets soiling communal parts, no rogue plants in your front garden, no painting your door pink ... I can't recall "having a moment" being prohibited under the lease, though. So there's no need to be sorry.'

'Well, that's a relief. In fact it's the highlight of a pretty crap day.'

'Want to talk about it? I was off for last orders when I saw you drive in. You're very welcome to join me.'

I'd like to drink the pub – any pub – dry, but I'm knackered. I haven't got the energy to traipse there, let alone make myself look half human. And, of course, there's the small matter of getting in the shower and spraying my 'baby' away. In fact, a long soak in the bath is the thing.

'Thanks, but ...' I pause. Jerome's gentle humour has already made me feel a tad lighter, so maybe company would be better than my own miserable thoughts. 'The terms of the lease ... Is inviting a neighbour in for a snifter past ten o'clock allowed?' I ask.

He theatrically sucks in air and squints at his watch. 'Probably not, but it's three minutes-to, so if you're willing to take the risk, so am I.'

'I'm in a rebellious mood. Follow me.'

Feeling observed from somewhere, I open my front door. When I turn to look, the only eyes on me are Jerome's, and as ever they're reflective, intuitive somehow.

'I need to nip upstairs,' I say. 'I'll be two minutes. Make yourself at home.'

'Will do.'

All fingers and thumbs, I hurriedly have a personal wash at the sink and try to avoid my flushed and guilty reflection. My lips twitch despite myself. It's truly ridiculous, but Jerome being here does feel illicit, a breach of *something*, if not the lease.

I brave my scrutiny to the mirror and speak to myself. 'It's hormones, that's all. That is all!'

The spread of pleasure at his being here is still really bad, though. I'm a married woman and he's Toby's friend, for heaven's sake! I steady myself with a few deep breaths. It's fine. After six weeks home alone, I'm allowed a neighbourly interlude and it's a welcome distraction from yet another baby disappointment.

Apparently far away in thought, Jerome's at the table and gazing through the window when I arrive in the kitchen. It gives me a couple of seconds to study his profile, those sculpted cheekbones made even more defined by his dark stubble. Why was he the prodigal son? Did he do something dreadful? I honestly can't buy that, so maybe it's as simple as him being gay.

'Oh, hi,' he says when he registers my presence. 'Everything OK?'

Sure his intent, dark-blue gaze can read my very soul, I turn away. 'Yup, fine. A drink, let me sort out that drink.'

Glad the blast of cold air will cool my burning cheeks, I open the fridge. Reality smacks me instead as I stare at the meagre contents: there are only a few bits and bobs of food for one solitary person, and they're pregnancy-friendly products at that. There's no booze for the very same reason. There isn't even a beer because my flaming husband is absent. What the hell was I thinking by inviting Jerome in?

I move to a cupboard and hunt through the hamper I was gifted by an appreciative client. I find a bottle at the bottom and drag it out. For fuck's sake, it's white.

Taking a steadying gulp of air, I rotate and present it like a sommelier. 'A nice Chablis, sir? It hasn't been chilled, I'm afraid. Can I tempt you to a tipple nonetheless?'

'Sure. Though tea or coffee will be fine too.'

'Let's do vino.' I place two glasses on the worktop. 'Warm wine is not ideal but, quite frankly, I need the hit. And we can add an ice cube, if that isn't too uncouth.' My fingers trembling, I snap the lid open and make to pour.

Jerome takes it from me. 'Hey, what's wrong?'

I can't look at him – or even speak – so it's a relief when he

144

wraps me in his arms and simply holds me. As I breathe in his appealing smell and the seconds pass, I'm aware of something happening to us both – an undeniable feeling of attraction, a stirring, a heat – and I know that if we kiss, it won't stop there. Isn't that precisely what I want, what I've secretly craved since first seeing him outside the gates? He only glanced at me that day, yet our eyes caught and I felt it. Just like I can feel his erection pressed against me right now.

'Come on, let's sit.' He gently releases me and tugs me to a seat. 'Talk to me. Something's happened. What is it?'

Though I'm mortified for misinterpreting his embrace, the words still rush out along with my tears. 'Apart from falling out with my mother, being abandoned by my husband, working with a load of cowardly men?'

He smiles a wonky smile. 'There's more?'

'I thought I might be pregnant,' I blurt. 'Or ridiculous hope told me I was. I wasn't. Or if I was, I'm not now.'

'I'm sorry to hear that.'

'Yeah, I got my period today, well over a month late.' He nods, his expression is so kind that I continue to ramble like a patient in the psychiatrist's chair. 'Or at least I bled. Spotting, I suppose, when I finally escaped the meeting, got to the ladies' and looked, you know, in my ... my underwear.' I groan. 'I'm so sorry; this is too much information. I have no idea why I'm telling you this.'

'It's fine.' He spreads his hands. 'Look, I've never had kids and I am but a lowly vet. However, as I understand it, light bleeding isn't uncommon in pregnancy.'

It's my turn to nod; from the reams of books and pamphlets I've read, I know this.

'And, call me a pragmatic old fool, but isn't it usual to take a test rather than rely on—'

'Hope.' And Minta's 'manifesting', but that would sound weird.

'I was going to say guesswork, but yes, maybe something more technical might be in order, so you know either way?'

Tears drip from my nose and I feel such a fool. I don't want him to think this is the usual me. Or at least the Frankie before the burglary and miscarriage. 'I lost a baby at ten weeks in February,' I say quietly. 'I didn't for a moment see it coming, so it's hard not to catastrophise.' I wipe my face and smile thinly. 'And I'm honestly dog tired. I could fall asleep in a basket.'

He returns the smile. 'Anything canine related can't be all bad.'

'Even though I resemble a knackered bulldog?'

'Maybe a touch weary. Still very pretty.' He stands. 'So my veterinary prescription is a good night's sleep and maybe a pregnancy test tomorrow.' His countenance cloudy, he pauses. 'I'm so sorry about your loss. It must have been dreadful.' He pecks the top of my head. 'I guess an early scan might be an option. You know, to give you an extra layer of reassurance.'

42

After a solid eight hours of rest, my analytical mind kicks in the moment I wake. My longing, my denial, my heightened sense of smell and emotion; my sheer tiredness, the blood in my undies ... How heavy was it? Spotting or a flood? Oh God, I no longer know. I do feel a little nauseous, even so. Is it really possible I could be pregnant?

I picture Jerome, his chivvying sweetness. He's right; I need to do a test. Guesswork – or hope, or manifesting – doesn't swing it, even if my breasts did feel tender as they pressed against his chest. With a nod of resolve, I make my way to the bathroom, pull out a strip from the packet and sit on the loo seat. My heart painfully thuds; I'm honestly so terrified I feel faint. The last time I did this, Toby was by my side. The concern etched on his face turned to pensive, soon followed by delight as the pink lines appeared. Why the hell isn't he here now to give me that same love and support? I know it's not his fault, yet I can't help feeling horribly let down by him, by circumstance, by my missing bloody mother.

Deeply sucking in some air, I search out the old resolute and fearless Frankie. I gasp out a sob. I can't find her. She's been replaced by this blubbering being who feels so abandoned, unloved and uncertain. I can't bring myself to pee on the stick; I can't bear the thought of it being negative. And suppose it is a yes but turns out to be wrong? False positives can happen where there's a loss soon after the fertilised egg attaches to the uterine lining. That could explain the spotting ...

I put a hand to my breasts and gently press. Yes, they are fuller and a little sore and, now I think about it, my tastebuds have been off for a couple of days. Which surely means ...

Oh, God, what to do? For the first time in my life I need someone to tell me. I pause at that thought. They have, actually. Jerome's 'extra layer of reassurance' is the thing. A scan would give me a definitive answer. I'd know either way; I can cope better with that.

Pleased to have a plan, I blow my nose, wipe my cheeks and search out my laptop. A private ultrasound won't be covered by insurance this time, but money hardly matters when I'm feeling this anxious. I'll pay whatever it takes for certainty and speed.

An internet search shows that several places do diagnostic services without a GP referral. A recommendation feels better, so I shake myself down and call Doctor Gauss' secretary. Her tone as chirpy as usual, she suggests the Spire Hospital again, and despite feeling a little winded at the thought of my last experience there, I call up and make an appointment for Saturday.

Though I notice a whole pile of new messages in my office inbox already, I snap close the lid. I'm going to take my working day easy. The stress I felt yesterday isn't worth it.

Glad the old Frankie is still around somewhere, I fill the bath, add bubbles and soak for a good half hour. Feeling a whole lot more positive, I dress, trot downstairs and unlatch a kitchen window. Not fancying tea or coffee, I help myself to apple juice, pour myself a bowl of muesli and pull out an old *Journalist* magazine I found in a drawer. It falls open at the obituary page, so I take that as I sign that work might be preferable after all. I'm about to log on when conversation echoes though the open pane. The voices are male and female, which surely means Pippa is back with her baby. I dash up to the box room and peer out of the glass. There's Scott, thank the Lord, strolling around his garden with a tiny newborn in his arms.

Buoyed even further, I join a Teams meeting.

'You look happy considering yesterday's bollocking,' a colleague says when we've finally finished.

'Yeah, no thanks to you. You could have come to my rescue.'

'I didn't need to. You were on impressive form.'

'Hmm. Weak excuse.'

He lifts his butty. 'Chicken and cranberry sauce on sourdough, here I come. What are you having for lunch?'

I'm actually bloody starving. 'That sounds delicious. Right, I'm off to the deli to buy the ingredients. If anyone wants me, I'm sure you'll manage to fill the breach.'

Once I've laced up my trainers and grabbed my shopper, I step outside and inhale the fragrant spring air. I move away, then turn back and eye up number one. No doubt poor Pippa will be exhausted, even asleep, but I'd love to offer help if I can. I gently lift the knocker and tap. To my surprise, the door's opened by the new mummy herself.

'Oh, hi, Pippa!' Then quickly, 'Don't worry, I'm not stopping. I'm on my way to the shops, so I thought I'd ask if there's anything you need whilst I'm there?'

'How kind.' Though the sun's beaming in, she pulls a cardigan from the stair rail and slips it on. 'Scott and Lucy are outside. Would you like to say hello?'

'Lucy? How lovely! I'd love a quick peep at her, if that's OK.'

'Of course. Come in.'

'I'm so pleased for you both.' I offer my arms. 'A quick hug for Mummy first?'

'Absolutely!'

'So, a little girl! One of each now; how wonderful.'

By the time we reach the kitchen, Scott has come inside. He hands Lucy over to his wife and pecks her forehead. 'Isn't my wife a clever girl?'

'She sure is.' My nose burning with emotion, I study the sleeping baby. The sheer miracle of new life; could I really have been blessed? 'She's simply perfect and what a cute hat. When did she decide to make her grand entrance?'

'Late last night.'

'Gosh, you're back home so soon.' I take in Pippa's rosy cheeks and her neatly-styled hair. 'You look amazing. I'm guessing everything went smoothly? Not too traumatic?'

She laughs. 'No, not at all. Would you like a cuddle?'

'Thank you, but no. I'd hate to wake her up.'

'I wouldn't worry about that.' She looks at her husband. 'She's just the same as Noah when he was born, isn't she? Another very good, sleepy baby.'

*

When I return from my outing, duly armed with a bouquet of flowers and a congratulations card, I pause at Pippa's door. It feels wrong not to hand them over in person, and yet ... Though I try to shake the image from my mind, I decide to text rather than take her by surprise again. Because, despite her looking as if she'd walked off the page of *Baby and Mum* magazine, Pippa was definitely caught short by my visit earlier.

I let myself into my house and absently scoop up another letter for Julia from the mat. Quite honestly, I feel horribly perturbed. Pippa has literally just given birth; she and Scott appear deliriously happy. However ... She soon covered them up with her cardigan, but I caught her injuries, nonetheless.

A profound shiver passes through me. My neighbour and friend has distinct purple-blue bruising on both her slim wrists. What the hell does that mean?

43

When Saturday morning comes around, I distract myself by vacuuming the whole house, cleaning the bathroom and polishing the kitchen granite until it gleams. My mind stays thankfully empty until it's time to leave, when worry thumps so badly in my ribcage, it robs me of breath. The scan appointment is in an hour. I'll be sitting in that same waiting room, lying on that same couch and searching the sonographer's face for the truth again. What if there's no heartbeat like before? Can I bear to go through that agony, this time all alone?

I picture Jerome, his steady kindness, the flash of concern which passed through his eyes when I told him about the miscarriage. Would it be odd to ask him to accompany me? I snort at my own ridiculousness. Well, that's a no-brainer; of course it would. I just have to summon up the brave Frankie and get on with this on my own.

Inhaling a lungful of balmy June air, I lift my chin and weave my way past The Gatehouse to the exit. As I wait for the gates to yawn open, I glance back to the red brick office block where I took my first breath and frown in thought. Not only had my dad died by then, he'd cheated on Mum and sired another child. How must that have felt? My stomach summersaults at the notion. I'm certain Toby wouldn't betray me, however ... How would I cope if I discovered he'd conceived a baby with someone else? Deeply hurt and angry, to say the least.

I finger my necklace and sigh. It doesn't lessen the fact Mum should have been honest from the start. I have no idea if I'll be able to fully forgive – or trust – her again, but I need her right now. God knows if the outcome will be laughter or tears, I need my mother's love, her solidarity, her humour and hugs today.

With a nod of resolve I set off, taking a shortcut through the familiar streets towards my childhood home. Breathing heavily when I arrive, I pause by the front wall and peer at the door plate. Funny how I've never thought of that before – I've swapped houses with the same digit. Lucky number three? Christ, I hope so.

My eyes shift to the front bay. The curtains are drawn, and when I look up to the sash window above, they're closed too. That's strange; it isn't late but Mum has always been an early bird. I shake my disquiet away. Save for those few weeks after the burglary, I haven't lived here properly since I left at eighteen. Maybe her habits have changed; perhaps the new boyfriend has moved in.

A thud of disappointment hits my chest. This is probably a sign I've made the wrong call. And time is ticking for my appointment. I really should turn tail and leave.

I stride up the path, press down the doorbell for several long seconds, then stand back to wait for my mother's shadow through the opaque glass. Nothing and no one stirs. She's clearly out – there's zilch untoward about that – yet I find myself trying again, tapping my foot with agitation as the seconds pass. Praying my key will still be in the side pocket, I dig in my bag and pull it out. Taking a huge gulp of air, I open up. 'Mum?' I call from the hallway. 'Mum? Are you in?'

Even as my words bounce back from the walls, the dankness, lack of warmth and aromas tell me she isn't; that she hasn't been here for days, if not weeks.

*

Panting from the dash and alarm, I trek across the Spire car park, check in at reception, then make my way on jelly legs to the ultrasound department. I've barely sat down in the waiting room when a voice cuts through my agitation.

'Francesca Whittle?'

'Yes, that's me.'

'OK. Come on through, please.'

The plump sonographer is different from the last time and her manner is brisk rather than loaded with pre-judged sympathy, which feels easier to cope with on my own.

'Take a pew,' she says.

I mutely obey.

Pen ready, she turns the first page of her form and efficiently goes through the usual questions from my current address to the date of my last period. I clear the clot of dread in my throat and duly reply.

'I'm assuming you've had a positive pregnancy test?' she finally asks over her glasses.

A ghost of myself, I nod my lie.

'Then we're looking at approximately eight to nine weeks. Any worries?'

It's too overwhelming to go into the miscarriage. Or my sheer terror it will happen again. 'A couple of days ago, I had a light bleed.'

Is that what it really was? Am I completely misinterpreting my tender breasts, my morning nausea and fatigue?

'Spotting?'

'I guess so.'

'That isn't usual in the first trimester, but let's see. Hop up on the bed. Top up and bottoms down.'

When I've done as I'm told, she adjusts the monitor for me to view, then squeezes a blob of gel onto my stomach. 'Is it a little cold?'

Though I'm icy with worry anyway, I nod and drag my eyes to the screen.

She lifts the transducer probe. 'Are you ready?'

44

As if a ten-ton truck has hit me, I tromp, heavy-limbed, past the police station and school. When I reach the top of the road, I finally tune into my surroundings. A car is parked outside the development in a space to one side of the gates. A guy wearing shorts is cleaning it with a soapy sponge. It takes me a moment to realise it's Jerome.

I'd like to skulk by, but his seeing me is unavoidable. 'Hi, you look busy,' I say.

'Morning!' He rakes back his hair with his sunglasses. 'No rest for the wicked so far today. An energetic run, then ...' He tilts his head. 'Hey, are you OK?'

Knowing I'll cry if I speak, I bite my lip.

'Ah.' His eyes seem to understand. Thank God he doesn't ask the question out here. Instead he motions to his handsome home behind us. 'Come in for drink? I'll show you around if you fancy.'

'Sure.' I manage. 'Sounds good. Thanks.'

To my surprise, he opens a pedestrian gate, hidden in the old wrought-iron railings. I clear my throat. 'You have your own private exit.'

'Or escape. Some sense of autonomy can only be a good thing.'

It's similar to what he's said before. Since the burglary, I've welcomed the sensation of being inside a safe cocoon, but I understand it's not for everyone, especially for someone who's clearly loath to take on the 'family legacy', as he put it.

'I don't know why I didn't twig it was there,' I say, to cover the embarrassing silence. 'I guess I've only focused on my side –

you know The Gatehouse, our quadrangle and so on, rather than the left half of the grounds.'

I follow him around the path to the front of the building. 'It depends on your viewpoint.' He gestures to the door and lifts his eyebrows. 'Voilà. The Lodge is actually on the right.'

He leads me through the hallway and along a corridor to a high-ceilinged kitchen. The straight, clean walls, granite surfaces, wooden flooring and brand-new appliances suggest the room has been recently refurbished, but there are no vases, photographs or personal mementos, which makes it feel a little soulless. I step to the window and look out to the sunlit garden. Like mine, high privet hedges and railings give it privacy from the abutting pavement, though it's at least four times the size.

I blink away the image of a paddling pool and a slide, then rotate and inhale to say something complimentary. Jerome speaks first with a faraway look. 'I know. It needs the warmth of a family.'

It's as if he's heard my deepest desires. Stuck for words, I don't reply.

'Family.' He seems to shake himself back. 'God, I'm sorry. Was that tactless?'

'Is it OK if I sit? I'm a bit—'

'Of course.' He pulls out a chair. 'Are you—'

'Woozy, I guess. Disorientated. And exhausted.' I try to describe how I feel. 'I have a friend called Anya who's a teacher. She says whenever she catches head lice from the kids, she's blissfully unaware of it until someone tells her about the outbreak, or she spots one, then the itching is overwhelming.'

I'm prattling, I know, still processing this morning. I take a calming breath. 'I'm just back from the hospital and ...' My nose burns. 'The sound was a bit ... well, whooshy, but the sonographer found a heartbeat.'

His serious expression is transformed by a smile. 'Really?'

I nod.

'That must have been a magical moment.'

'It truly was.'

'So everything's fine after your ... worries?'

'Yes. So far, so good, at least.' My fingers trembling, I carefully remove the ultrasound photograph from my handbag and pass it to him. 'Nine weeks, apparently.'

His brow creasing, he studies the image. 'Wow, awesome. That's fantastic news. Congratulations.' Though I long for a hug, he hands it back and peers at me. 'Then why so sad?'

'I'm not, I'm really not. Seeing my ... my tiny baby on the screen was incredible. I'm so thankful, delighted, grateful.' Tears squeeze from my eyes. It's tempting to admit how lonely I felt, but that would be self-indulgent when I have been blessed by this miracle. 'Ignore me, it's sheer relief and hormones. And I'm shattered.' I give a wonky smile. 'I was tired the last time, but nothing like this. Make sure to hide the dog baskets!'

I expect him to respond with a quip. Instead his brow creases. 'You must have missed having Toby with you today.'

'I did. I know it's not his fault he's away, but ...' I check myself short. The two guys are friends; it's wrong to whinge. 'Well, I missed his hand-holding.'

'If ever the need for a hand arises again, give me a shout.'

'I will. Thanks.'

'I'm serious, please do.' He snorts wryly. 'Even if I'm fully aware a substitute isn't quite the same thing.'

Though he turns to fill the kettle, I catch his flinch of anguish. 'I'm so sorry about your brother,' I blurt. 'It must be tough losing him and then having to be, well, the substitute, as you put it.'

'Yeah. Tea or coffee or something cold?' He opens a cupboard. 'There are all sorts of herbal and fruit infusions in here, so help yourself. I can't guarantee if they'll be in date, though.'

Conscious of both his grief and proximity, I move next to his broad shoulders and select a sachet.

'I'll give this a go.' I inhale the distinct tang of peppermint. 'It's funny how these things creep up on you without you realising. Now I know that I'm pregnant, the signs are there. Taste, smell, fatigue, as well as ... well, perhaps I'm a touch teary.' And my wholly inappropriate draw to this man. I will my blushes away. 'The aroma of those coffee beans, for example ...'

'Infinitely preferable to head lice.'

'Ha, you were listening!'

'Always. I'm so pleased for you, Frankie.'

'Thank you. I am too.' The image of Pippa's bruised wrists flashes in. 'I think I'll keep it under wraps for now. You know, early days and all that.'

'Good plan.' He hands over a mug. 'Ready for the tour?'

'If you trust me not to spill.'

Our footsteps echoey, we enter a lofty dining room, a study and a spacious lounge. They're elegantly furnished with tables, chairs and standard lamps, yet there's no hint of them being used, or any clues of the occupant's personality. Though I itch to scatter the leather sofa with colourful cushions and add holiday curios, funny cards and thumbed paperbacks to the bookshelves, I nod and murmur, 'It's all very lovely.'

'Thanks. Upstairs is much of the same but ...' He motions me ahead, so I self-consciously climb to the top and peer into the first open chamber. From the pile of books by the divan, the dented pillows and yes, that citrus smell of his aftershave or deodorant, it's clearly Jerome's. As if embarrassed by the slight disarray, he kicks his khaki vet's bag to one side, slots an ironed shirt and a checked jacket into the wardrobe, then smooths out the rumpled duvet.

Feeling myself blush at the notion of me entwined with him beneath the sheets, I quickly gabble to fill the awkward moment. 'The house – or should I say lodge – is beautiful and the rooms are huge,' I say. 'I've only ever lived in a terrace or a flat, so I wouldn't know what to do with the space.'

He seems pensive, far away. 'Fill it with children?'

I picture two boys, scuffling and play-fighting, as he described at the water park. 'That would be nice.'

When we've looked into the other bedrooms and an ultra-modern bathroom, he opens the only closed door. Just knowing this was Stefan's, I peer around the jamb. It's as empty as the rest, yet I clearly see that navy cot, snug beneath the sash window.

Blinking the image away, I turn to Jerome and lightly touch his arm. 'What happened to your brother?' I ask quietly.

'This life wasn't for him.' He blinks a tear away. 'So he did what he had to do.'

45

Feeling a whole lot calmer than I was when I walked into the hospital foyer this morning, and indeed when I left, I wave goodbye to Jerome, scuttle back to the right – or left – side of Pavilion Gardens and let myself into my home. I spend a few minutes hunting for my water bottle to quench my thirst. It's nowhere to be seen, so I fill a glass instead and settle down on the sofa.

My heart gallops afresh, so I lower my head and steady my breathing. God knows how I'd have coped if the baby had died in the womb again, yet the smiley relief I'd expected to feel simply wasn't there. At least not until I shared my news with someone who understood how terrified I'd been about the bleeding and possible miscarriage. That person just happened to be Jerome. I feel a bit bad about his hearing the news before Toby, but his delight for me was infectious, perfect for the moment – this moment – when I break the news to the daddy!

Already inanely grinning, I open up FaceTime and tap Toby's icon. Frustratingly he doesn't answer, so I follow with a call.

He picks up straight away. 'Frankie!'

'Can you talk?'

'Sure. I'm on my way out to dinner with a couple of people from the office, so an excuse to be late suits me.'

I'd rather see his face. 'It's fine, you go and I'll speak to you later.'

'No, go for it. There's a bench over the road. One tick.' The sound of his footsteps and traffic filters through. 'I'm back. What time is it there?'

'Half twelve.'

'So what have you been up to so far today?'

'Well ...' I consider how to say it. 'I feel we need a drum roll ...'

'OK ... Why?'

'Guess! It's good news. In fact, it's a million times better than that.'

He pauses. 'Tell me, Frankie. I don't want to guess wrong.'

'It's early days, obviously, but your superlative performance was indeed ... well, superlative!'

'You're—?'

'Yes!'

'Oh, my God, that's amazing. So ... so are you certain? Why didn't you say anything before now?'

He sounds a touch peevish and, in hindsight, I don't blame him; it's his pregnancy as much as mine. Yet explaining about denial and spotting and fear is too complicated over the phone. 'I wanted to be sure. You know, after the last time. So I decided a scan was the thing and I went this morning. I saw our baby, Toby! Apparently, he or she is the size of a strawberry.'

'And was everything—'

'Yes, all was as it should be for nine weeks' gestation, including a steady heartbeat.'

'Thank Christ for that.'

'I know. Me too. I have a photo. I'll send it over now.' I wait for several seconds for his reaction. 'Toby? Are you still there?'

'Yeah.' His voice sounds choked. 'I'm lost for words. It's ... it's amazing news. Exactly what I needed to hear. I'm so pleased for you, Frankie. I know how badly you want this.'

'You too, I hope?'

'Yes, me too.'

'Are you sure?'

'Completely. Why wouldn't I be?'

'I just wish you'd been here. Any news on when you'll be home?'

'You'll be the first to know when I have. Look, I'd better go. I do love you, Frankie. You know that, right?'

'Of course. I love you too.'

'OK, speak tomorrow.'

'Hey, Toby?'

'Yeah?'

'It's still only nine weeks, so ...'

'Keep it under my hat and keep everything crossed. Don't worry, I've got it.'

46

I was as high as a kite as I sliced tomatoes, shredded lettuce and grated cheese for my lunch. Now I've woken from a nap, reality has settled on my shoulders. I'm still in the early stages of pregnancy, so it's back to the grind with my head down and trying to act normally. Although I'm still convinced my miscarriage and the burglary were connected, it happened at ten weeks, so I can't risk spreading the news further than Jerome and Toby until the end of my first trimester.

Then there's my diversion to Matlock Avenue this morning. With all the excitement, I'd almost forgotten it. My subconscious has clearly been mulling on it, as Mum figured heavily in my daydream. It dissolved on waking, but a huge sense of loss is still stuck in my chest. Save for a couple of drinks that had formed a mouldy skin, I found nothing suspicious or worrying in any room of her house. However ... where on earth is she?

I reach for my necklace and smooth the sparkling gem with my thumb. Away for the weekend? Unlikely, as the house felt uninhabited for longer than that. Has she moved in with that Colin bloke? Hmm, really? My independent man-phobic mum? My stomach churns with disquiet. An accident or illness? No; I'd have heard about it, surely? Though if it was something she could have treated on the quiet, I could see her doing that rather than worry anyone ...

I slide from the sofa and tug on my trainers; aimlessly speculating will drive me nuts and the walk will do me good. I nod, decision made; I'll pay Gran a visit and find out.

I briskly walk the pavements and, by the time I reach Withington Baths, I have to pause to catch my breath. After an argument with Mum as a teenager, I'd be here like a shot, running the mile or so journey to Old Moat Lane in ten minutes. It seems much longer today, so maybe I'm not as fit as I was. Or perhaps it's because I'm carrying my strawberry-sized baby ...

Groaning out loud, I snap an invisible rubber band on my wrist. I've swung from astonished pleasure to wheezy terror since I left Pavilion Gardens. Neither is good for me, so I really must stop. Yet when I reach my grandparents' semi, my stress levels go up another notch.

I take a gulp of air and rap with the knocker. The door cracks open and a woman I don't recognise peers out.

'I'm so sorry ...' I begin. Mum's black cat slithers out. 'Gran?'

'Oh hello, love. It's you.'

I try not to gape at this withered person. She's aged a decade since I saw her ten weeks ago. A horrible sense of dread sizzles in the pit of my belly. Mum; something dreadful has happened to my mum.

Gran speaks, thank God, words she'd surely not utter if her daughter was dead: 'Are you coming in, then? Or are you here to gawp on the doorstep?'

'Yes, I am, thanks.'

'Who's that?' I hear my grandad call. 'Is everything all right?'

'It's our Frankie,' Gran replies. 'So make sure you're looking decent and on your best manners.'

I frown. Was there a warning note in her tone? I follow her through to the back room and kiss Baba's papery cheek. 'Hi, Baba. How are you doing?'

His eyes slide to his wife. 'Good. We're good, aren't we, Sylvia.'

'We are.' She sits on the sofa and pats the cushion by her side. 'How come we have the honour of a visit?'

Their behaviour is decidedly odd. I'm usually welcomed with

tight hugs and plied with tea and cake. Maybe they're pissed off with me for not visiting them sooner, or think I was wrong to walk out on Mum ... No, something more is going on, I'm sure of it.

'I went to Matlock Avenue this morning ...' Still as statues, they both stare. 'Mum wasn't there. The house has clearly not been lived in for a while. Where is she?'

'Spain,' Sylvia says.

'Spain? Whereabouts in Spain?'

'Barcelona.'

'With that bloke?' The bloke I've never bloody met. 'Calum or Colin or whatever he's called.'

Gran's eyes flicker. 'No. She's gone for work. What do they call it?'

'A secondment,' Baba pipes up.

'With the library?'

'Yes, that's it.'

Resentment replaces my relief. 'She's gone abroad. Why didn't she tell me? Why didn't you tell me?'

'Your mum thought you needed time to settle in without worrying about her.'

I narrow my eyes. 'Why would I worry about her?'

'Not her, then.' Gran lifts her shoulders. 'Worry about things, then.'

'Right, I get it. Things being the family she hid from me. Specifically a half-sister. Did you know?' I don't wait for an answer. 'Of course you did. How could you not.'

Baba looks fit to cry and Gran reaches out a shaky hand. 'Come on, chicken. We're your family, me and Baba. We only ever want what's best for you. We love you. You know that.'

But hurt has already lodged like a ball of rough string in my gullet. 'I'm sorry, I don't believe you.' Though I stand to leave, neither of them move. 'If this is what you call love, you can keep it.'

47

The twine horribly unravels as I schlep past the bustling shops on Burton Road. I'm angry, for sure, yet the searing disappointment is so much worse. Maybe I've gone about my new home and friendships with a dash of high-moral-ground pride – and perhaps a touch of stubbornness – but I've always been sure that, come hell or high water, Mum would be on her doorstep with open arms. Gran too. When I got myself into a fug, or a set-to with Mum, she'd be the first person I'd turn to. She'd cluck and fuss and tut without judgement and offer a sleepover. Yet today her cosy and welcoming semi had seemed raggedy, chilly and indifferent, just like her. Baba hardly even looked at me. I so wanted to stamp my foot and say: *I'm your only grandchild. You've always made me feel special. Why have you stopped caring?'*

As I walk past my railings, consternation hits me afresh. Nina has gone to Barcelona without a bloody word! It beggars belief. She's buggered off to work in her favourite city in the world without even a text, let alone sending me a postcard. Colin is clearly somewhere in the mix, which makes my sense of rejection worse. I have amazing news to share. Who else to tell but your mum?

The aroma of baking hits my nostrils even as I wait for the gates to open. As they clank satisfyingly behind me, I allow myself a small smile. The acute sense of smell shows I'm astonishingly, wonderfully pregnant and that this time I'll be safe.

As I round the corner, I almost bump headlong into Ursula.

'Francesca! Hello. How lovely to see you,' she rushes. 'I've been meaning to pop round to see how you are, but time flies, doesn't it? One gets immersed in one thing, then before one can take breath, something else comes along. From midwifery to planting seeds to spring cleaning, not to mention getting the correct jigsaw piece in the right box, which takes an age, I can tell you. Sorry, I'm prattling.' She drags me to her bosom, squeezes, then releases me. 'Don't you look as pretty as a picture! Are you well? Settled in?' She peers at her watch. 'Flapjack due out! I have to dash. It's one of those delicacies that can turn to the dark side in a moment.'

'Of course, you go.'

'Thank you, dear.' She bustles up to her door and rotates at the top. 'Come back in five minutes; it'll still be warm. Then we can have a good old catch-up. I'll put on the kettle. Don't worry about knocking; it's always unlocked.'

Smiling at the woman's insistent energy, I continue to my house and open up. As I pick up the post, I pause in thought. That brief encounter with Ursula has made me feel more cared for – and yes, special – than my own grandparents just did.

'Hi, Frankie.'

I turn to Minta, on my doorstep.

'How are you doing?' she asks. 'I've barely seen you all week.'

'Good, thanks. I've been ...' If I was being honest, where the heck would I start? 'I've been for a stroll.'

'Same here.' She gestures to her shopping bag and grins. 'Walking off the goodies I'm going to eat later, if you know what I mean.' She hands over a bunch of flowers. 'I bought some for Pippa and thought you deserved some too.'

The gesture brings a burn to my nose. 'That's so sweet of you! I love tulips. Thank you.'

'Always a pleasure.'

'I would invite you in, but I have an invitation for tea and flapjack at The Gatehouse.'

'Then you'd better not be late.' She pecks my cheek. 'See you for a natter soon.'

Keeping an eye on the time, I have a quick pee and check myself in the mirror. Though nothing is visible, it feels as if my tears have left a stain, so I thoroughly wash my face and look again. That's definitely better and ...

I stare at the sapphire pendant in the hollow of my throat. Save for schooldays when no jewellery was allowed, I've worn this chain since Mum gave it to me at thirteen. Lifting my chin with resolve, I reach around my neck and unclasp it, then drop it on a cabinet shelf and consider how that feels. Symbolically satisfied, actually, a sign that I'm strong on my own.

On the way out, I scoop up the latest letters for Julia, then hurry to The Gatehouse and hop up the steps. It goes against the grain not to use the cherub knocker, but I do as I'm told and walk straight in. Though the smell of home cooking pervades the air, there's an underlying dank aroma of bygone days.

I catch my nervy breath and look around the hallway. From what I can glean, it's the same set-up as Jerome's. In contrast to his plain elevations, framed images take up every inch of the burgundy wallpaper, and although it's dusky without light from the elaborate chandelier, sheer nosiness takes over, so I step to the antique sideboard and peer at the section above. These photographs are in colour, so I start at the top, taking in the poses of various white-toothed, smiley 2.4 family groups. I stop at one and try to place the familiar looking quartet. Though the father's face is hidden by a rakish hat, the mother's icy gaze gives her away. It's the sophisticated older 'cousin' who took a fancy to Toby. Chuckling at the memory of his terrified look, I move to the next row. My eyes rest on a snap of two solemn-looking boys with fishing tackle. My stomach squeezes with intrigue. Could this be Jerome and Stefan, off for a day by the River Mersey?

'Jerome says it's more like a gallery than a home.'

A palm to my chest, I jerk around to Ursula. 'Sorry, I've just arrived. You said to come in without ...' Embarrassed to be caught snooping, I push Julia's mail at her. 'Before I forget, these came to number three. I think Fabian redirected the others, so if he doesn't mind ...'

'He did indeed.' She props them on the radiator shelf, flicks on a lamp and views her vast collection with shiny eyes. 'Despite what my son says, I think I have a balance between museum and residence.'

'Wow.' Most of the historic images are in monochrome or sepia. 'They look fascinating.'

'And so they are. Despite modernisation, not a lot changes. I have to say, I like that. Someone has to be the keeper of tradition, don't you think?' She bustles over and taps one. 'This is circa nineteen-ten.'

Amazed that horses and carriages were used outside this very building not so very long ago, I study it. I almost mention Mum's love of history, then I remember she's in bloody Barcelona, undoubtedly taking in a dose of sunshine and romance, as well as the past.

'Gosh, you're right about change, or the lack of it. There's the chapel and this house and Jerome's next door.' I search out my own little townhouse. 'And there's me. Astonishing, really. It could have been taken today.'

I move onto another image with a similar backdrop. This one sports stony-faced, stiff-uniformed nurses standing outside the iron gates like guards. Reminding myself our plush homes were once part of a workhouse for poor and destitute 'inmates', I give a little shiver.

Ursula's warm tones smooth it away. 'Fascinating, no?' She points to the far wall. 'That's the architect's plan of the original construction in the mid-eighteen-hundreds.' She beams proudly. 'Built on a greenfield site, no less. Come on through to the kitchen. Next time I'll give you the grand tour. For now, fresh scones and healthy oat bars are awaiting.'

She slips her arm into mine. 'Between you and me, I've been perfecting my home-grown herbal tea. You can be the first to give me your verdict.'

48

I thought they would drag but, interspersed with trips to Lincoln, another nine working days flash by. My new 'I'm bloody good at my job and if you can't see that, I don't give a damn' attitude is paradoxically paying off, as I feel a lot less stressed and the mansplaining client is treating me with more respect. Which just goes to show that determination or leadership, or whatever the word is, comes from within; internally set out your stall, then show people your mettle and self-worth. It's a win–win situation I'd like to share with Toby, but he's still in the doldrums whenever we speak and I don't want to make his negativity worse.

Minta calls round at Thursday teatime with a heap of homemade teacakes. Perhaps because she's so small, her bump suddenly seems huge.

'Look at you, shaping up so nicely,' I say, as I make us a cold drink. 'How are you feeling?'

'Really well. Staying positive. Still manifesting a completely pain-free birth.'

Though I smile, that's a projection too far for me. My current goal is the relative safety net of twelve weeks. I'm so nearly there; looking further feels like I'm tempting fate. And at the end of the day, if a woman wants to procreate, severe discomfort at some point surely goes with the territory.

Minta seems to read my mind. 'I know some people think that torture is part of the birthing "experience" and that those who have epidurals or similar are cheats, but not me. Whatever is on offer, I'm having it.'

Feeling rotten for not coming clean about my own pregnancy,

I chuckle unsteadily. 'I guess when my day comes, I'll go for whatever's safe for both mother and child.'

She audibly harrumphs. 'As if they'd use anything that wasn't. You can bet your bottom dollar that the "unsafe" lobbyists are men. If it were them who had to do the hours of agonising labour and pushing, well, there'd be more people using it.'

'You sound like my mum,' I find myself saying. I don't want to go down that rabbit hole either, so I quickly change the subject. 'It's so sunny. Shall we take these outside?'

'Sorry. I'm going on, aren't I?' Minta says when we're settled in deckchairs. She rubs her bump. 'This is what comes of being tiny. Sheer terror about getting him or her out. Why am I even worrying about it? Look at Pippa; she's a flaming role model.'

I picture the nasty bruising on her wrists. To my surprise a different thought comes out. 'I hardly know any babies, so who am I to judge, but little Lucy is so quiet,' I say, lowering my voice. 'I'm not complaining for a moment, yet I don't think I've ever heard her cry. Is that normal or has Pippa just got lucky?'

'Manifesting, of course! You need to get with it, Frankie. An easy birth and a sleepy baby is what every new mother wants.'

I smile ruefully. 'Not, I'm guessing, what every new mother gets.'

Apparently losing interest, she shrugs. 'Maybe it depends on who your obstetrician is.' She animates again. 'Oh, so you do know about Midsummer's Day?'

'What about it?'

'It's on Saturday.'

'So ...'

'So there's a party, of course.'

'Oh, right. You mean here?'

'Where else?' She rolls her eyes. 'The solstice traditionally involves gathering with family and friends, so yes. Have you never done it before?'

What family? I'm tempted to say, but the idea is warming. It's something to do at the weekend, especially as Toby still hasn't been given his 'parole date', as he puts it. And it'll be nice to chat with Jerome; though I've searched him out around The Lodge and on the Sunday walks, I haven't seen him in ages.

I cover my flush of excitement with a sardonic tone. 'No, I have to confess that I haven't participated in a pagan ritual before. It sounds like fun, though. What do I need to do, make or bring?'

'Probably nothing if Ursula hasn't already provided you with a "to-do" list.' She looks at me pointedly. 'I'm not sure if it's because you're a newbie or her favourite, she seems to have a soft spot for you.'

'Ha!' Ridiculous though it is, I'm pleased. 'Glad to hear I'm in the headmistress' good books.'

'Matron, more like. Just be sure to pay attention and make suitably admiring noises when she gives you the grand tour of The Gatehouse and all its treasures.'

'Good tip. I can't turn up empty-handed on Saturday, though.'

Minta gives it some thought. 'Candles.'

'Sorry?'

'Bring candles, then you'll have fire to represent the sun. Be sure to write down any wishes for the coming months and bring them with you.'

I guffaw. 'So I'll be sharing my deep, dark desires with my neighbours.'

'No. You burn them to ash. Then they'll come true.'

'Ha. Really?'

'Why not? I love the old myths. Another is to sleep with a special concoction of herbs beneath your pillow in the hope you'll dream of your future partner.' She chuckles. 'I would suggest you pick some from Ursula's garden, but you already have Toby, so maybe that would be inappropriate.'

Jerome's chiselled profile flashes in. 'Yup, I'd better stick with flames. Will we have a maypole on the green and prance around it wearing flowers in our hair?'

'That's another phallic reference. But yes and, believe it or not, we're allowed to put blankets on the grass. No heels though, so remember to leave your dancing shoes at home!'

171

49

It rains on and off all day Friday. By Saturday, the hot sunshine has sucked up every last drop of moisture. Even at eight o'clock, I can still feel the brush of heady warmth on my bare arms and legs. I haven't touched even a smidgen of alcohol, yet I feel contented and a little drunk from Ursula's homemade juices and merriment. The crèche is being used as a base for food and drink, and the lawn at the centre of our quadrangle has been a hive of busy activity for the kids. Supervised by Ursula, they've made flower garlands, acted out simple charades, picnicked on healthy goodies and played musical cushions.

Though I have repeatedly tried to dampen my dreams, I've spotted my own dark-haired children amongst them, joyful, laughing, carefree and safe. I wryly laugh to myself. Whatever happened to the grounded, pragmatic Francesca Whittle? It seems I've got so used to manifesting these days that I do it without trying. Or maybe it's because I wrote my wishes down and burned them. As I watched the flames turn them to ash, I sensed Jerome's eyes on me and felt a flip in my belly. That was surely subliminal thoughts of my growing baby inside, rather than the strange pull I feel whenever he's near. And anyway, his intense gaze was simply because he knew what I'd be longing for, and nothing to do with the arousing dream I had about him only last night.

I fan my hot cheeks. Bloody hell, the power of suggestion or what! I glance at Minta, efficiently demonstrating the moves for a barn dance now the children have gone to bed. In my old life I'd have shared the erotic fantasy with one of my friends, a 'Oh, my God, I feel really guilty, however ...' conversation but, quite honestly, I'm embarrassed by own unconscious mind. I'm married and pregnant, for goodness' sake! And no, I didn't put a special concoction of herbs beneath my pillow before sleep.

I now turn to Pippa, as neat and demure and sweetly smiley as ever. 'Noah looked like he was having fun,' I say.

'Too much! I think Scott will struggle to persuade him to go to bed.'

My eyes slip to her wrists. Albeit feint, the bruising is still there if you look for it. Could she really be in an abusive relationship?

She takes my hand and squeezes. 'It's fine, Frankie. Really. I honestly can't remember anything.'

'Sorry?' Oh God, she clearly noticed me ogling. And what on earth does 'can't remember' mean? I swallow. 'Sorry, I'm not following—'

A shadow, then a voice interrupts. 'May I have the pleasure of this dance, Francesca?'

It's the father rather than the mind-reading son, thank God. Fabian decorously offers his elbow and Pippa moves away, so I accept it and try to follow the steps to the *Dashing White Sergeant* without treading on his bare toes. Once I get the hang of it, I shrug away the peculiar exchange with Pippa, let the folk song wash over me and go with the moment.

'Do you have a due date?' Fabian asks amiably after a while.

My joyfulness crumbling, I almost stop in my tracks. Bloody hell, Jerome has clearly told his dad about the pregnancy. So much for the special friendship I was building in my head. I try to search him out, but he's nowhere to be seen and, on reflection, I haven't spotted him for a good hour or so. It isn't the first time he's disappeared mid- 'Pavilion' activity, so perhaps his dry quips about feeling trapped by his 'legacy' are really true.

Or maybe he has other things to do, such as seeing a girlfriend. Or boyfriend, perhaps.

I revert to Fabian, still studying me politely.

'Sorry, badly phrased,' he says. He wafts a hand in the direction of the chapel. 'A linguistic occupational hazard, I'm afraid. What I meant to say is do you have a date for the conveyancing completion on number three?'

'Ah, I see.' The music plays in my ears again. 'No, I haven't. In fact, we haven't even exchanged. Last I heard, the solicitor was waiting for some answers to our enquiries before contract. It's been full on at work. I'll get in touch and ask him to chase them.'

'A good plan. And I'll give Julia a nudge the next time we speak.'

'Thanks. And her husband? I guess they'll both need to sign the transfer and so on.' I have no idea where that question came from. I go with it, nonetheless. 'Ben, I think Julia called him. I noticed the wedding portrait of them when I came to view. A handsome couple.'

'Yes. Ben.' He smiles thinly. 'Another woman, I suspect. Leaving poor Julia somewhat floundering and lost. Have you thought about whether you'll want the blinds, the furniture, the beds and so on? She has no need for them now, so I suspect you'll get them at a snip.'

'Oh, right.'

I haven't thought about that. Or the legal aspects at all. From curtains to pots and pans, and everything in between, my day-to-day living needs have been presented on a plate. My social life too. Indeed, since Toby left for Hong Kong, life has passed by very smoothly without him, including our growing strawberry, hopefully now the size of a plum.

Feeling guilty at my disloyal thoughts, I clear my throat. 'That's the sort of thing I'll need to discuss with Toby.'

Fabian twirls me around. 'You could ask him right now.'

'Hong Kong is eight hours ahead; he'll probably be fast asleep. I will give him a call in ...' I begin, but there's something about the twinkle in Fabian's eyes. Though I come to a stop, the world continues to spin. For a moment I honestly wonder if I'm hallucinating. Smiling and chatting like old friends, Toby and Jerome are strolling towards me.

50

I prop my head on my hand and check whether Toby is awake.

'Why didn't you tell me you were coming back? You promised to keep me posted.'

'I wanted to make you smile.' He opens an eye. 'I thought you'd enjoy it. You know, similar to a surprise birthday party.'

I resist saying *Don't you know me at all?* Instead I say, 'Fair enough. Bit embarrassing with everyone staring, though.'

'It was only for two minutes. Lucky for you to be the centre of attention, is what I say.'

I have to chuckle at that comment. Ursula ran over with a chilled lager and plate of pastries for him, then all but finger-fed him like a prince. 'Says the golden boy. Fabian even shook your hand.'

'They were pleased to see me!'

'Hmm. That cousin woman will arrive next and seduce you with her obvious ...' I briefly pause. Did I really glimpse her cold scrutiny at some point during the evening? God knows; the whole event was so surreal and frenetic, it felt as if I was on speed. 'Her obvious wealth.'

'Meryl?'

'Oh, she even has a name!'

He laughs. 'Are you jealous?'

I snuggle against him. 'Might be.'

'Glad to hear it. And we had fun, didn't we? Dancing the night away ...'

'Giving me away, more like.'

'I could tell he wanted a whirl with my beautiful spouse.' He pecks my lips. 'And who can blame him.'

I cringe at the memory. Sure, Toby had had a few drinks by then, but at some stage he theatrically handed me over to Jerome like some weird wife-selling custom from the seventeenth century. Jerome looked as embarrassed as I felt, yet it was nice to feel his warm palm against mine as he guided me through the moves for *Flirtation Reel*, of all things.

'And I needed to show him who was boss.'

I frown at that. 'Excuse me? Boss of me?'

'God, no!'

'Then what, exactly?'

'I'm just kidding. I think he likes you, though.'

I return to my shoulder nest. 'I thought you two were best buddies,' I say, to cover the smattering of pleasure. 'You know, the "I'll secretly tell you when I'm back in the UK and get a lift from the airport" type of besties.'

'I misjudged that and I'm sorry, OK? I did arrive bearing gifts, so you'll be pleased when I have the energy to unpack.'

I grin. 'Oh yeah? So ...'

'Later.' He yawns. 'I'm unbelievably tired. Ten long weeks in prison followed by bloody jet lag.'

'Fingers crossed your incarceration will have its rewards.'

'It had bloody better.' He falls quiet for a few moments. 'I can't tell you how knackered I feel. Doubt I'll be up to a Sunday walk.'

'Fair enough.'

As his breathing becomes regular and deep, I consider what to do with my morning. I have no Toby-appropriate food, let alone alcohol, in the fridge, so a supermarket shop is definitely in order if he's here for the foreseeable. Once sunset passed and darkness descended, the celebrations went on for a while. When we finally came home, we flopped into bed and immediately fell asleep, so we haven't had a chance to discuss what's happening in any respect – house-wise, office-wise, future-wise.

My smile waning, I stroke my stomach thoughtfully. No one else would notice, but there's definitely a bump. And the food faddiness, morning nausea and tender boobs are ongoing, so things are looking good in that respect. The fact Toby didn't say anything in company about our growing baby is unsurprising, yet is it odd he didn't whisper a sweet something about it last night? Has his absence made him feel detached? I bite my lip. Or am I projecting my own feelings of guilt?

'Hey, Frankie ...'

The sound of his voice splinters my thoughts.

I rock my head towards his. 'Yes?'

'Love you.'

'Love you, too.'

'The twelve-week scan must be soon.'

'It's booked for Thursday.'

'Thursday. Fantastic.'

'Is it though?' pops out of my mouth. 'Is it fantastic?'

'Hey ...' He hitches across and gently kisses my belly. 'Yeah, completely. Why would you think otherwise?'

'I've just missed you, that's all.' I puff out my clashing emotions. 'Are you going to take a few days off work now you're back? They must owe you some slack after doing them the huge favour.'

'Yeah, you'd think.' He strokes a strand of hair from my forehead. 'But it'll be fun having you as my office mate again.' He seems wistful, almost sad. 'You know, looking at you longingly across the room. Wondering if I'll ever gather the courage to ask out a ten out of ten. Would she say yes, or would I end up humiliated again.'

'Humiliated's a big word. Surely *disappointed* is more the thing ...'

'Not when Marcus Penny is in the running.'

'He was never in the running, as you put it! Give a girl some credit. I chose you, Toby. And, hopefully, we'll have this little miracle as proof of our love.'

'Yeah. So this scan is a follow-up to the last one?'

'Yes, it was sort of a package deal price, so I thought why not.'

'And after that?'

'I'll go via the NHS. I'll need to register with my old GP.'

'Well, I think we should stick with private healthcare. I'm sure the NHS are mostly brilliant, but looking at the newspapers ...'

'Childbirth isn't covered by BUPA, Toby. It'll cost a shedload of money.'

'I know.' As if I'm a precious package, he gently kisses my forehead. 'But some things are worth it.'

51

I squeeze Toby's knee reassuringly. He's been tapping his foot since we arrived at the Spire Hospital. I'm apprehensive too, but I was nauseous then actually sick only this morning, so that felt a good sign, a wave from our baby: *I'm here, Mummy, and I'm thriving!*

'We're paying for this,' he murmurs in a low voice. 'You'd think we'd walk straight in.'

I take in the other tense faces surrounding us in the waiting room. 'I guess we're not the only ones. Do you fancy a cold drink or something?'

He doesn't reply, so I study him. He's as groomed and as handsome as always, yet he still looks a shadow of himself. Though I've been out like a light every night this week, I sense he's been fidgety and awake with jet lag. 'Are you OK?'

He gives me a thin smile. 'Just nervous.'

'Yeah, me too.' I peck his lips. I've done this two times before and I know what's involved, whereas he is squeamish at the best of times. 'Everything will be fine, OK? In fact, more than fine. You'll see your baby!'

I inwardly cringe. Am I tempting fate by being so chipper? All the symptoms are there and at times I'm so exhausted, I can barely keep my eyes open, so ...

He looks lost. 'Yes, hopefully.'

I wrap my arms around him. 'I know it's stressful. As you said, some things are worth it.'

'Yeah.' He nods. 'Yeah. That's true.'

'Francesca Whittle?'

My stomach lurches. 'Yes, that's us.' Trying for a confident smile, I hold out my hand. 'Are you ready?'

Toby nods. 'Yeah, I am.'

It's a different sonographer, yet again. She introduces herself as Mary and offers Toby a chair. Then she addresses me, her manner calm and reassuring.

'If you could lie down on your back and make yourself comfortable, then pull up your clothes to expose your tummy. I'll be applying some cool, lubricating gel to your skin to help us get a clear picture. Once I do, I'll turn the monitor to you. OK?'

It's a struggle to find my voice, so I nod and hold my breath as Mary presses the ultrasound probe across my abdomen at different angles.

'You came here at the beginning of the month?' she eventually says.

'Yes.'

'At around a gestation of nine weeks?'

'Yes.'

I stare at the woman's intent eyes. She's taking far longer than the sonographer took the last time and she keeps glancing at the notes on her chart with a hint of a frown.

Words burst out of me, making Toby literally jump from his seat. 'What's wrong?' I demand, so loudly the whole clinic will have heard. I want to scream the place down. This cannot be happening to me again. I was certain, so sure. How could I have got it so very wrong?

Though a huge effort, I try to temper the volume and my fear. 'Something's wrong, isn't it? Just tell me.'

'Nothing. Nothing at all.' Mary turns the screen towards me. 'Did you know you're having twins?'

52

Barely exchanging a word, we make our way outside and gulp in the late June air.

I don't know about Toby, but I'm still reeling from the shock.

'A hidden twin happens from time to time,' Mary explained. 'Despite modern technology, scans aren't perfect. Because they're sonographic images of what's going on beneath the surface, there's always some room for error, especially early in pregnancy.' She smiled. 'The little rascal was clearly reluctant to make his or her ultrasound debut the last time.'

'My legs feel like jelly. Maybe we shouldn't have walked here after all,' I comment, as we amble across the car park. 'A hidden twin! I had no idea there was such a thing.'

'Me neither, but wow.' Toby's voice catches. 'Seeing two of them on the screen. Well, that was pretty awesome.'

'It was, wasn't it!' I turn to study him. I have a horrible feeling this development will either make or break us. 'So what do you think about double trouble?'

He looks at the sky, then wipes a tear from his eye. 'Single, double, it's all brilliant news.'

Relieved and touched by his emotion, I slip my arms around his chest. 'I'm so glad. It feels surreal to me, so goodness knows how you're feeling.' I give him a soft kiss. 'Thank you.'

'For what?'

I smile. 'Your superlative performance, amongst other things.'

'Yeah.' He frowns. 'She – Mary – was happy with the heartbeats and measurements, right?'

'She was.'

'And what was that about a trimester?'

'It's what each third of the pregnancy is called. I'm nearly thirteen weeks, so I'm just in the second. The risk of miscarriage drops dramatically but ...' Though I pull a face, I feel wonderfully calm. 'Having twins is still that little bit more risky than having one.'

'Right. So all is good?'

'Yes!'

'Thank God.' He seems to shake himself down and hear my comment from earlier. 'Jelly legs. OK, you stay here. I'm going to fetch the car.'

'The surprise made me wobbly.' My heart sings at his sweetly crinkled brow. 'I'm fine. I have the use of my limbs now.'

'Nope. You're having freaking twins, Frankie! You go back inside and wait there. I'll be ten minutes, tops.'

53

I sit in the Spire reception and simply breathe. Twins, I'm having twins. I laugh out loud. It's amazing, astonishing, unbelievable. And yet it's true. I saw it for myself on the screen. Two tiny tots, topping and tailing in their own little sacs, with their perfect walnut brains, their beautiful hearts beating and each with two arms and two legs.

Carefully pulling the scan photograph from my bag, I say a silent prayer of thanks. Then, remembering what Minta said about sacrifice and parenthood, I whisper to my babies, words I know will be my mantra. 'From this moment, I'll do whatever is best for you. You will always, always come first.'

Though the 'ten minutes' turns out to be forty, I can't complain when Toby arrives with pink cheeks and an apology.

'Sorry! I stopped off at the florists and there was a huge queue ...'

Almost detecting the smell of each exquisite flower, I hold the spectacular bouquet on my lap as he drives the short journey home. He hops out and inputs the code for the gates.

'I must remind Fabian about the remote,' I say when he returns. 'I don't know about you but I'm starving.'

'Me too.' He drives in, parks up and dashes around to my side to open up.

I chuckle and climb out. 'Very gallant, though you might be fed up of it by the end of the weekend.'

'Ah, about that—'

'Francesca!' As though she's been watching for our arrival, Ursula bounds over from the chapel. 'Such wonderful news!' She pulls me into an embrace. 'Twins, I believe? Which means two Christmas babies, an extra delight.'

I try not to take umbrage. Toby's lived here all of two minutes and he's told a veritable town crier the news when I'd have preferred to announce it myself. In fairness, the woman's beam of pleasure and enthusiasm is heartwarming.

She slips her arm into mine and guides me home as Toby follows like a bridesmaid. 'Of course, every mum has to think of her diet, but with twins an iron supplement might be in order,' she rushes. 'Be aware that constipation can be a side effect of using it. Nevertheless, with exercise, water and high-fibre food, one can get the old bowels going.' She puts a finger to her chin. 'That's right. There's a marvellous dish with prunes and figs, so that can be on the menu and, of course, I shall consult my recipe books for more.' She releases me at my front door. 'Take the weight off your feet for a few minutes. I'll be back shortly.'

'Oh, OK. For ...?'

'To bring your celebratory lunch!'

When she's gone, I fall onto the sofa and roll my eyes. 'Thank God she said "celebratory". I couldn't be doing with this every day.'

'She means well.'

'I know that, Toby. I was only joking.' I look at him pointedly. 'It would have been nice to tell people together, though.'

'Come on, don't be like that, it wasn't intentional. I called Jerome while I was in the florist's and she must have been earwigging.'

'Right.'

'He is my mate, Frankie.'

'OK, fair enough.'

A tang of petulance catches in my throat. I have no right to be miffed that the two men have rekindled their friendship, but I liked my special relationship with Jerome, our confidential exchanges and his blue-eyed concern when I was struggling, and there's a strange sense of loss now the pregnancy is public. I swallow it down. Toby's attachment to him is a good thing; today is an amazing day, one for celebrating indeed.

I revert to him. 'You started to say something about the weekend before Ursula appeared.'

'Yeah.' He smooths back his hair. 'It was only to say that I'll probably catch the train down to London this evening.'

I sit forward. 'Already? Why?'

'To see Mum and stay over for a couple of nights. Call in at Dad's too.'

'But we've literally only just found out—'

'I haven't seen them in person for over two months, Frankie.'

My initial impulse is to protest. On reflection he does have a point. 'Yeah sorry, I didn't think about that.'

'No you didn't. Not everyone is the same as you.'

'What's that supposed to mean?'

'Nothing.'

The flash of anger in his eyes hits my chest. 'Seriously, Toby, I have no idea what you're on about.'

'Your tunnel vision.'

'And that is?'

'Forget it; it's fine.'

Alarm fizzes through me. Out of nowhere, our relationship feels like it's built on sand. 'No, really, please explain.'

His shoulders seem to slump. 'You always succeed and get exactly what you want. And mostly without even trying.'

A rap at the door breaks the uncomfortable silence. I make to stand, but he holds out a palm.

'You stay, I'll get it.'

Still shocked at his snap of temper, I watch him open up, amiably chat for a few moments, then bring in a huge platter of food.

'From Ursula.' He places it on the coffee table. 'I'll be another minute. Apparently, there's more to come.'

'OK.'

My heart thrashing, I try to work out what just happened. Getting what I want? Really? It beggars belief; how quickly he's forgotten that I lost a baby after being held at knifepoint. And as for succeeding ... Well, I understand he has confidence issues when it comes to work, but he has to stop wanting it so much. Being adulated career-wise isn't everything. There's so much more, such as our incredible discovery today. Trust bloody Toby to put a downer on the most special day of my life.

He soon returns, slowly shouldering through the door with a tray laden with a teapot, cups, plates and a cake stand piled with mini tarts, scones and buns. He carefully places it down next to the cold food. 'This crockery is Georgian, apparently. Thank God I didn't drop it on the path. Can you imagine?'

I can't help but smile at his look of relief. 'Blacklisted for sure.'

He sits next to me. 'Sorry about earlier.' He rubs his eyes. 'I'm still so tired from the jet lag. And Mum's been nagging me. As you know, it's hard to say no and—'

I take his hand. 'And you've missed her. I understand; she's your mum.'

'True. But you're right about dashing off tonight. She can wait another day.'

'It's honestly fine. You go.' I pat my tummy. 'It isn't as though we don't have another six months of enjoying these two. God willing.'

'Yeah, God willing.'

I clear the clot of emotion from my throat. 'Earlier you said ...'

'Forget it, Frankie. Really. It was just exhaustion speaking.'

My lips twitch. '"Tunnel vision's" a bit harsh.'

'I know, and it's only because I wish I could be more like you.'

'Hmm, as in?'

He narrows his eyes in thought. 'Innately resolute, I guess. Having conviction. You make a decision and you go with it without picking it apart in here.' He taps his temple. 'And that's a rare talent.'

'So, you were actually giving me a compliment?'

He grins. 'Exactly. My kick-ass woman. My ten out of ten. The love of my life.'

'Haha.' I return the smile. 'OK, you're forgiven.'

I inspect the buffet Ursula has sweetly prepared. Hard cheeses, smoked salmon, sun-dried tomatoes, leafy salad and stuffed figs to boot. Not an item on the banned list in sight, bless her. 'Looks delicious,' I say. 'Let's dig in.'

54

I wrap my wet hair in a towel and turn on the TV, hoping for something to distract me from my slump after watching Toby bump his suitcase across the train station cobbles until he disappeared. Why I feel abandoned, I have no idea. We had a tender exchange and this time it's only for a week. And, despite that tiny blip, we did have a wonderful day.

My lips curve into a smile. We companionably marked each dish Ursula had prepared out of ten and, at some stage, she appeared with a saucer of yellow butter, a basket of bread and a profuse apology for the delay. The hot rolls were so delicious, we couldn't manage all the cakes.

'Why don't you invite Minta and Pippa round to enjoy them?' Toby later suggested. 'I'll make myself scarce so you can break the news.' He grinned. 'I know you're gagging to have an all mummies moment.'

His sweetness was touching and so was their response to my announcement. I suspect they'd already heard, yet they both feigned surprise and their delight was genuine.

'Ooh, they'll all be playmates. Can you imagine the midsummer's party in a couple of years with them all toddling around?' Pippa said.

'We'd better not put herbs beneath their pillows the night before when they're older, though,' I quipped.

'Good point,' Minta said with wide eyes. 'That would be a step too far.'

It was so nice to talk about how I was feeling, what size the tiny babies will be now, the shock of discovering it was twins, whether they'll be fraternal or identical, girls or boys, if there's any history of them in the family.

I groan out loud at that particular thought. *Family*. I've tried to stay in denial, yet I miss my gran and I really, really miss my mother. Maybe Toby was right about me being resolute about my decisions; that doesn't mean they're always the right ones. She's my mum for goodness' sake; I should be reaching out and sharing my amazing news, but I honestly don't know if I can.

As if in reply, the doorbell rings. Expecting it to be the closest thing I have to a mother, I drag the towel off my head and tighten the belt of my dressing gown. Donning a polite, appreciative demeanour, I open up. It isn't Ursula to collect her tea service. It's her son.

'Oh, hi. Sorry, I thought it was your mum.'

He looks down at his linen shirt. 'Was it the floral dress?'

'Ha!'

'Before the day's over I wanted to say ...' He clocks my own attire. 'Ah, I've come at a bad time.'

'No, it's fine. I had an early shower. I felt a bit sticky from the ...' I scrunch my curls self-consciously. God, I must look a sight. I turn to hide my blushes. 'Come in and I'll get us a drink,' I say over my shoulder.

He follows me to the kitchen and I open the fridge. 'I can offer something cold this time thanks to Toby being home.' Pulling out a bottle in each hand, I finally rotate and meet my visitor's blue gaze. 'Wine or beer?'

He lifts a gift bag. 'Or champagne?' He leans in to peck my cheek. 'Congratulations, Frankie. Not just one but two! That's incredible news. You must be thrilled.'

'I'm still a bit stunned, to be honest. If I didn't have the photograph as proof, I'd think I was dreaming.'

He seems thrown. 'The photograph?'

'The sonogram image?'

'Ah, of course.'

I feel myself flushing again. 'Would you like a peep?'

'Absolutely.'

I collect it from the lounge and hand it over. 'The sonographer called the second baby a hidden twin.'

'Back in the day some mothers didn't know they were having two until the second one appeared. Can you imagine?'

'I know; incredible.' I glance around. 'I want to compare it with the first picture. Toby must have put it somewhere.'

He studies the printout with a thoughtful frown. 'Just awesome, especially to see two. Having a sibling is great, but being together from the very start of their existence ... They'll always have a special bond.'

I nod. Mum kept my half-sister a secret, yet somehow my anger has dissipated completely. I'm grateful I've found sanctuary and friendship here; I so wish she was part of it too.

'Hey ...' Jerome dips his head to peer at me. 'Are you OK? You look sad.'

'I'm fine. It's hormones, I expect.' I try for a smile. 'God, I sound like a broken record.'

'That's allowed.' He doesn't break eye contact. 'Just hormones or ...?'

'I'm really missing my mum.' His expression's so tender, the words tumble out. 'She doesn't even know I'm pregnant, let alone ... We fell out and I haven't spoken to her for weeks. The breach between us is so huge that it feels fatal, somehow. I miss her, I miss her humour, her laughter, her hugs. But I can't bring myself to simply send her a single text.'

'Why not?'

My heart thrashes as I consider the question. Rejection. That's it, that's my deep-seated fear. Gran's drawn features flash in. Or even something worse. 'I'm frightened she won't reply.'

Jerome offers his arms. 'At least I can help with the hug.'

He folds me in for an age and, though I'd love to stay in his solid embrace forever, even lift up my head for that longed-for kiss, I make myself step away. 'Thanks.'

'You're welcome.' He hands over my phone. 'Now send your mum that sonogram photo.' He grins. 'I guarantee she'll be in touch.'

55

I feel light and carefree on Friday morning. After Jerome left last night, I settled myself on the sofa, took a deep breath and typed out a text to Mum. The one message became many as I deleted and composed to get it word perfect. My attempts continued until I could barely keep my eyes open so, in the end, it comprised two simple words:

Hi Mum.

To my delight, her response was almost immediate:

Frankie! How lovely to hear from you. How is everything going? Have you settled in? xx

My weariness was replaced by burning tears of relief and, though we both walked on eggshells, we had a brief exchange about the basics – Pavilion Gardens, Toby, work. I considered asking about Barcelona or mentioning Gran and Baba, but I didn't want to spoil our tentative reconciliation. Besides, I was desperate to share my excitement.

So, I have news ...

Oh?

I'm pregnant!

Music to my ears! How far along?

Thirteen weeks!

I'm SO happy for you! That's wonderful news.

There's more ...

Go on.

It's twins!

OMG!!

I know. Initially I thought there was just one, but the other was hiding ...

I'll send the scan pic ...

Now, finishing my breakfast, I consider what to do with my day. Assuming Toby would be around, I booked it off work and, though I could log on and say there's been a change of plan, I don't fancy the miserable faces of the guys in my team bringing me down from this buzzing high.

I thrum my fingers on the table top. Is it too early in the pregnancy to stalk Instagram and see what's on trend for twin cots and accessories, decor and furniture? I catch the pile of Ursula's Georgian crockery. I'd hate anything to get broken, so I'll deliver them first, enjoy a saunter along the riverbank and buy something healthy for lunch on the way back. Then maybe I'll allow myself a snoop on the internet ...

The sunshine warm on my shoulders, I take in the gorgeous colours of the world – the purple rhododendrons lining my pathway, the vanilla strawberry hydrangeas surrounding the chapel and the shades of vibrant green in the bushes and trees – as I cautiously transport Ursula's precious belongings to The Gatehouse. Thankfully the front door is ajar, so I elbow it open.

'Hello? Ursula? Anyone home?' I call.

From the lack of response, it appears not, so I move further in and lower the tray onto the sideboard. Though I intended to slip out as quietly as I came, the treasures of the 'gallery' call to me, so I tiptoe around the high elevations, absorbing what I can in the shaft of light from outside. The photographs, drawings and ancient plans of the workhouse are as fascinating – and if I'm honest, a little creepy – as they were the last time. I briefly peer at more snaps of young Jerome and his brother dressed in cute mix-and-match outfits and, though I'd love to study them closely, it wouldn't do to be caught gawping.

I make for the exit, then remember Ursula's antique napkin rings, still in my shoulder bag. As I deposit them on the dresser, I stop for a further moment to squint into an old wooden display case, apparently containing a vintage surgical pouch, complete with scissors, scalpels, tweezers, pliers and pins. And, somewhat alarmingly, a folded blood-soaked apron and a copper poker.

Pondering a doctor's need for an ancient soldering iron, my eyes rest on a partially opened top drawer. I frown. It can't be the greetings card which arrived for Julia all those weeks ago, surely? Carefully tugging it out, I inspect the white envelope. A German stamp, the same handwriting and the name: Mrs J Logan. And there are more letters addressed to her beneath. What on earth? Ursula definitely said they'd been redirected ...

Hearing the echo of footsteps, I hurriedly slot it back, fixing a smile just in time for Fabian's entrance.

'Hi.' I gesture to the delicate teacups and saucers. 'I was returning these. Please would you thank Ursula for our special treat yesterday. It was very kind of her to make such a fuss of us.'

'If you wait a minute or two, you can thank her yourself.' His lips curve. 'Gratitude goes a long way with my wife, if you take my meaning.'

'Yes, of course.' Despite his avuncular look, the hairs on my arms stand erect and I want to get the hell out of this stuffy hallway. 'I have a chore to do right now. I'll look in later.'

'Excellent. I believe you haven't had the grand tour.'

'That's right.' I inch towards fresh air. 'I'm looking forward to it, though.'

'Very good. We'll see you later.'

The chill of something being off runs through me, so I dart out of the gates and set a brisk pace to throw off my agitation. When I arrive on the riverbank, I find a boulder to sit on, then I organise my thoughts as the water glides by. Why the heck hasn't Fabian delivered Julia's mail as promised? Why hide it away in a drawer? I chuckle eventually. There could be any number of reasons and none of them menacing. The older couple have never been anything other than kind and supportive, even loving towards me. They're Jerome's parents, for goodness' sake!

I find myself squinting in the direction of Didsbury village, nonetheless. What did Julia say about her sister when I viewed number three? That she lived in a gated development, in a house on the outside. I can't remember its name, but I'm fairly sure I know where she meant.

I take a deep breath. I'd intended to get some exercise, so why not?

56

Wondering what on earth I'm doing and what I'll say if Julia answers the door, I walk past the park entrance and along a tall wall surrounding the Cheshire brick-built housing estate. When I finally turn the corner and take in the scene, the metal barriers are considerably newer than the ones at Pavilion Gardens. Side gates allow entry by foot here, but I don't need to do that. From what she told me, my landlady lives at either number one or number two.

I glance from one elegant newish build to the other. The curtains are drawn on the left so I opt for the right, quickly striding across the driveway before I change my mind.

Taking a sharp breath, I rap with the knocker. The door is soon opened and a woman eyes me suspiciously. 'Yes?'

'I'm so sorry to bother you, but does Julia live here?'

'Julia?'

'Julia Logan.'

'No, she doesn't. What address were you looking for?'

I gesture across the small roadway. 'I'm guessing your neighbour's.'

'Hmm.'

She's clearly dubious, so I quickly speak before she closes me out. 'Sorry, I'm not being clear. Julia Logan is the sister. I'm buying her house and already live there, as it happens, so I want to hand over some letters which came for her.' It sounds lame, even to my own ears. 'It's probably just junk mail. Still, you never know, and as I was passing ...'

'Ah.' The penny clearly drops who I'm referring to. 'Well

you're very welcome to knock on and try but, if I were you, I'd post them through the letterbox.'

'Oh, OK. Could I ask why?'

'Hazel's gone a bit ... reclusive, I suppose. Life and soul one minute, then ... Well, you only need to look at the state of the house now. Closed blinds, the weed-strewn side garden.' She sucks in her cheeks. 'It's the first thing passers-by or visitors see, so it isn't a good look.'

'Right. Is she still actually living there?'

'She is indeed, so she has no excuses. She opens up for her supermarket deliveries and to put out the bins, but that's it. That poor dog never gets a walk. No wonder she had to call out the vet.'

I feel a spread of discomfort. Why would poor Hazel go from 'life and soul' to a recluse? 'Maybe she has a disability. I don't know, a physical one or something like agoraphobia.'

The woman blushes and steps further into her hallway. 'I have no idea. It's not the sort of thing one asks when passing.'

'Of course not.' I try to backtrack with a winning smile. 'Have you seen Julia – the sister – at all?'

'I'm afraid I'm not the neighbourhood watch, and I think that's the telephone. Feel free to post the letters whilst you're here.'

'Good plan, thanks.'

Though I'm sure she's watching through her bay window, I can hardly dispatch correspondence I don't have, so I make a show of searching my handbag and tapping my brow in a 'I can't believe I forgot them' manner.

Setting off the way I've come, I pull out my phone and call Toby.

'Hey, have you forgiven me?' he immediately says.

'There's nothing to forgive.' There isn't. Now I've reconciled with Mum, I understand that more than ever. 'How is Felicia?'

'She's good. She's here now and says hello.'

Hmm, 'hello' rather than congratulations or excitement about the baby news? I shrug; that's typical of Felicia and not Toby's fault. It's also a huge improvement on her being a masked burglar; why I thought that, I'll never know. 'Hello back to her.'

'You sound breathless. Are you on a walk?'

'Yeah.' My stomach is fizzing with alarm. 'You know Julia, the vendor? Well, something peculiar has happened ...'

57

By the time I reach Pavilion Gardens, I'm laughing at my own fervid imagination. I told Toby the whole story about Julia, her sister and my concerns, and he laughingly said I was 'as nuts as they are'. And now I'm back here, I no longer know why I had that weird spasm of uncertainty when I've always felt so safe. It's clearly my hormones. Again. My 'broken record' comment is so very true and, from what I've read, I'll have way more of them than with a single baby.

As I pass The Gatehouse, I stop. I'm exhausted and need a rest, but the goody-two-shoes – or perhaps the simply pragmatic – pupil within knows it's best to keep on the right side of the headmistress if I want to retain my top grades, so I rap on the door and push it open.

'Hello? Anyone home?'

'Francesca, is that you?' echoes back. Then Ursula herself appears with a tea towel over her shoulder. 'You're here! Wonderful. Fabian said you'd be popping in.'

'Yes, I just wanted to say thank you for—'

'Always a pleasure.' She cocks her head. 'Goodness, you look as though you need a sit down, young lady. Let's have a nice a pot of tea.'

She flicks a switch and the hallway floods with light. As if there might be evidence of my snooping, I avoid looking at the dresser and point at the photographs I briefly looked at earlier. 'Are these of Jerome and his brother?'

Ursula puts a hand to her ample breast. 'Yes. My dearest Stefan. Look at them both. So beautiful and such a special bond between them.'

'Yes, I can see that. I'm so sorry for your loss.'

'Thank you.' She sniffs, then dons a bright smile. 'But there's no need to dwell on the past when there's so much to look forward to.'

She shows no sign of moving, so I gesture to the framed map on the far wall. 'I think you said that's the original architect's plan of the workhouse?'

'Indeed, yes it is.' She walks over and studies it, so I join her. 'Men and women, girls and boys, young and old were separated in dormitories back then. Chief Medical Officer Baden was paid thirty pounds a year from which he had to tend his many patients and pay for all medicines.' She glances at me. 'Except for trusses and leeches, apparently.'

The thought of being treated with bloodsucking parasites brings on a shudder. 'Trusses?' I ask.

'A hernia belt. We have one in a display cabinet which I'll show you when we have the tour. Though, I confess, it looks more like an instrument of torture than a surgical appliance.' She steps to the showcase I glimpsed earlier. 'One or two of his nick-nacks are also here.' She points them out. 'A somewhat bloody garment, not laundered yet worn with pride, chloroform if you were lucky and a hot iron for cauterising wounds.'

She clearly sees me flinch as she studies me reprovingly. 'To stop profuse bleeding, Francesca. Given that or death, when one's amputated limb is still leaking juices in a tray of sawdust, I know which I'd choose.'

As I shape how best to reply, Ursula returns to the chart and continues to point out landmarks with an avid glint in her eyes.

'The female imbecile ward was here, the lunatic, the itch and isolation wards just there, and adjacent to them, somewhat conveniently, was the mortuary.' She loudly sucks in her breath. 'The mortality rates for the inmates was, sadly, high. What was termed "ward fever" accounted for much of it. In those days, even the most foul smelling post-surgical pus was considered a sign the wound was healing rather than a bacterial infection.' She tuts.

'Lack of hand and surgical instrument washing, let alone general hygiene, I'm afraid.'

She spins around to another image. 'This rather splendid photograph is of an inmate who spent her whole adult life making shrouds for the dead.'

I swallow hard. 'I guess someone had to do it.'

'Correct. Far worse was the job of the mortuary keeper, as he had to strip the diseased or malnourished body and prepare it for burial in the cheapest possible casket. That would go into an unmarked grave, often along with several other coffins. If the corpse was unclaimed for forty-eight hours it could be donated for use in medical research and training. Needless to say, that's never a bad thing, and it was especially convenient for Medical Officer Baden, as he could do the dissections and analyses on-site.'

'God, really? Here at Pavilion Gardens?'

'Yes, of course. Enhancing his knowledge was altruistic and beneficial for everyone, Francesca. And having a burial ground within the estate was most fortunate, too. Few workhouses had their own.'

'So ...' An icy sensation down my spine, I return to the chart for the cemetery's location. 'Oh my word. So the lawn ...? We were dancing on a graveyard last week?'

'We were indeed. However, the remains were dug up at some point and rehoused in Southern Cemetery, so let's hope we didn't upset any spirits.' She drags her finger to a spot beyond the chapel, and beams. 'This is the part you'll like, Francesca. The baby house was here. Can you imagine those newborns under the care of nurses, some rolling about on the floor, some warming their little toes at the fire, whilst others with rosy cheeks and flaxen curls lay sound asleep, looking the very incarnation of beauty and innocence?' She gently pats my stomach. 'Well, as I say, thankfully some wonders of life don't change. Now off you go into the parlour and get comfortable on the settee. I'll pop on the kettle and be a minute or two.'

I search for an excuse to escape more relics from the past. Just as I draw a blank, my mobile peals. 'Oh, it's Toby. I'd better ...' I say.

Inwardly chuckling at Ursula's 'well, seeing as it's Toby' expression, I rub the goosebumps from my arms and trundle back to my abode. At my door I turn and squint at the green, moving my head from the group of grubby, shaven-haired and morose ragamuffins at one side, to the joyous, shiny infants dancing around a maypole on the other. Blinking the vision away, I nod in acknowledgement. Ursula's zealous résumés about the past are undoubtedly disconcerting, but they bring home my staggering good fortune in comparison to the deprived people who once lived here.

58

What with telling friends and colleagues about my – our – astonishing news, catching up with a backlog of work tasks, attending daily Teams meetings, and the usual overnight stay in Lincoln, the week flashes by. Making the most of our final rental payment, Toby has stayed in Fulham, but he'll be home tonight and I'm buzzing. I've already packed the kitchen cupboards and fridge with hubby-friendly provisions, so I turn to my next errand of making room for his stuff.

Wrapping my hair into a high bun, I collect cloths and cleaning products from under the sink, snap on a pair of rubber gloves, then set about my brisk housework, starting downstairs. My back aches after a time, so I lie on the sofa to rest for ten minutes.

When I wake an hour later, I laugh. 'So this is the way it's going to be, eh?' I say to my babies. 'And I'm starving too!'

After ambling to the shops to buy fresh ingredients for lunch, I wait for the hint of heartburn to pass, then resume my chores upstairs. When I first moved in, I hung my clothes on the right side of the wardrobe and took the lower shelves from force of habit, so I polish the accessible ones for Toby, then look up to the high cupboards above. Will he need those? He does have a *lot* of clothes, yet would he really be prepared to fold his designer gear and have to climb up to access them? Nope. On the other hand, there'll be bedding and a whole load of miscellaneous stuff from the flat that'll need to be stored.

I rub my stomach. 'Well, you guys will only get bigger, so I guess now is the time ...'

Placing the dressing table stool in situ, I test it for strength, carefully mount it and tug at the cabinet knob. On first inspection it's empty but, when I apply the spray and reach in my sponge, it catches a metallic object. I pull it out, dismount and examine my find with a puzzled frown. What on earth ...? It's clearly the missing remote control for the gates. Yet it's accompanied by a photo keyring of a smiling couple, that same wedding portrait which had hung on the landing wall. A car key, too. And they're sticky ...

Instinctively dropping the bunch, I step back and stare, then I gingerly pick it up with a tea towel. Whatever is smeared on it – which is surely only grease – might soil the cream carpet. Though would oil leave a rusty red stain? And who the heck does it belong to? Well, that's a silly thought; it has to be Julia or her errant husband ...

Prickles of unease stab my skin. The fob is Mercedes and fairly new looking. Wouldn't the owner have some sort of finding device app? And irrespective of that, what would it be doing at the very back of a built-in closet?

My shoulders jerk at the sudden peal of my mobile. It's a FaceTime from Toby.

I swipe it open. 'I'm glad you've called. Something really odd has just ...' I begin. But his pallid face and haunted expression catches me short. 'Oh God, what's happened?' I ask.

He flattens his hair. 'Bloody hell.'

'What is it, Toby? You're as white as a sheet.'

'Bloody hell!'

Alarm shoots through me. 'Tell me. What's happened?'

'Daniel Blewitt's just called.'

'As in work Dan?'

'Yes. I'm still taking it in.'

'Taking in what?'

'It's awful.'

'Toby! For Christ's sake ...'

'Marcus was in a hit and run accident. On Thursday lunchtime, apparently.'

'Our Marcus? Marcus Penny?'

'Yes.' His gaze is hollow. 'Rumour has it that the car drove straight at him.'

'Oh, my God. Is he OK?'

'Apparently a witness said he was tossed in the air like a rag doll.'

The image hits the back of my eyes. 'He's alive, right?'

'No. They put him on life support for his relatives to say goodbye. According to Dan, they've now turned it off.' He rubs his face. 'It's unbelievable.'

'Christ, his poor family.'

'Yeah, exactly.' Seeming to look right through me, he falls quiet for several seconds. Then he sighs. 'Thing is, I feel really bad but ... Well, his new project starts on Monday and Dan needs an answer from me today.'

'Whose project? Marcus'?'

'Yeah, exactly. It's London-based, high profile and the role is director. So I'll—'

There's a lead weight in my stomach. 'Get the promotion you wanted?'

'Yes.' He puffs out his cheeks. 'As I say, Dan needs a reply PDQ.'

'Right.'

'They'll backdate the salary to the start of the year. You know, as a sweetener.'

'Wow.'

'I know.' Although he smiles thinly, I sense he's sitting a little straighter and has a certain gravitas about him already. 'The circumstances aren't ideal, and, of course, I wish it could have happened another way, but this is my moment, Frankie, a chance to prove my worth and shine. I hate to put it so crudely, but the loss of Marcus is my gain, and I'd be a fool not to take it.'

59

Almost in a fugue state, I stand at the bedroom window and watch the rain bounce on the pathways.

'I understand. You have to take it,' I said to Toby at the end of our conversation.

And I do get it completely; I work in the same industry, for the same company. I know how the system works: the generous offer shows how urgent the need for a substitute director is; the client is a merchant bank; Toby's career would badly suffer, or even end, if he didn't grab the opportunity with both hands – indeed, grasp it with the resoluteness and conviction he thought he was lacking. And besides, he wants it, he needs it, he's hungry for it; this very scenario is just what he's been manifesting – not the death of a man he's known since childhood, of course – but a miracle.

I also comprehend it's the end of our marriage.

'I can still come up at weekends,' he said. Yet it was a feeble attempt to appease me. We both know how full on the role will be, how the last thing he'll need is a schlep to Manchester, even if he happens to have a day or two free, let alone help with the care of …

I look down to my small mound. Twins. I completely adore them already, but I have no delusions about how hard it will be with two babies to feed, nurse and cuddle, change nappies, bathe and dress. And even before that, I have to carry them to term and look after myself to give them the best chance in the womb, then give painful birth. Will Toby be there for that? Will any period of parental leave be compatible with his new job? Will he want it, even if it is?

Although a huge effort, I focus my fuddled mind and go through our FaceTime exchange frame by frame. Did he mention the pregnancy at all, or acknowledge his paternal responsibilities, other than saying, 'It'll be a massive increase in salary, Frankie ...'

So what does that mean? Hire a full-time nanny to live with me in my flaming house? No way. There's no substitute for an actual father, the role model a child needs. I, of all people, know that.

Realisation hits, like a blow to my chin, making me physically wobble. A single parent; I'll be a single parent, same as my mum.

I look down to my mobile, still glued to my hand. Mum, I'll call Mum. Yet what will I say at this stage? So many things are whirring in my mind – not just the dreadful, tragic news about Marcus – also my life here, which suddenly feels shaky. Both would take a huge amount of explaining. She's in Barcelona, for God's sake, and she might be at work. I nod. Yes, I need to calm down and sort out my worries before passing them onto her.

But it's so hard to concentrate. My heart is wildly thrashing, the walls caving in.

I lower my head and try to suck in some air. Am I ill, even dying? No, I can't be. My babies; I have to live for my babies. Help, I need help. Minta and Pippa; stagger to them. Or Jerome. Phone Jerome.

My fingers fumbling, I call his number. The line is engaged, so I slither to the ground and slowly count tummy breaths, in and out, in and out, for several long seconds. The fog gradually clears and reason seeps in. I'm panicking, not dying; I've had a nasty shock and my blood sugar is low.

Glad I've avoided embarrassing myself by a whisker, I eventually stand, eat a cereal bar and head outside. Homing in on the positives, I put one foot in front of the other and walk towards the gates. After the longing and loss, I'm pregnant with twins; I'm over the danger period and my waistline is expanding every day. It's precisely what I wanted, prayed for, manifested.

Yet the negatives are so overwhelming ...

'Hey, Frankie. Frankie?'

The sound of my name filters through. I look up to Jerome at the bottom of his steps. He wafts his mobile. 'You phoned. I've just seen it.'

'Oh, sorry. A pocket call.' I can't cope with his blue-eyed concern today. 'I need to buy an avocado for tonight's dinner, so ...'

'Are you OK?'

I bridle at the question. Toby's clearly been in touch with his bestie already. 'Yes. Why do you ask?'

'It's raining and you're not wearing a coat.' He gestures to his door. 'Come in until it passes or at least borrow an umbrella?'

I want to bolt; I'm afraid I'll cry; I hate being this weak and frail version of myself. Yet I nod and follow him into to the modern, bright hallway, tastefully decorated in muted colours, without, thank God, an eerie artefact or ancient image in sight.

'First things first.' He nips into the downstairs toilet, then hands me a towel. 'There you go.'

I self-consciously pad my face and hair. 'Thanks.'

'You've missed a bit.'

He takes the cloth and gently taps beneath my eyes. So very close, I can almost sense his lips gently pressing against mine.

Thankfully, a bubble of humour rises up through my embarrassment. 'Streaked mascara?' I say, stepping back. 'How charming.'

'Always charming. Especially when you smile.' He motions towards the kitchen. 'A coffee before you go? Or just the brolly?'

Emotion prickles behind my eyes. I want to stay here, curl up against him and bask in the feeling of being special. And if I'm honest, a whole lot more. I'd like him to hold me in his arms and kiss me, really kiss me, then take me to bed. Somehow I know that's what he wants too, what his offer of a coffee really means. But my life is already beyond complicated. And I have my babies to think of.

60

'Francesca! Hello!'

Hidden beneath Jerome's huge umbrella, I rotate to Ursula. I thought I'd managed to stealthily bypass The Gatehouse. No such bloody luck.

Ridiculously needing to justify my desultory walk, I waft the avocado in my free hand. 'Oh, hi. Popped out for this.'

'In such dreadful weather.' She tilts her head and studies me. 'Looks like you could do with a hot drink and a sit down.'

It's on the tip of my tongue to say no, but I honestly could do with her genial company, even be given a dose of her enthusiasm and energy. Amused by the notion, despite myself, I graciously dip my head. 'That would be lovely, thank you.'

The fusty lobby is in darkness as usual and, though I ready myself for more buttock-clenching tales from bygone times, she gestures to a door on the left. 'Let's sit in the parlour like genteel Edwardian ladies taking tea, shall we? Of course teashops were an integral part of the women's liberation movement. Perhaps we can also set the world to rights.'

If only. My world still feels at a perilous angle. 'Sounds good to me.'

'Wonderful. I'll be with you shortly.'

I enter the refreshingly bright room and look around the elegant quarters. It's cluttered with antique pieces, which all look pristine, and the three-piece suite adds a touch of art deco glamour. Wondering if it was made by the poor inmate who'd been tasked to sew shrouds, I peer at a framed tapestry above the bronze and black hearth. The intricate wording appears to be in

Latin, so maybe not. Or perhaps one of the wealthy masters wrote it down and watched over her shoulder as she neatly, and perhaps fearfully, crafted each letter. Yes, somehow, I can visualise that.

Turning to yet another 'gallery', I take in the neatly hung arrays either side of the door. One elevation is dedicated to the workhouse days, so I spend a few moments looking at the dour group photographs – grim-faced women wearing mobcaps and shawls; broken, bearded men holding sticks to support themselves; bonny toddlers nursed by wrinkled, toothless nannies. And the rows of shaven-haired boys and girls, not even cracking one smile between them.

The last image makes me pause and turn to the embroidery again. The Latin is signed off by the name 'Cognati' and, though I can't remember where I've heard the word before, the serif script capital 'C' is too similar to be a coincidence, so perhaps the Peppercorns are involved in the charity too. Supporting disabled children is a warming thought, yet it brings into stark contrast the grinning kids on the Hundred Club pamphlet and those solemnly staring from the walls.

I move on to a list of rules the 'Poor in the House' were to observe, my eyes sliding from *Obey the Governor and Matron in all their reasonable commands* to *WHOEVER shall offend ... will be punished by confinement in the stocks, or in the dungeon, or by distinction of dress, by abatement of diet, loss of gratuity, by such corporal or other punishment ...*

Swallowing hard, I step over to the other half. Thank God this display is more contemporary and of people in colour film. Drawn by their delighted countenances, I lean closer and scan each bright beam. After a few moments, I frown and start again. The whole collage comprises different women holding their babies. I squint at the first, then switch from one portrait to the next and the next. Each shows a mother with a tiny newborn. But the common denominator isn't just their happy broad smiles. It's the man amidst them, looking as proud as punch.

I blink and peer again. Though older in some images than in others, there's absolutely no doubt.

It's Fabian.

My tongue burned from slurping the boiling tea so fast, I scuttle back to the silence of number three to think straight. I managed to mutter something about taking a casserole out of the oven to break free from Ursula and that oppressive room, but I'm honesty gobsmacked. Fabian is – or was – an obstetrician. Even if the photographs of him and those delighted mothers hadn't been a huge clue, his framed certificates on the parlour wall had confirmed it.

Wrapping the throw around my shivering body, I climb onto the sofa and curl into a ball. I'm wholly shocked at my discovery. Precisely why, I don't know. Jerome told me his father was from a family of medics weeks ago. In fact, he said something about him still working part-time, which makes sense, as he doesn't always seem to be around. So why do I feel so confused and so thrown? So unstable, so out of control?

I slow my breathing and reason with myself. This horrible feeling of discombobulation is actually my own fault. I've been in a blinkered state since the burglary, if I'm honest, a sort of high anxiety I've managed by looking only at what I've wanted to. So perhaps Toby's comments about my 'tunnel vision' were actually justified. Maybe I should have made a bigger effort with him, even moved back to London when he asked.

Tears stinging my eyes, I cup my tummy. Oh God; have I made the right decisions here? Or has my pigheadedness blindsided me?

61

So incredibly tired, I flop onto the mattress at nine and immediately fall into a superficial sleep. My subconscious mind rumbles with snapshots, moving images and dreams that could be fantasy, memories or real-life events: ultrasound scans and silent little Lucy next door, keys in a pool of glistening blood, Julia's tense expression and that beautiful bouquet of lilies, Pippa's bruised wrists and Minta's sunny smile. The Gatehouse gallery of photos: from those severe nurse guards at the gates to young Stefan, from Fabian's beaming grin to his 'new mummy' fans. And that huge workhouse map with the chapel at the centre of the cruciform design, everything in shadow save those bouncing, curly-haired infants in the baby house. Then, finally, me dancing on gravestones with Jerome, his solid hand warm in mine, tugging me with a smile towards his crumpled divan.

I burst to the surface at that point, relieved it was only a dream, yet still wanting to retrieve the fantasy, to feel him move inside me until I climax.

Sitting upright, I sigh. God, what a mess inside my head. A shrink would have a field day. Needing to shake off the haunting image of the cemetery from my psyche, I climb out of bed and open the curtains. There are no ancient headstones nor starving children with hollow eyes staring from the grimy workhouse windows like prisoners, thank the Lord. It's just a square of grass, fully recovered from the imprint of midsummer's bare feet. If I do the same with my equilibrium, all will be fine.

I rotate my shoulders and stretch. From the depths of panic earlier, I'm actually OK. The strong, resolute Frankie is still inside.

I'll draw on that moving forwards. Do whatever is best for my babies. Getting a handle on my hormonally-induced and lavish imagination would be a good start.

As I make to close out the night, a light from an upper chapel window is gradually blocked out. Someone is clearly in the penthouse flat, lowering a blind. I frown in puzzlement. Who the heck lives there and why have I never met them in all the weeks I've lived here? Determined to ignore it and not give my mind the chance to gear up and speculate, I amble to the bathroom for a pee. Then, instead of retreating to my duvet, I pad downstairs, pop on a thin mac and slip into my loafers.

'Imagination killer needed before sleep,' I mutter to myself. 'And there's no time like the present.'

Almost chuckling at my own daring, I ease open the door and step out. My smile falls as I peer into the black night. The stillness and silence feel oppressive and, despite the balmy air, I have a horrible sensation that someone is behind me, their bony fingers reaching to drape an icy blanket across my spine. Suddenly terrified it's a stony-faced matron or an inmate risen from the dead, I force my feet to inch around. Only emptiness ricochets off the old buildings and bricks, the walkways and the perfect maze of trimmed green, thank God. Yet my stomach clenches at the thought. Emptiness, isolation, *seclusion* ...

I shake off the ridiculous alarm and reinstate my resolve. But as I put one foot in front of the other, the notion of someone or something watching and wheezing from the ancient enclosures again prickles my skin. I creep past the sleeping Gatehouse, along the silvery path to the chapel, then I climb up the steps and peer through the panelled window. Though my hot, nervy breath clouds the glass, there's no one in the lobby area from what I can glean, so I shift across to the entrance and cautiously press down the handle. The door that's never locked reassuringly opens, so I enter and listen for movement. Satisfied that nobody is on the ground level, I tiptoe across the plush carpet, past the aged font to the open staircase at the rear.

As noiselessly as I'm able, I steal up in the darkness to a first-floor landing. Voices echo from the walls so I stop, stock still, and strain to hear over the loud thud of apprehension in my ears. The conversation's too muffled to make out, but it's coming from the right, so I turn the other way and squint through the gloom. Part of me wants to bolt out and escape whilst I can, but there's a doorway and it's ajar ...

My pulse revving from intrigue and fear, I sneak across the floorboards, edge into the vaulted room and glance around. Though moonlight shines through the arched casement, it takes moments to adapt to what I'm seeing. The centre contains an adult-sized cot, for want of a better description. I stare, bemused. Is it a disabled person's bedroom? That would explain why I've never seen hide nor hair of them. No, it's too whitewashed and clinical for that and, besides, the bed is adjustable and surrounded by monitors and machines. I take in a wheeled unit with a Perspex rectangle on the top and a wall-mounted fridge beyond it. Almost mesmerised, I move to the glass door and squint at the rows of drug vials inside. The labels are handwritten and, as I strain to read them, foreboding trickles through me. What the hell? They're neatly marked with percentages of 'morphine' and 'scopolamine' and someone's initials ...

Rotating again, my gaze lands on a tray of methodically placed surgical items: suture packets, kidney bowls, scissors and a row of metal tools. I pick one up and frown. They appear to be very large spoons or tongs, but why would they be freeze-wrapped? Realisation finally cracking, I drop them. Good God, they're birthing forceps and this is a delivery suite.

My eyes slide to what I've already seen, yet not fully absorbed. Noise-cancelling earphones, a padded head restraint and blindfold, harnesses and straps for wrists, ankles and knees.

I swallow hard. Though it looks more like a ward in a lunatic asylum, this room is a secret venue for childbirth. I gape at the leather shackles again. Why the hell would any woman agree to these?

'Francesca?' I snap around to Fabian's eloquent tones. 'It is you. I thought I heard something.' He turns to the person behind him. 'No need to come in here, dear. The end and not the means is what we focus on, remember?'

I have already caught a glimpse of my friend. 'Minta?' I push past him. 'What are you doing here?'

'Hi Frankie.' She takes my hands in hers. 'You're shaking! I'm just here for an antenatal appointment. Come through and see for yourself. There's nothing at all to be worried about.'

I carefully pull my fingers away. 'An antenatal appointment at this hour?'

'It's only half past eleven and ...' She gestures to Fabian and beams. 'Having an obstetrician of such renown is wonderful, but it means he's in great demand. We're lucky to have him here now he's gone part-time.'

Struggling to catch up with this astonishing development, I gape at my friend's placid expression. Then I spiral to him. 'So all your patients come here in the flaming dead of night to have their check-ups?'

'Goodness, no.'

He chuckles amiably, strides across the landing to the other entrance, opens it up and gestures me in. I'm still rigid with shock yet I duly follow and absorb my surroundings. This office-style room doesn't contain wires and instruments – or fucking restraints – but it does have an examination couch and an ultrasound machine against one wall.

He grins with clear pleasure. 'This extra, shall we call it, is simply a bonus for those living in our community. I see my other ladies at my rooms in town.'

A shudder passes through me and, though I'm horribly sure of the answer, I still ask. 'And they are where?'

'St John Street. I believe you've met my very able colleague, Doctor Gauss?'

As if I'm an infant, Minta rubs my arm. 'Honestly, Frankie. Having Fabian – Doctor Baden – and his specialist care is an incredible privilege for us all. It's on-site and he offers his services to us for, well, free.'

'I think *pro bono* is a nicer expression,' he adds.

Despite their friendly countenances, nothing feels right. In fact, it's downright abnormal. 'Why?' I demand. I glare at Fabian. 'Why would you do that?'

He answers easily. 'Family tradition; philanthropy passed down the line from son to son for many years. Similar to an entail, if you like. And, God willing, long may that bloodline last.'

'What? So you've all been ... baby doctors?'

He seems to think about that. 'In one form or another.'

'Right.' Minta's words from earlier trickle back. 'Doctor *Baden*? I thought you were called Peppercorn?'

His eyes sparkle with amusement. 'An old nickname that stuck; I rather like it.' He cocks his head. 'The old peppercorn rents? Peppercorn being a metaphor for a very small cash payment or other nominal consideration used to satisfy the requirements of a legal contract. It's generally not demanded by the landlord.'

'I see.' The surname 'Baden' nags; I've heard it before ... Too weary to work it out now, I turn away to retreat from this too, too bizarre situation. Then Pippa's injuries flash in, so I jab at the opposite room. 'Did Pippa give birth to Lucy in there?'

'Indeed she did. Noah too. A very relaxed, pain-free experience from my perfected combination of medicines that she was most grateful for. Only a little sore down below for a day or two, but otherwise up and about hours later, which you saw for yourself.'

'And I'm having the same,' Minta says. 'Which was a huge relief from the very start.'

'Then why the ...' I don't want to freak her out, but bloody hell, who gives birth strapped down? And using those sodding huge forceps? 'Then why the set-up in the delivery suite?'

'The treatment I offer from start to finish is a matter of trust, Francesca. I promise the fairytale ending, and I always keep that promise, which Pippa will gladly attest to.' He peers over his glasses. 'You look a touch weary. You have two little ones thriving in there, so I expect it's past their bedtime.'

Minta slides her arm through mine. 'I'll come with you,' she says, gently tugging me away.

When we reach the lobby, she studies me with luminous eyes. 'Look, I know it seems a little odd at first, and there's no way I'm looking it up on the internet, but I'm personally all for a pain-free birth. If that's what a woman wants, she should be allowed to have it.'

It's more than bloody 'odd'. 'What do you mean, exactly? Something similar to an epidural?'

'No, not really. It's called twilight birth,' she whispers. 'Or more appropriately twilight sleep. You know, sort of semi-awake yet feeling nothing? I mean, come on, if men were giving birth, it would be used every blinking time, wouldn't it? And it isn't something you'd get on the NHS, is it? Which is why the other mums here were so fortunate, why I will be and you, when your time comes! Doctor Baden does a bespoke – well, procedure, if you like – for every patient. You know, so the doses are the perfect balance for each individual.' She smooths the font stone and sighs. 'I'm so glad we live here, aren't you? Not every obstetrician-gynaecologist undergoes that extra training.'

'Extra training for what? Plying women in labour with zombie drugs?'

'No.' Minta looks offended. 'You know perfectly well what I mean.'

'No, I don't.'

She looks meaningfully at my stomach. 'Ah, I see. You're teasing me.' She laughs. 'The proof's in the pudding, as they say. So yes, we're very lucky to have an all-in-one obstetrician-gynaecologist and reproduction endocrinologist on our very doorstep.' She taps her nose. 'All on the QT, of course, otherwise every couple in Manchester would want to live here. You know, those with fertility problems.'

62

After a frustrating, sleepless night of internal wrangling – without finding even one logical answer to my host of concerns – I was up, showered and dressed by six o'clock. I knew I had to bide my time until a civilised hour, so I paced the small confines of the house and tried to rationally list all of the questions I want to ask Julia. Now I'm here at the entrance to Heritage Grove, my heart is wildly thrashing and my head feels like it's stuffed with cotton wool.

I summon up the resolve I need for this mission, turn to the house on the left and stride across the driveway. Then I post the note I wrote earlier through the letterbox:

'Hello. My name is Francesca Whittle. I've been renting 3 Pavilion Gardens from Julia Logan and I'm due to buy it. I believe you are her sister. Please may I speak to her or to you? It's urgent. Many thanks.'

I gently tap with the knocker and wait. When there's no reply, I step back, look up to the bedroom bay window and, in the hope that someone might be peeping through the drawn curtains, I press my palms together like a prayer.

I've almost given up when my ears prick to the scrape of keys. The door parts a crack. 'Julia isn't here.'

'Please can I talk to you instead?' My voice catches with emotion. 'I'm worried and confused and I don't know who else to ask.'

The woman stares, but her eyes eventually soften and she opens up fully. 'OK, five minutes.' She gestures beyond the staircase. 'This way.'

I follow her slim frame to a conservatory. In contrast to the dim hallway, it's filled with early sunshine and warmth.

'I'm Julia's sister, Hazel,' she says. 'I'm not sure how I can help, but ...' Her gaze slides to my protective palm on my stomach. 'You're pregnant?'

'Yes.' I swallow hard. The word 'pregnant' already feels horribly loaded. I consider where to start. 'I'm supposed to be buying Julia's house.'

Hazel wafts the note. 'Yes, it says.'

'Where is she?' I blurt. 'If she isn't here, where is she? I have her mail and ... and a key that I think may belong to her.'

'Please sit.' Though she looks inordinately weary, Hazel smiles a thin smile. 'This might sound ridiculous but I honestly don't know where Julia is. She came here for a while after moving out, then she left to ... to find herself.'

Questions tumble out. 'In a car? Does she drive? What make does she have?'

'No, she never passed her test. Ben did all the driving.'

'Did?' The *sorry for your loss* greeting hits my chest. 'You mean before he left her?'

'He didn't leave her.' A spasm of pain passes through Hazel's face. 'He died.'

'Oh God.' I cover my mouth. I said that too loudly; I need to stay calm. 'I'm so sorry to hear that. May I ask what happened? I know it's personal and I'm sorry to press.' I inhale deeply. 'It's important that I know.'

'He died in hospital. Complications after surgery.'

I feel my shoulders relax. 'Gosh, how awful. That must have been a dreadful shock.'

'It was; one stunning blow after the other.'

'Oh, so ...'

'The operation was to fix his broken femur, or maybe I should say shattered leg; he had multiple fractures which needed metal plates and so on.'

'He was in an accident?'

'Yes. He was hit by a vehicle of some sort.' She sighs. 'He was drunk when it happened, so who knows, but Julia saw him before he was taken into theatre and he was convinced it was deliberate. She chided him for being his usual dramatic self. Little did she know they'd be their last words.'

'Oh no.'

'He never came round from the anaesthetic. She's been lost ever since.' She smiles ruefully. 'If she'd had a child, she'd have had something to hold on to. I suspect that's where she is now.'

'Where?'

'Turkey, is my guess.'

'For?'

'IVF or similar.'

'I see.' I try to organise my thoughts. My throat is so dry, it's a struggle to speak. I need to get to the real crux of why I'm in some stranger's home, attempting to get a handle on my erratic fears. 'You commented on, well, this.' I touch my tummy. 'So Julia was never pregnant?'

'No, she dearly wanted to be, which is why ...' She bites her lip. 'You must be so pleased about your situation. I don't want to speak out of turn, and anyway I don't know that much about it.'

'Please do.' I look at her intently. 'Please do. That's why I'm here. I'm totally in the dark, imagining all sorts of things, and I need some answers.'

'I can see that. In all honesty, I don't know if they'll be answers or speculation. Ben was a newspaper hack. He'd latch onto a conspiracy theory and not let go. He called it "journalistic intuition", but, at times, it felt more like obsession.'

My heart thumps. 'Understood. Please go on.'

'OK.' Hazel takes a big breath. 'So ... Julia wanted kids from the start. Eventually they found a problem with Ben's sperm; a low count or not viable or similar. A donor and artificial insemination was the only way forward. He understandably railed against the idea, and it took some time to get his head around it, so perhaps that's why he was looking for an excuse not to go ahead.'

Despite the warmth, I shiver. 'Did he find one?'

'Yes. Julia was led to believe the donors would be sourced

through the usual channels and be screened for basic blood typing and viruses such as HIV, hepatitis and so on.'

'And they weren't?'

'I truly don't know. Ben's theory was that the sperm came from what he called a "private collection".'

The word *trust* echoes in my ears. I suck in some air and brace myself. 'Do you know who she consulted about the infertility?'

Hazel nods. 'Doctor Baden.'

Though his name was inevitable, I can't help visibly flinching.

She reaches out a hand. 'I'm sorry, that's maybe not what you want to hear. In fairness, Julia liked him and had every faith in him. He was extremely professional and, at the end of the day, she wanted that baby and, if anything felt a little odd about the set-up in Pavilion Gardens, she was willing to turn a blind eye.' Her gaze slides away. 'As I'm sure you are too.'

'OK, thank you for talking to me.' My limbs insubstantial, I stand and make for the exit. There are more queries, I know, but I already have an information overload I need to process.

As I press down the handle to leave, Hazel's final comment lands. I turn with a frown. 'What do you mean by "as I'm sure you do too"?'

Her pale cheeks colour. 'Sorry, I didn't mean to say anything out of turn. I just assumed – like the other couples who live at Pavilion Gardens – that you'd had, well, treatment from Doctor Baden yourself.'

'No, not at all. It was a natural conception.' I need to bolt and breathe in unsullied air. But the woman has been kind and I don't want to be rude. 'It's lovely out there; a nice day to walk your dog.'

'Sammy died eight months or so ago. I'd love to have another. Sadly the antidepressants I'm on make me sluggish, and I worry I wouldn't have the energy to walk it every day.'

'So why did the vet visit a few weeks ago?' I struggle to inhale. 'Sorry to ask. Your neighbour said one had called round.'

'I don't think so. Unless I was out or asleep and Julia answered. Why would one call when we don't have a pet, though?' She gestures over the way. 'And how would she even know it was a vet?'

'I have no idea. Maybe he drove a van with the name of the practice on it. Or perhaps he ...' An image flares in my head and my words trail off. It's of two men chatting outside Pavilion Gardens. One is my absent husband and the other ... 'Never mind. Thanks so much again for talking to me.'

I wave a leaden arm and force my legs to work. Maybe the vet did drive a business vehicle. I grimace. Or perhaps he was carrying a khaki veterinarian's bag.

63

Frantically searching for explanations, I tromp blindly up Wilmslow Road. Something is seriously amiss at Pavilion Gardens. The ancient baby house and former hospital, the penthouse-cum-clinic, that squeaky clean crèche, the constant jolly, smiley faces of the residents and the Peppercorns – and, yes, their weird control — let alone bloody sperm donations and twilight births behind closed doors. What the fuck? Why did I never see it?

I attempt to absorb the information I learned just now. It was Hazel's understanding that every couple in the community had had fertility issues or treatment. Yet what about me, Francesca Whittle? Sure, I had one miscarriage, but I conceived naturally. So why have me and Toby been so embraced by the Peppercorns? Not that it's their real bloody name, of course.

Trying to steady my thudding heart, I put a gentle hand on my belly. There has to be a logical explanation for everything. And my imagination has been in overdrive. Ben died from complications in a hospital; Hazel's reclusive behaviour wasn't because she was hiding away or in fear, as I'd supposed from the neighbour's description, but because she's struggling with her mental health and medication; Julia isn't dead in a ditch, but in Turkey, and in all probability still desperately trying for a baby out there. Then there's the 'private collection' of sperm insinuation made by Ben, a man who was positively looking for an excuse not to go down the donor route and who revelled in conspiracy theories to boot. Fabian's a respected doctor in his field; as well as his many delighted 'new mummy' fans, he has all the certificates hanging on the parlour wall, and one would assume he has the appropriate licences, insurance and suchlike for both his rooms in central Manchester and his clinic at Pavilion Gardens.

And yet, and yet ... Fabian implied that Ben had left Julia for another woman. Ursula said he'd forwarded her post. Why the hell would they lie about either? Then there's the road traffic accident which put Ben in hospital in the first place. He was convinced he'd been deliberately run down ...

Another thought strikes me like a knock-out blow. Christ, it wasn't only Ben who was hit by a driver who didn't stop. What did Toby say about Marcus Penny? That a witness said the car drove straight at him. It has to be coincidental, surely? One happened miles away in London, the other around here.

Sheer panic threatening again, I flop down at a bus shelter and drag in some air. Who can I honestly trust? My husband, who couldn't wait to get back to London, and his mother, despite just discovering he was the father of unborn twins? Avuncular Fabian or scatty Ursula, who're clearly not just the benevolent retired occupants of The Gatehouse? My pals Pippa and Minta who omitted to mention they were having their antenatal care in the penthouse above the flaming chapel. And what about Jerome, who seems the most trustworthy of them all ... Can he really have been the vet who visited Julia and, if so, why?

When my pulse stars to slow, I summon up a reality check. I don't know anything; I have no actual facts. And there's no reason to suppose 'fertility treatment' only comprises donor sperm and insemination; it might involve medicines, surgical procedures or other assisted conception.

With that thought in mind, I inhale and call Minta.

'Frankie! I'm so glad you've called. Are you OK after last night? You looked a bit shellshocked. Honestly, there's nothing to worry about, I promise. If there's anything you want to ask me, please feel free.'

'I do, actually.'

'Great. Fire away!'

Her tone is so sweet, I lose my resolve to challenge my 'friend' about the multiple things she hasn't mentioned so far. Yet I do need information. 'Look, you don't have to say if you don't want to, but did you undergo artificial insemination for your pregnancy?'

'Yes, I did, and I'm honestly not embarrassed to tell you about it. After losing our first three, both Dominic and I were all for it. We did it by IUI, so it was all very straightforward. We waited until around the time of ovulation, then the sperm was inserted directly into ... well, my uterus, I suppose is the correct term.'

'By Fabian ... Doctor Baden?'

'Yes. And it miraculously worked the first time.' She laughs. 'Super sperm, as he called it!'

I shudder at the thought of the man's 'private collection'. What exactly does it mean? That he provides the semen himself? I picture the Pavilion Gardens children dancing around the maypole at the solstice. Christ, do they all really bear a resemblance to him?

Pushing away the shocking notion, I go back to Minta. 'And was it the same for Pippa? The IUI?'

'Yes, for both babies, though it did take a little longer to conceive with Lucy.' She pauses. 'I'm assuming you didn't go down that route, then?'

'No, Minta, I didn't. I had one miscarriage, otherwise it was ...' I steel myself. 'Last night you thought I'd had, well, the same treatment as you. Why did you think that?'

'I just assumed we were all in the same boat. And what Ursula said, I guess. But she always says sentimental stuff like that.'

'What stuff?'

'Well, she's always going on about our little family community, isn't she.'

I try not to shout. 'What did she say, Minta?'

'Something about adding another set of twins to our tribe.'

64

Despite my whole psyche imploding with flashes of memories, moments, aromas, my body is frozen solid. I know I have to stand up and move. I can clearly picture a car coming for me if I don't – not to run me down – but to carefully bundle me inside with gentle hands and take me back to my incubating nest behind that damned *sallyport*. Although I have no idea why, I've been chosen as some sort of surrogate. That can be the only explanation why I'm having my babies, my twins, the new additions to 'the tribe'.

Nausea burns like acid as I walk. The Baden family tradition of philanthropy, passing the bloodline baton from father to son to fulfil the 'entail'. Those solemn photographs of Jerome and his brother. Only they weren't just brothers, were they? They had the 'special bond' both he and his mother mentioned. They were fraternal twins. Stefan was born first but he died, so Jerome was called in to do his 'baby doctor' duty and instead of rebelling, of calling it out, he disgustingly complied.

'*Duty.*' The very word and the connotations repulse me. Christ, I liked him, I trusted him. And not only that. I fancied, I craved, I desired him. How could I after what he'd committed? How did I get him so very wrong? Because he was attentive and nice. Because he made me feel special. How bloody shallow was I?

I want to block out the night of conception, scrub it with a steel scourer until it's obliterated. I'm certain I never will. I'm stained, I've been branded, invaded. And I didn't fucking know it when I should have. The clues were there if only I'd opened my eyes. His citrus aftershave aroma on the sheets the next day, the sense I already knew the feel of his lips and his skin on mine.

I halt, bend double and retch. Something else is prodding, something else isn't right. I strain my fuddled mind but it's hopping and jumping and all I really know is that I need refuge to rest and think. Though I long to curl into a ball and simply disappear, there are my babies to consider. If I piece everything together, I can work out the why. Why the hell did they pick on me?

I look up to take in my bearings. Like a homing pigeon, I've instinctively headed towards Mum's. I nod in acknowledgement. The comforts of my old bedroom will help calm my hammering heart. Pray God, I have the spare key in my bag. Glad of a plan, I doggedly tromp along Lapwing Lane and focus on staying upright. Almost there, I glance down Burton Road before crossing, then stop in my tracks as realisation snaps. Oh, my God, that's it, the thing that was nagging. The day I met Anya beneath the outdoor heaters at Folk. I can picture the bubbles of tonic water on the shoulder of a man's jacket quite clearly. Only he wasn't some random guy who happened to be on the next table to us. It was Jerome. That's why he seemed familiar from the start. But my date with Anya was weeks before I'd even heard of Pavilion Gardens ...

Fear shudders through me. What the fuck does that mean?

I hurriedly weave through the traffic, then break into a run, thundering past my old school and childhood park until I reach the top of Mum's avenue. I frantically reach into my bag to search out the key, then do another take. Her curtains are open. Not daring to hope she'll be here, I belt over the street, push past the gate and rap on the front door. The next thing I know, I'm sobbing in her arms.

Her own eyes heavy with tears, she helps me in and sits me down in the lounge like an invalid. I expect her to ask me what's wrong, but she simply rubs my back until my panting and the convulsions from crying have passed. I try to read her loaded, apprehensive air. Despite our friendly text exchange, is she angry with me?

'You're back,' I say, stuck for other words.

'Only just. You're shivering.' She pulls down the throw and carefully gathers it around me. 'We need to get you warmed up. I'll make you a hot drink. Tea? Or I could do a cocoa. I have milk.' She stands. 'Let me put on the kettle and then—'

'No.' I grab her hand and tug her back down by my side. 'Don't go.' I grope to find words which would even begin to cover what I'm slowly comprehending about my time at Pavilion Gardens. 'Blindsided. Blind. I've been horrendously blind.'

She bites her lip. 'Oh, love—'

'I was raped, Mum.' She sharply inhales and my words jumble out. 'We had a welcome party at our place. My drink must have been spiked. Toby knew I was ovulating; I showed him the test. He must have agreed to it. I remembered bits in the morning but ... Christ. My own fucking husband.' Needing to just say it, I put my hand to my stomach and take a quick breath. 'We didn't have sex after that because he had to go to Hong Kong. Out of nowhere, he was told to go as a replacement for someone who ... Oh God, who'd been in hospital.'

Her eyes like shiny brown pebbles, Mum quietly waits for more.

'It doesn't make sense. Toby hated his time there. Constantly complained. But now ... now he's been offered his dream job ... Bloody hell, they held back "payment", didn't they? They waited until twelve weeks had passed; they wanted to make sure there was a viable pregnancy. That's why he was so pleased and relieved about the scan.'

I pause. He was troubled too. Yet any regrets he might have had were too bloody late. The loss of Marcus – and me – was his gain.

I go back to Mum. 'I thought it was strange Felicia wasn't interfering, or on the phone or even here like a shot. Then poor Marcus ... It doesn't bear thinking about. They must have killed an innocent man for Toby as a trade. That's unreal, isn't it? Cold blooded murder? Just to get a job?'

I look at her pleadingly. 'Tell me I'm crazy. Tell me I have pregnancy-induced psychosis and paranoia, that I'm imagining things. That these babies I love aren't the product of some weird, malign tribal ritual.' The need to know why sizzles in my chest like heartburn. 'I thought Jerome was nice, I thought everyone was nice, but they were grooming me, weren't they? What for? Something to do with having twins? Passing on the gene, same as Jerome and his brother? That was risky, surely. I guess some twins are hereditary, but not every time.'

Mum sucks in some air to finally speak. I expect her to tell me I've lost it, that I'm ranting or delirious, but her expression is wretched. 'Fraternal twins actually go through the female line,' she says. 'They're determined by the mother's – your – genetics.'

'What?' I stare, confused. 'So we have twins in our family?'

'Your family, yes.' She takes both my hands and tightly squeezes. 'I'm so, so sorry, love.'

It feels as if my throat is lined with sandpaper. 'Sorry for what, Mum?' I croak.

She inhales deeply. 'I lied.'

PART 3 - THE CONCEPTION

Nina

32 Years Ago

65

I don't bother with my brand-new bra and matching knickers, the stockings and suspenders today. They're still snowy white and wrapped in silver tissue paper in my bottom drawer. After all, it's only a try on, and the dressmaker warned me the gown might be a bit soiled.

'How are you doing up there?' I hear from downstairs. It's Mum, of course, almost as excited – and nervous – as I am. She wants me to have the very best for the wedding, to 'look a million dollars', when sadly we don't have even a spare penny. The three of us work, but we're not hugely paid – me at the library, Mum cleaning every morning and stacking shelves in Sainsbury's most afternoons, and Baba doing whatever he can to supplement his benefits after the Royal Mail made him redundant. And though getting married is supposed to be the most joyous thing ever, it's hugely expensive, not least the cost of the flaming dress.

'It's the focal point of the day,' Mum said every time I recoiled at the ridiculous prices of the equally ridiculous frocks in the local boutiques.

'Um, I think that would be me, and not whatever I'm wearing,' I dryly replied.

'You'd look stunning if you wore a black bin liner, you know that, Nina, but the bride's outfit is the nuptials. It's what people talk about, during and afterwards. Then, of course, there's the photographs which'll be there forever. If it's a disaster, there'll be no getting away from them. "What were you thinking?" your kids will say when they look at them one day.' She chuckled. 'You need to think about their future well-being.'

It was a joke. Those were precisely the words I'd used when I'd leafed through her wedding album. I'd been a post-punk-rocker teenager who'd based her whole look on Poly Styrene from X-Ray Spex at the time. Now, at twenty-three, I'm far more discerning – and tactful – than I was then.

I raised my eyebrows. 'Future kids being the point, Mum. I don't know why Greg's insisting on this big fuss of a church and a formal reception. I'd gladly go for a smart trouser suit at the register office, followed by the pub, a dance and the conception of our first baby.'

Mum laughed. 'Well that's an easy answer. Greg worships the very ground you walk on; you're his princess and he wants to show you off.'

I smile at that thought. My fiancé does love me very much and if the 'complete works' is what he wants, who am I to object? He'll be ditching that bloody condom on our wedding night, though.

'Hello? Nina?' Mum repeats. 'Do you need any help?'

'Nope. I'll be another five minutes. You've time to make a cuppa before my grand entrance.'

I open the press-studs of the Berketex bag. I'd almost given up hope of finding anything within even a reasonable budget, or indeed a creation that wasn't an overblown Bo Peep or Disney Princess style, yet there it was on a sale rail in Lewis' bridal department. Ivory raw silk, long sleeved and a fitted style. And, save for the tiny roses around the Bardot neckline, simple.

I carefully pull the shimmering fabric out. It's badly creased and perhaps a little grubby, but it'll go to the dry cleaners this afternoon. The correct fit is the main thing for now, so I quickly step into it, slip in my arms and look in the mirror. Though I can't reach each and every tiny button all the way down to my bum, I'm immediately pleased with what I see, so I climb into a hooped underskirt to give it some width, then take out the matching satin heels from their box and pop them on.

Somewhat giddily, I make my way out to the landing. 'Mum? Baba? Are you ready? I'm coming down.'

It takes a few moments to spread the train out behind me, and by the time my parents arrive in the hallway below, I'm swaying down the stairs like Naomi Campbell.

Their delighted beams match mine. 'A million dollars,' Mum says.

Baba pads his eyes with a hanky. 'My girl. What a beaut. Always was and always will be.'

I'm nearly at the bottom when the doorbell rings. 'The post gets later every flaming day.' Mum gives Baba a nudge. 'Let's hope it's one of your lot, so we can show off our Nina.'

When the door swings open, we all frown in surprise. It's not a postman but a ginger-haired woman around my age.

'Oh, hello. Can we help you?' Mum asks politely.

She ignores her and glares up at me. 'Has he told you?'

'Sorry?' Her tone is challenging. 'Has who told me what?' I ask.

She looks me up and down. 'Clearly not,' she says with something of a sneer.

Mum steps forward. 'Excuse me. Whoever you are, you can't just—'

'Yes, I bloody well can.' She eyeballs me. 'Greg. So despite his promises, he hasn't had the decency to tell you. I thought not.' She sets her jaw. 'So that's why I'm here to inform you in person.'

My parents' mouths are slack and I'm struggling to work out what's going on too. Is it some sort of new kissagram or stripagram or similar joke? Or even mistaken identity? But she mentioned Greg by name and she's unbuttoning her coat ...

Her cheeks are as red as her hair. Yet her eyes gleam with determination. 'As you can see for yourself, I'm four months gone. It's Greg's and I'm keeping it.'

66

Even as I'm all but carried by Mum and Baba to our back room and sat down on the sofa, I just don't believe it.

'I'm Lindsay from work,' the woman said before turning tail and marching away. 'Phone Greg and ask him.'

Mum perches next to me. Her face is pallid; she's clearly as incredulous and stunned as I am. She passes over the telephone. 'There's only one way to find out, love.'

I stare at the dial. I don't know if I can do it. I'm still certain there has been some sort of mix-up. Me and Greg have dated since we were seventeen; he's devoted to me. He started at the recruitment company after school and, though I went to uni, I chose Manchester because he was worried about the male attention I'd get. But I've only ever wanted Greg. He's my soulmate and my ticket to a family – three kids at least, we've always said – because we're both only children and that's what we want. What I still desperately want!

Mum chivvies me. 'Come on, love. You need to find out. Then you'll have decisions to make.'

I look at her with horror. 'What decisions?'

Her eyes well with tears. 'That'll be down to you.' She fingers a silk rose on the cuff of my dress. 'I know how much you want that first baby, but if it's true ... Well, Greg has clearly cheated, which happens, but he's also kept the ... the outcome from you. Would you ever be able to trust him again? You don't want to make a mistake, love. You're young and gorgeous; there'll be suitors knocking on the door day and night.' She turns to my dad. 'Won't there, Baba?'

His face stricken with emotion, he nods. 'Too right, there will.'

'I don't want anyone else; I love Greg.' Then realising what she means, 'What are you suggesting? That I don't go ahead with the wedding? That I finish with him? For God's sake, Mum. It isn't even true. I know it. Who the hell says it's his?'

'That's why you have to call him.'

I shake my head. 'No. I can't just ask if he's been shagging someone at work. We're getting married in five weeks!'

'Exactly.' Mum lifts the receiver. 'Either way, you need to know.'

'For Christ's sake, OK.' My hands are shaking. 'You do it for me, my fingers won't work.'

She punches in the number without looking it up. Because that's how well we know Greg and his parents. Then she gives it to me and motions to Baba to leave the room.

He answers. 'Hello?'

'Greg? It's me. I've had a visitor this morning ...'

He doesn't reply.

'Don't you want to know who?'

'I know; she just called me.'

'Who did?'

'Lindsay.'

His tone is flat. And the way he said her name ... Cramp pulls at my belly. I force the words out of my mouth. 'Is it true? Is what she said true?'

'Yes.'

I'm stupefied afresh. 'What the fuck, Greg? We're getting married in a month.'

'No, we're not.'

'What?'

'We're not going to get married, Nina.'

My mind is spinning; I can't think straight. 'It's such short notice; I don't know if they'll let us postpone.'

'We're not getting married in a month or ever. I'm sorry.'

I fumble for words to stop the avalanche of devastation. 'It was a fling, a one-night stand, right? We can't let that stop what

235

we've planned for years. The wedding and the house ...'

'That's not going to happen. Not with me, anyway. Lindsay's got a new job in Norwich. I'm going to transfer mine, move in with her and give it a try.'

It takes moments to make my mouth move again. 'What, after two minutes of knowing someone, you're going to throw away everything.'

'Me and Lindsay. It's been longer than that. Months.'

'Months?' I'm reeling again. 'Why would you do that? You love me. You tell me that all the time. We go out, we have fun, we laugh, we have sex. What has she got that I haven't?'

'Nothing. That's probably the point. I'm good enough for her.'

'You're good enough for me! When have I ever said—'

'You've never needed to say it, Nina. The university student, the first class honours graduate, the girl who reads a different book every day said it.'

'Those things didn't mean—'

'They do. Just like you being standoffish or sneery to my mates and having clever opinions about fucking everything.'

'I didn't do it deliberately. If you'd said—'

'It was never going to work.'

My heart thuds. My baby; my first baby; the baby I so badly crave. 'What about the family we planned?'

'Yeah, that too. Pecking my head about it day and night.'

Anger finally bursts through my fugue. 'You and Lindsay are doing exactly that, you bloody idiot.'

'I know. But with her, at least I'll be number one.'

67

Fighting the constant urge to cry, I fix a polite smile, take members of the public's library cards, open book covers and stamp in dates on autopilot behind the main borrowing counter. The bubbling anger, indignation and outrage at Greg's shocking decision to call off the wedding lasted all weekend, seeing me through it. I stomped upstairs, bundled the dress and accessories into the Berkatex bag, then shoved it in a suitcase and stowed it under the bed, whilst Mum went about tactfully cancelling the flowers and the cake. Then, my blood boiling, I called Greg back and told him in no uncertain terms that he was to deal with – and pay for – the rest, including any further instalments for the cars, the church, the venue and so on.

Although I kicked myself for my lack of pride by even entertaining the thought of going through with the ceremony, let alone continuing my relationship with the cheating bastard, the rage all Saturday evening and Sunday felt good. I'd been humiliated, betrayed, lied to, virtually stood up at the altar because I was apparently too flaming good for him. Well, actually, I was. In fact, I'd spent the last six years trying my hardest not to outwit, outsmart, outgrow, outrun or outdo the bloody man. And yes, now I thought about it, his sexual prowess had vastly improved over the past few months. He'd finally discovered a woman had a clitoris, so I guess I had something to be grateful to Lindsay for.

Now it's Monday, the violence of the unexpected has hit me like a rock. I'm going about my working day at Central Library and trying to act normal, but the reality of what has happened winds me whenever my mind has a moment to wander. And even when I start respiring again, the ground shakes beneath my feet as though there's an earthquake. I was so certain, so sure about Greg. I had my life mapped out. I'd have put Mum's 'million dollars' on marrying him and staying wed until the day one or the other of us dies. The shock of what he has done is simply stunning, yet the hollow devastation in the pit of my stomach is the loss of my babies. That grief is so sharp, tears fall with a will of their own and it's all I can do to stop them before they splatter on a page.

I managed a few halting words to my co-worker, Mel, when I hung up my coat this morning. 'The wedding is off,' I said quietly. 'I'll explain another time, but could you pass it on, so everyone knows not to ask me about it.'

She now rubs my shoulder. 'Do you want to go home?' she asks in a low voice. 'I'll make an excuse for you and cover your afternoon shift.'

'That's really kind, but it's fine. I think I'm better staying busy.' I look at her sympathetic gaze and sharply inhale. 'Besides, being dumped a month before my wedding isn't something that will improve if I lie on the sofa and watch inane TV, is it?'

'I guess not. However, one thing that does help with heartache is time, it honestly does. When he divorced me, I was certain I'd never smile or laugh again. Now the very thought of being rid of him makes me positively delirious.' She nudges me. 'Let's face it, blokes are only good for one thing and most of them aren't even good at that.'

I want to challenge her and say that she's had her kids, that men are good for their sperm as well as for sex. Yet I know she means well, and I haven't ever confided in her – or anyone else other than my mum – about this nagging, compelling, desperate broodiness for a child.

'Thanks, Mel,' I reply. 'You're right. I just need to get a grip.' I transfer the latest batch of returns to the trolley. 'I'll take these back. Having a walkabout will do me good.'

Lifting my chin and saying the usual bright hellos to my male colleague fans, I wheel the books along corridors and into various sub-libraries and chambers, so I'm fine for the next hour. I save one tome until the last drop off. Inevitably somehow, it's Doctor Miriam Stoppard's *Pregnancy & Birth Book*. Not a week goes by without someone borrowing it, and it usually brings on a secret smile. Today my nose badly stings with sadness and regret, and I have to lower my head and puff out the anguish before slotting it back on the shelf of similar reads. My plans for *pregnancy and birth* have gone horribly, horribly awry. I know I'm only in my early twenties and have plenty of years ahead of me, but this dream is something I've been wanting and planning for years.

Aware of eyes burning my spine, I turn to a blonde-haired woman who's peering at me intently. 'Morning,' I say in the usual library-hushed tones. 'Are you looking for something in particular I can help you to find?'

If she's after reading matter about conception, I suspect it isn't for her. Though polished and wrinkle-free, I'd guess she's in her mid- to late-forties.

'No, I was passing through to the reference section and I couldn't help noticing your ... well, distress.' Her cheeks pink apologetically. 'Then I saw which book caused it. It's absolutely none of my business, of course, but I've been there, if you take my meaning, and my heart went out to you.'

'Thank you,' I croak. I manage to blink the hot tears away. 'It's not what you probably think, so I actually have no right to feel this ...' I gulp in some air. What the hell is wrong with me? People are watching. 'This grief,' I whisper.

She smiles softly. 'We all have a right to feel what we feel and not be judged.' She looks at the gold watch dangling from her slim wrist. 'I was planning to go downstairs for refreshments soon. How about joining me for ten minutes? Maybe a little break would do you good?' She holds out an elegant hand. 'I'm Meryl.'

68

Although I question my own sanity about meeting a complete stranger, the need to share my misery with someone who might understand is overwhelming, so I sneak down the spiral staircase to the basement café and spot my sophisticated new friend sitting at a round table with a cup and saucer.

'Let me get you a drink,' she says when she greets me. 'What would you like?'

'A cappuccino would be great, please.'

'A slice of gateau?'

Picturing the tiered affair me and Mum chose from the bakery's catalogue, the blow ricochets through me again. 'No, thanks,' I manage. The nauseous way I feel, I doubt I'll ever have an appetite for food, let alone cake, again.

When she returns with my coffee, Meryl sips her tea and fills the silence by politely asking questions about how I came to work here, what I studied at university and where.

'History, how interesting,' she says. 'Something tells me you got a first class honours degree,' she adds sweetly. She tilts her head. 'And with your physique, I bet you're sporty too.'

Though I know she's just being courteous, it's so nice to have someone build up my abilities rather than use them as a reason to dump me. 'Yes, to both,' I say, struggling to hold in the emotion. 'I did athletics at school and with Sale Harriers, then netball at uni, but ...'

My sentence trails away. I basically gave up sport and the other social activities to hang out with Greg, and to stop him feeling threatened; even emasculated, I suppose.

Meryl peers at me. 'But ...?'

The one word unlocks any remaining restraint. I spill out both my tears and the last six years of my life in a few choice sentences, then I graphically describe the astonishing call at our front door on Saturday.

'I'm so sorry,' I finish, using the paper napkin to blow my nose. 'I don't know what's wrong with me. There are a hundred things to get upset and angry about – Greg's duplicity, his dumping me, all the money me and my parents have lost, let alone the whole embarrassing and humiliating jilted bride parts – but I honestly thought I'd be pushing a pram this time next year and I can't stop obsessing about it. It's like I've lost a baby.' I glance at her attentive expression. 'Which I know is wholly unfair when there are so many women who have miscarried an actual child, rather than ... well, the dream of one, I guess.' I hate my snivelling self-pity, yet I can't help it. 'Made all the worse by *her* being pregnant.' Kicking myself at my lack of tact, I hurry to apologise. 'I'm sorry, you said that you've had ... difficulties?'

'Yes, many years ago now, so don't feel you're offending me. In my case it was on the fertility side, so I do understand those feelings of desperation and frustration, and yes absolutely, the grief you mentioned. Every one of those emotions is completely valid and you shouldn't ask for pardon.' She pats my hand and smiles. 'But it all came good for me once I ... took control.'

'How so?' I ask.

'Rather than waiting for another month and the next excruciatingly disappointing period, I mulled on what I really wanted and decided to deal with it head on. A friend recommended a reproductive endocrinologist she herself had consulted, so I steeled myself, went to see him to find out what was wrong, and he got to the bottom of the problem within weeks.' She beams. 'I now have a handsome son and a beautiful daughter. We couldn't be more proud of what talented and wonderful people they've turned out to be.'

Though I try to rise above the word 'we', I can't. That's the crux of my sheer exasperation: I'm not in a couple any more. My nose sharply stings as the unfairness of my situation whips me again. No Greg, no wedding, no home, no family. He's pulled the rug from beneath me in the very worst way, and he gets the happy ending *and* the baby.

'I'm glad it all came good for you,' I say stiffly. 'I bet you're a lovely mother.'

'Thank you; I certainly hope so.' She smiles softly. 'You will be too one day. And you're so personable, eloquent and intelligent, I'm sure you'll find your real soulmate soon.'

'I don't want a soulmate,' I blurt. Then more quietly, 'Sorry, I know you mean well but I thought Greg was that and look what he did to me. Someone he was meant to love. It's so shocking, I don't think I'll ever trust a man again.' I grope to explain the emptiness I feel in my belly. I know I sound like some spoilt child who's stamping her feet because she hasn't got her own way but, in all honesty, it does feel as if I've miscarried. 'He's more than just cheated on me; he took away my ... my future, my expectations, my aspirations. He promised to be the father of my children.'

As though analysing my very being, Meryl scrutinises me for several long seconds. Then she lifts her slender shoulders.

'Maybe he could still be,' she says.

69

My heart thudding like a drum, I walk down the row of three-storey Georgian terraces, all occupied, it would seem, by the medical or legal profession. When I reach the last one, I compare the name on the brass plaque with the details Meryl gave me. She made me promise to wait a week and carefully think about it before making any decisions and, as it happened, Doctor Raymond had a cancellation at five o'clock today.

Almost guffawing with nerves, I hop up the step and push open the panelled black door. *Thinking* about it was an understatement. For the past seven days, I have been unable to do anything else; I've gone to bed at night with it rotating in my head like a thirty-degree wash and I've woken each morning to the spin cycle. I've tried to step back and think about it rationally, logically, pragmatically, but my excitement has repeatedly doused the many, many downsides of Meryl's suggestion. As I inhale the smell of ancient cigar smoke and old leather, I find myself smiling at the possibility again: time is of the essence, yet Nina Whittle could have Greg Ward's baby after all.

I give my name to the receptionist, perch on a Chesterfield-style armchair and finger the small box in my pocket. The rub with this outlandish plan is money. This first consultation is pro bono; after that there'll be a fee. How much, I have no idea, but I'll go to the second-hand jewellers in St Ann's Square and see how much they'll offer for my engagement ring. If there's enough to split it between this tempting possibility and what I owe Mum and Baba, it'll be a no brainer; if not, I honestly don't know what I'll do.

'Ms Nina Whittle?' The mellow voice makes me jump from my skin. A tall, suited bloke offers his hand and a smile. 'Hello, I'm Doctor Raymond. Would you like to come through?'

I clear my throat. 'Yes. Thank you.'

He gestures to a chair opposite an old-fashioned desk, takes his seat and politely observes me. 'How are you today? May I call you Nina?'

It takes a moment to adjust my expectations. Rather than an elderly balding man with a bow tie and half rimmed spectacles, he's a well-turned-out guy in his forties with laughter lines, sparkling blue eyes and a full head of hair.

'Yes, that's fine. Nervous, if I'm honest,' I reply.

'There's really no need to be. Anything discussed within these four walls stays here. And rest assured, I've heard everything before, so don't shy away from being completely frank. I won't be embarrassed and nor should you be. OK?'

'OK,' I reply, yet I feel my cheeks burning. Telling Meryl my life story was one thing; sharing it with an undeniably attractive older man is another.

'So ...' he says, leaning forward attentively. 'How can I help you?'

'Well,' I begin, looking down at my lap. 'I understand from a ... a friend who you treated a while back, that you might be able to help with my ... peculiar situation.' I snap up my head. It was the first thing I promised myself to ask. 'This first chat is free, right?'

'It is, so don't worry about that.' He waits for a few moments. 'So, your situation ... What is it and why is it peculiar?'

I inhale to explain. Instead of words, traitorous tears trickle out.

'It's fine,' he says, pouring water from a jug and passing the glass over. 'Take your time.'

Aware of his solid gaze, I sip my drink and get ahold of my emotions. To my surprise, he stands.

'Oh, so ...'

He collects an umbrella from the coat stand in the corner. 'I believe rain is due, but let's brave the weather and walk.'

70

By the time we've done three laps of St John's Gardens, I've learned that Doctor Raymond went to Oxford University on a competitive scholarship, that he's infinitely better with dogs than human beings when it comes to long-term relationships, that he makes the best omelette this side of the Pennines and that he's now had twenty-plus years of clinical experience, so he's heard every tall, short, shape and size of human story.

He glances up to the moody sky. 'Oops, it looks like a deluge is on its way.' Then, motioning to a bench by a flowerbed, he says, 'Let's sit before it gets wet.'

'OK.'

Shoulder to shoulder, we shelter beneath his brolly and watch the drizzle surround us. I don't know whether it's the fresh air or his easy chatter but, as though I've imbibed a stiff gin and tonic, a sensation of calm and relaxation replaces my earlier agitation. Even, dare I say it, a feeling of giddy hope.

'So, back to business ...' he says, briefly looking at me. 'I specialise in helping people become and stay pregnant and, to do this, I diagnose causes of infertility such as PCOS, endometriosis, anovulation and male-factor infertility, along with many other issues. I have an NHS practice but, if the funding isn't there, I charge privately for my treatment. OK so far?'

'Yes.'

'So how can I help you?'

I picture Meryl and her words of wisdom: *What do you want, really want, Nina? That's all you need to focus on. It will empower you, give you the strength to follow it through.*

'The becoming pregnant bit.'

'OK.' He smiles. 'That wasn't so bad, was it?'

'No.' I pull a rueful face. 'But the rest is.' I take a big breath and the words rush out. 'I'm after intra-uterine insemination and for reasons I won't bore you with, I don't have a husband or boyfriend to provide the semen.'

'So we're talking donor sperm?'

'Yes. I wouldn't qualify under the NHS for obvious reasons and ... well, the thing is, I'd need to do it very soon. Would that be something you could facilitate?'

'Yes, it is.'

'Great.' I bite my lip. Enquiring about finances is bloody humiliating, yet I have no choice. 'Could I ask how much would it cost, please?'

'You can indeed. We charge for the IUI itself – either one cycle or a package – then there's the cost of the sperm if it isn't from a partner, I'm afraid. My secretary can give you specific prices, but we're talking a tidy sum.'

'Over a thousand pounds?'

'Yes.'

I swallow. 'And how likely is pregnancy the first time. You know, from just one cycle?'

'I'll be honest, not great. People assume artificial insemination is simply a matter of placing sperm into a vagina for conception to take place. In its very simplest form, this can happen, but it's a little more complicated than that. If there's spontaneous ovulation, the woman has a higher chance, but ovarian stimulation treatment may be needed.'

My stomach turns at the thought of the additional expense. 'What's that? What does it involve?'

'The stimulation phase lasts around ten days, during which ultrasound scans and blood tests evaluate the follicle growth. Then thirty-six hours before the insemination itself, we give an injection of human chorionic gonadotropin, which triggers ovulation.'

'So what per cent are we talking about?'

'At your age – fifteen per cent, per cycle. Overall, over half of women having IUI become pregnant over the first six cycles.'

'Six cycles?' I gasp. 'Six months and six lots of money?'

'Yes.' He spreads his hands and smiles ruefully. 'Cost aside, if you're healthy and fertile – which in all probability you are – there's no better way to get pregnant than by having normal sexual intercourse with, well, your donor.'

71

My mind spinning, I accompany Doctor Raymond back to his rooms. I appreciate his candour, but where does it leave me? Even if a miracle happened and the IUI worked the first time, the proceeds of an engagement ring wouldn't even begin to cover the cost. A final demand envelope fired through the postbox for my parents only this morning, so whatever cash I get, it should go to them. What are my other options? The obvious solution is Greg. Can I seduce him or get him back? Or come clean, play the pity card or even bloody beg?

Sheer anger shudders back. No way on earth will I do that; the thought of being civil with him makes me feel nauseous, let alone any intimacy. Besides, I know his choice of Lindsay is final; he isn't one for changing his mind once it's set, hence the bloody wedding he insisted on.

Doctor Raymond's mellow tones filter through my dismay. 'Oh dear, it looks like we're locked out,' he says. Handsome and somehow boyish, he pats his pockets and pulls out a latch key with a wry smile. 'Thank goodness for that. My faithful secretary probably slipped it in when I wasn't looking. She knows my proclivity for forgetting the hour. She wants to leave on time and who can blame her?'

His self-deprecating manner brings on a smile. 'Not me.'

Once we're inside, he pauses in thought. 'That reminds me: paperwork! Let me jot down a few details – dates of birth and last period, address, GP and so on – before you go.'

'OK, no problem.'

I follow him through to his office, give the brief answers and hover by the door as he notes them on a pad. Even before he lifts his head, I'm aware of a flutter of attraction for this slightly chaotic, yet incredibly attractive and self-assured man. When he finally stands upright and fixes his blue gaze on mine, my belly turns in a way I've never experienced before. As if he knows, he shrugs off his blazer, unknots his tie and loosens his shirt buttons. Winded of speech, I just gawp, but instead of stripping off more layers as I'd both feared and hoped, he scoops a leather bomber from the coat stand and slips it on.

'That always feels better.' He flashes a smile. 'Off duty at last. Are you rushing off or can I buy you a drink before you go home?'

I shake myself back to reality. I thought he was making a move to seduce me, and quite honestly, I might not have said no. Laughing at my own vanity, I nod. 'Sure, why not.'

72

I'm literally closing the front door on Friday morning when the telephone rings. I consider leaving it for Baba to answer. Thank God I don't, as it's Raymond's secretary.

'Oh, hi,' I say, surprised. She hasn't called me before.

'Sorry to bother you. I've just looked at the diary and noticed your follow-up consultation with Doctor Raymond is at seven, which means you'll have to ring the intercom to gain entry. Is that OK?'

'Yes, no problem. Thanks for letting me know.'

I'm already running late for work, so I have to belt for the bus. Once I'm squashed on the back seat, I have time to let my mind wander. An out-of-hours appointment at Raymond's rooms ... Despite the sweaty men either side of me, my belly flips with pleasure. Could tonight be the night something happens between us? A kiss or cuddle, or even more?

Inanely grinning to myself, I go back to Monday evening. Once we left his clinic, we huddled beneath his umbrella and headed to a wine bar on Deansgate. I thought that would be it, but he asked me if I'd ever eaten at San Carlos. When I said no, he offered his arm and said, 'Then you must and there's no time like the present.'

So charming, witty and erudite, he brought out the best in me. I felt pretty and funny and smart. And though there's an age gap of nearly twenty-five years, it didn't seem that way. He's good looking, slim and sporty, an eternal bachelor type. Plus he's a doctor, an Oxbridge graduate, no less! It was so nice to lap up his every word, buzz from his subtle compliments and prove to myself that I'm worthy, that I won't be defined by what Greg has done to me. But I was nervous too. Was this a prelude to sex? Could this educated, handsome man be the father of my baby?

I look out of the grimy window and sigh. Nope, not then nor when we had action repeat on Wednesday. The perfect gent each time, he walked me to the bus stop, waited until the 142 arrived, then waved me off as though I was precious cargo. I try to dampen my excitement for tonight's 'consultation'. I'm sure he finds me attractive, but maybe I'm letting conceit get the better of me.

*

As we saunter arm-in-arm beneath the streetlights, I fear this man has me hooked. My whole body is pumping with anticipation and desire. I've been flattered and fed in San Carlos again but, this time, he's asked if I'd like a nightcap in his rooms.

As he opens up, I study his profile. God, I so want romance and if that results in more, it'll be the icing on the cake. Yet I still feel horribly shy as I've only ever had sex with Greg.

He gestures to the Chesterfield sofa. 'Have a seat. How about an Amaretto? With or without ice?'

My throat is so dry with nerves, my voice is a croak. 'However you have it.'

When he returns, he sits by my side and flirts with those blue, crinkled eyes as we sip our liqueurs. Though he looks at my mouth, sweeps stray hair from my face and appraises my figure when I stretch, he frustratingly doesn't make a move. Suddenly not giving a hoot about my inexperience or gender niceties, I lean forward and press my lips against his. Quite honestly, I don't know what has got into me as I haven't drunk *that* much, but when he kisses me back, there's no stopping my urgent need, and before I can reprimand myself for my bold, almost uninhibited moves, I've stripped to my bra and undone his belt.

As I make to unzip his flies, he puts his hand on top of mine. 'Are you sure about this, Nina?' he asks.

A little stunned by his question, when his desire is plain to see, I sit back. 'I am. Don't you want to?'

He gazes at me reflectively for a moment or two. Then his smile spreads. 'Yes, I do. You are just perfect; how can I possibly resist?'

73

Clutching the scan photograph, I thank the clinician and find my way back to the glassy exit. But instead of leaving the private hospital with a grin on my face, I'm so winded I need to sit down. Despite the morning sickness, fatigue and the slight rounding of my stomach, this conception hasn't felt tangible until now. It isn't a fantasy, playtime or a pipe dream any more; it really is happening. I saw the evidence for myself on the monitor just now. A mouth, button nose, two arms and two legs.

'Just one foetus of approximately twelve weeks' gestation,' the woman said, as if she'd expected two. 'A strong heartbeat and everything developing normally. All lovely news. Enjoy the rest of your pregnancy.'

I look at my clenched hands. I should be happy; I am happy. Utterly overwhelmed and scared too. This is a huge, life-changing event. I'll be responsible for a living, breathing, helpless little baby in six months and, though it's precisely what I asked for, the notion is suddenly terrifying. And I'll be doing it alone.

'Congratulations, darling,' Raymond said when the test was positive. 'I'm exceptionally happy for you as a daddy donor, but not as a daddy. OK?'

Though his words dented my elation for a moment or two, the pragmatic me got a grip. He looked bloody good for a bloke in his forties, but he was twice my age. Would I still fancy him at sixty, sixty-five, seventy? I doubted it and, anyway, did I want a man putting in his oar about how I should bring up my child? No. Not him, nor indeed my ex-fiancé. Which was why, in hindsight, Greg had been right to make himself 'number one' with Lindsay.

Now reality is here, things I've blissfully ignored are tumbling on my shoulders. I'll be a single mum. How will I cope practically, financially, emotionally, once the little one is born? And even before that, there's the birth itself. As a result of complications, I only survived by a whisker, and Mum couldn't have more kids. Because it was so traumatic, so horribly painful, it's a tale I've only heard from her friend. Quite frankly, the prospect petrifies me.

Tears prodding, I cover my face. Where's Raymond when I need the loving reassurance he's given me over the past three months? Yet I knew I'd be on my own from hereon in. Albeit in his ruefully sweet way, he'd said as much in his rooms last week.

'We'll organise you a private scan at the Alexandra, then you can go to your GP and get referred through the usual NHS channels. It'll be an exciting time. Once your first trimester is up, you'll get bigger by the day, the sickness will recede and you'll be able to share your news with family and friends.' He must have sensed my disappointment as he gently lifted my chin. 'You're special, Nina. Your baby will be special. You can do this. OK?'

I finally stand and force my legs to move. It has to be OK; I have no choice. Trying to work out how on earth I'll spin the pregnant-by-Greg falsehood to my mother, I meander towards the bus stop. So deep in thought, I jolt from surprise as a car pulls up beside me. When the window winds down, I expect someone to ask for directions. It's Raymond.

He leans over. 'Hop in.'

A little stunned, I do as I'm told. 'What are you doing here?' I ask.

'As though I'd miss such an important day. Let's go for a spin and chat.'

'OK,' I reply, my mind already analysing what this unexpected development means. Has he changed his mind? Does he want in, after all?

He smoothly drives until we hit the Cheshire countryside, then he pulls over in a lay-by in the middle of nowhere and turns off the engine.

'For you,' he says, handing over a velvet box.

His expression is so attentive that for a heart-stopping moment, I think it's a proposal. But the jewellery case is slim and rectangular.

'Open it,' he says.

'Oh, OK ...' A gold chain with a pendant is nestled in the silk bed.

'For you,' he says. 'Then you can pass it on when she's old enough to wear it.'

'How do you know it's a girl?'

He smiles. 'Just a guess. Do you like it?'

'Yes, I do.' The sapphire stone is the colour of his eyes. 'It's beautiful. Thank you.' So choked with emotion and those feelings of misplacement, it's all I can manage.

He takes my hand and squeezes. 'This isn't the finish but the start, Nina. Through sheer providence, you've found yourself pregnant by your ex-fiancé. It's the fairy tale you wanted, and I guarantee it'll have a happy and pain-free ending.'

74

The jubilation will surely come, yet as I traipse back to our house, I feel stripped of emotion. Although I've literally just stepped out of Raymond's prestige car, the whole episode from chancing upon Meryl to meeting him feels fictitious already. The grainy pixelated image in my handbag tells me otherwise, of course, and I know the moment has finally come to deal with my future – our future – head on.

Once at our gate, I take a deep breath and fix my face into a suitable expression, somewhere between tentative excitement and shock. I bought a pregnancy testing kit several days ago, so all I have to do is pee on it and show the result to Mum.

And tell a barefaced lie.

Can I do it? Can I really, really do this?

The front door fires open before I've had chance to use my keys. Mum props a hand on her waist. 'What's going on, Nina?'

My heart literally stops. Oh, my God, she must know what I've done.

'What do you mean?' I squeeze past her and pray for a miracle. 'Why? What's happened?'

'This.' She pushes a sheet of paper at me.

'What is it?'

'A credit receipt.'

I ease out my relief; it has nothing to do with the web of deceit I'm about to convey. 'What for?'

'The deposit we paid for the reception. It's gone straight in our bank account, apparently.'

'Oh. I thought it was non-refundable.'

'Indeed, me as well. I assumed they must have had a new booking and taken pity on us, so that felt good for all of thirty seconds.'

'It's better than good, surely?'

Her lips are still pursed. 'You'd think. There were two envelopes on the doormat. I opened this one, then Baba turned to his. It was from a firm of solicitors.'

'Oh, God, Mum, is money that tight?'

'My thoughts exactly. Someone had clearly meant business after sending a final demand.'

My stomach churns with guilt. I've been so self-absorbed, I've overlooked their wedding debts. 'I'm so sorry, I didn't realise things had got so bad. I'll go into the jewellers with the—'

'Just listen. The letter to Baba says the Royal Mail didn't do whatever they were obliged to do when they made him redundant.' She gives me an odd look. 'So apparently he can have his job back if he likes.'

'Really? That's fantastic news.' Discomfort spreading, I stare at my mother. This will give Baba a new lease of life. Why is she so unimpressed? 'Isn't it?'

'No, not when it's accompanied by a banker's draft as "compensation".'

'Money as well? I don't understand, Mum. Why aren't you—'

'Fifty thousand pounds, Nina.'

'You're joking?'

'I'm not. Tell me which postie even earns that in five years?'

'Fifty grand? What the hell?'

'My words precisely.'

'A mistake, surely?' Heat fires up from my toes to my cheeks. A sum of money like that could buy a house. 'Was the cheque definitely payable to him?'

'Yes. He called the number and spoke to someone. There'd been a breach of procedures, protocol or similar, which made his and the other workers' redundancies unfair.'

'Who else? Anyone we know?'

'They weren't at liberty to say.'

'I see.' I feel horribly sweaty. None of this feels right. 'So he's going to take up the offer?'

'Part-time.' She tuts. 'I suppose that's good news. Get him out of my hair.'

'And give him a sense of purpose again. So where is he now?'

'He's gone to the building society to pay it in. He said only a fool would look a gift horse in the mouth.' She folds her arms. 'I don't like it and I, for one, won't be spending it.'

Now clearly isn't the time to waft a positive pregnancy result along with a falsehood. 'I'm parched. Do you fancy a—'

'Because the solicitor said something peculiar. I listened in and caught a few words. Baba says it was a joke because he's a postal worker but ...'

Alarm fizzles in my chest. 'What was it?'

'The man said we'd likely need it.'

'For what?'

She looks at my stomach meaningfully. 'To help out with our new "precious package".'

PART 4 - THE COGNATI

Frankie

75

I'm so shell-shocked by Mum's confession I gape, disbelieving and in denial, for seconds. Yet as I take in her cowed, guilty and ashamed demeanour, sheer outrage fires through me.

'For fuck's sake, Mum. How could you? How could you do that? You *prostituted* yourself for a baby.'

She flinches at my choice of words. Deep down, I know I'm being unfair – that desire, the lure, the desperate need for a child – but I'm reeling, shocked, aggrieved and scared. Anger consumes me right now. 'Tell me! How could you?'

Instead of answering, she stands. 'I'm parched. Let me make us that cuppa.'

I sharply inhale to protest, to say that tea won't cure this living nightmare, but I'm caught short by the stark fear in her eyes. There's more she hasn't yet shared.

I follow her to the kitchen and yank out a chair. 'You need to tell me everything. Brutal truth, Mum. There's no room for evasions or omissions or lies any more.'

'I know.'

She makes the drinks, sits opposite me and takes a gulp of air.

'So Greg ... I didn't for a moment plan to deceive him or ask him to play the role of a father, contribute child support or anything like that. He'd already said he was moving away with Lindsay, so it all felt ...' She smiles thinly. 'Serendipitous.'

That fucking word. I shake it away.

'And Raymond ...' she continues, rubbing the knots in the table. 'It was me who instigated sex the first time. I basically made the moves, put all the fantasies I'd had in my head into practice, I guess, but it wasn't just a one night—'

'Maybe it was more than simple alcohol in your nightcap.'

She looks up at that. 'What do you mean?'

'Never mind for now. Go on.'

'Are you sure?'

I grimly guffaw. 'It's the story of my creation, so why not.'

'OK.' She sighs. 'It wasn't just a one-night stand. It was relationship. I had a secret older lover, even a potential boyfriend, who couldn't get enough of me.'

I can't help snapping. 'You were ovulating, Mum. He wanted to make sure the conception worked.'

'Yes. I didn't see it at the time but, yes, you're right.' She spreads her arms. 'I honestly thought he liked me; it even felt like love.'

Though the expression knocks me sick, crippling hurt hits my chest. 'It wasn't; I can assure you of that.' Willing it away, I focus on facts. 'They – whoever the fuck *they* are – are veritable professionals at it. It was grooming, Mum, grooming by flattery, friendliness, pleasantness, charm. You were simply a vessel, a surrogate, same as me.' I glare at her. 'So why you?'

'I honestly don't know. Random? A candidate ripe for procreation in the right place at the right time. When it was happening, I was utterly blind to it.' Her eyes glisten with tears. 'All I can say is I'm so, so sorry.'

I lean back and try to release the tension in my jaw. Part of me wants to continue shooting Mum's meek justifications down, but I should probably give her some slack. She was foolish, self-absorbed and dogged, same as me. The real question is where we go from here.

I stand and pace. 'So Greg wasn't my dad and I don't have an Uncle Billy or a half-sister?'

'Correct.'

'My real father is a fertility doctor called Doctor Raymond?'

'Yes. At least, he was practising as one then.'

A bloody fertility doctor who provided his own sperm ... Like poison, a thought spreads. Christ, could Raymond and Fabian be father and son? Praying it isn't so, I look at my belly. Dare I even ask? I have to; whatever the reply, the time has come to face the realities of my situation. 'Is Raymond his first name or surname?'

Mum squints. 'I assumed first, but the plaque said Doctor Raymond, so I'm not sure. Why do you ask?'

I shake my head. Information gathering for now is the thing. Then I can fall apart if I need to.

'So the letter from the solicitor. Was that when you told Gran about the pregnancy?'

'Yes. She'd already guessed.'

'Did you go with the fake Greg story or ...?'

'No. She knew something was wrong and, quite honestly, I needed to offload, so I came clean about everything.'

'How about Baba?'

'No. He was so pleased about his job and having the means to look after his family again. It seemed wrong to belittle that.'

Making mental notes I can examine and absorb later, I nod. 'What about the money? It came from Raymond, surely. Weren't you freaked out?'

'A little, but ...' She flushes. 'Whether deliberately or not, I convinced myself it was per the paperwork. And if the occasional doubt seeped in, I reasoned I had a wealthy and kind benefactor who was looking out for his child. Besides, I had you to focus on, love, worry about and provide for.' She studies her trembling hands. 'I know I was in profound denial for ... well, years. I'm so—'

'So did Greg really die?'

'Yes, he did. He was hit by a car outside his office in Norwich. Apparently, the driver didn't stop.'

The very words take my breath. 'Didn't you think it was odd?'

'Not at the time.' She stifles a gasp with her palm. 'Poor man. He didn't deserve that. Nor did Lindsay and their daughter.' Her hollow eyes slide to me. 'I do now. Not only think but know.'

Alarm shoots through me. My mother's gaze is both certain and frightened. 'Tell me,' I whisper.

She peers at me intently. 'This is why you, why we both have to play it smart, Frankie. I'm not sure who *they* are, but they're dangerous.

76

They're dangerous. I already knew this, of course I did. Yet, until now, it's been pure speculation in my head. As if preparing for the blow, I press my feet against the floor tiles.

'What do you mean?' I ask.

Mum covers her face, then lifts her chin, the old Nina back.

'That letter came from Billy Malloy and I didn't know what to do, so I hid it. Why I didn't just burn it or bin it later, I don't know.' She laughs without mirth. 'Actually I do. Denial, shelving, the usual. Why change the habits of a lifetime? Anyhow, you found it and, even though I was caught on the hop, I did consider telling you the truth. Where would I even begin?' She bites her lip. 'If I had, you wouldn't have left and—'

'Don't go there, Mum. God knows why, but I'd already fixated on living at Pavilion Gardens. Tell me. Why are they dangerous? What happened?'

'So you were understandably angry when you left here. I was distraught; I didn't know what to do for the best. You thought I'd hidden your family from you and—'

'It's fine. Just tell me.'

'The decision was taken out of my hands.' She shivers. 'Remember Col? Colin.'

The boyfriend I've never met. I steady myself for another curveball. 'Yes ...'

'When he came here on the Friday, he could tell I was down, so he suggested we go to the pub for a change. We had a nice meal and a few drinks, then on the way home ...' Her voice cracks with emotion. 'A car drove straight at him.'

'Shit.'

'I was right there. I saw it with my own eyes.'

'Was he badly hurt? Is he OK?'

Thank God, she nods. 'As OK as compound fractures can be. It all happened so quickly. My assumption was a drunk driver or joy riding. Someone called the police, an ambulance came and I was allowed to go with him. I waited in A & E, totally shaken up but thanking my lucky stars it wasn't any worse.' She glances at me. 'It made me realise how much I cared for him, how devastated I'd be if I lost him ... Anyway, I was almost asleep when I sensed – or smelled – a person sitting by my side. A particular cologne I hadn't inhaled since the day you were born.'

'Oh God ...'

'Yes, Raymond. Now grey-haired but not so very different, especially those eyes.'

I touch the hollow of my throat. 'What did he say?'

'I was so surprised, I can't recall his exact greeting. He was friendly, apparently pleased to see me. I assumed he was there in a professional capacity of some sort, then it dawned that someone was in the other seat beside me.'

'OK ... Who was it?'

'It was Meryl.' She puffs out a long breath of air. 'God, what an utter fool. Until that very moment I hadn't known of her involvement. All those years I'd assumed the ... the serendipitous encounter at the library was just that – accidental, random, lucky.'

I slowly nod. 'So she was Raymond's pimp.'

'Yes.' Mum blinks. 'And, it turns out, also his wife.'

'Bloody hell. You're joking.'

'Nope. "Hello Nina," she said. "My husband and I haven't seen you for quite some years!"' As though picturing the woman, she squints. 'She was superficially as pleasant as she'd been the last time, yet she was unrecognisable too. Her glassy eyes were as cold as ice cubes.'

With a jolt I realise I've met her. Yes, Meryl the older 'cousin' who was so keen on Toby.

But Mum is still speaking, with a thoughtful frown. 'Her

loathing of me positively dripped from her. Rich considering she'd found me, vetted me, approved me. Anyhow, she continued to chat in an oh-so charming way about how we were related and how wonderful it was that "family" looked out for each other, which was why an offer for a secondment to *Biblioteca Pública Arús* would be dropping into my inbox. It was a job I'd always coveted, wasn't it? And staying away, incommunicado for a while, would give "our precious package" a chance to properly settle in at Pavilion Gardens. They were dreadfully sorry to hear about poor Colin's accident. Thankfully it wasn't *fatal*.'

Mum's expression is grim; fearful too. 'She didn't need to say the words *this time*, Frankie. They must have been watching me. It was honestly a last-minute decision to go to the Metropolitan. Then Meryl added her *pièce de résistance*: I didn't need to worry about Gran and Baba in my absence. She'd be sure to keep a careful eye on them.'

I think of my spat words to my grandparents. No wonder they'd looked frail and so scared. The surge of guilt is immediately superseded by anger. 'The bastards. They're fucking evil.'

Mum tugs me back to the chair and firmly holds me by the shoulders. 'I know you're alarmed, frightened, furious,' she says. 'There must be a million other emotions churning inside, but you need to listen to me, Frankie. Now isn't the time for hot-headed or impulsive decisions. You have to play it smart for your babies as well as yourself. So that means taking it easy and carefully thinking things through. I completely get the need to kick out; I want to charge in, rail against them, rage and scream too. You can't. These people are powerful, and if Greg's death wasn't simply a dreadful coincidence, they have influence as far as Norwich, so that means you have to—'

'What? Play along with those manipulative perverts and the rest of the Stepford wives who're supposed to be my friends? And *him*?' The thought of Jerome brings tears of fury to my eyes. 'The kind, helpful vet, who just happens to be a fucking rapist?'

'Look ...' She peers at me beseechingly. 'I know it's not what you want to hear, but yes. I've spent the past three months mulling on it night and day and I can't see any other way out.' She kisses my cheek. 'At least we have each other again. Come on, let's have a hug of solidarity, then I'll give you a ride home.'

77

Play it smart, Frankie, beats in my head as I stride away from Mum's house. Needing to suck in the untainted fresh air for as long as I can, I declined her offer of a lift. I slow my pace after a minute or two. I need to preserve my energy. I need my wits to be razor-sharp. Though I baulked at the word 'home', let alone Mum's suggestion of playing along with the freaks behind those closed gates, she's right. Until I figure a way out of this nightmare, I have no alternative.

'Homeward' bound, I cross at the traffic lights, tromp past the vibrant bedding plants outside Blagg's and glance at the Metropolitan's Elizabethan facade. Colin's accident must have happened around here ... I stop. God, of course. That's what the police 'Accident Here' placard was about all those weeks ago. I frown in thought. What did Toby say about his Friday night out with Jerome? That they'd seen Nina with a bloke.

My heart races at the notion, yet it makes complete sense. Jerome must have called it in to whoever pulls the ... the bloody *cult's* strings. Because that's surely what these evil people are. And it's how they'd known Mum and Colin were there. My husband and my friend. How could they? How *could* they?

I lower my head and puff in and out. I have to get a handle on this. I already know that Jerome is a rapist and that Toby has sold his soul to the devil. This is more of the same. But as I trek further down the street and eye up Folk's canopy, my contemplation takes an even darker turn. Jerome was the man at the next table, I'm sure of it. I picture Anya eyeing him up and saying ... Christ, yes. Something about him being with a woman who looked old enough to be his mother.

As I fix another piece of the jigsaw, my world rocks again. It was Ursula, wasn't it, listening in to the conversation about me being 'preggers'. If the cult's influence stretches as far as Norwich, what about Fulham? Of course it does. They *murdered* Marcus Penny, so arranging a burglary to scare the shit out of me would be small fry.

Sheer outrage sizzling, I stalk to Pavilion Gardens. Catching my breath at the keypad, I nod grimly. The sticky substance on the remote control was blood, wasn't it? Someone must have retrieved it when Ben Logan was splayed on a road in agony. Why incur the cost of replacing it for muggings here, the numpty who was played and manipulated from the moment she stepped into Folk that February night.

Once the gates part, I don't scuttle back to my padded prison cell. Instead I snap left, march to The Lodge, climb up the steps and yank down the handle. Why I'm surprised the door swings open, I have no idea. These apparently benign, considerate and benevolent villains have been hiding in plain sight. I've been an utter, utter fool to be so taken in, yet some parts have been imposed and there's no way I'll pretend they haven't happened.

An embroidered tapestry has been added to the far wall since last I was here. Though I don't have the headspace to consider what the Latin wording might mean, I draw breath to holler for Jerome. Before I have chance to, he silently steps from the kitchen into the hallway.

I jab a finger. 'Why me? Why the fuck did you choose me? Because I was earmarked that night, wasn't I? You or Ursula saw me and said "yes she'll do" to carry on the fucking family entail. Only there was a wee problem. I was already pregnant. So what did you do, Jerome? You sent your minions to frighten me so badly that I'd miscarry. Have you any idea how terrified I was? And yes, I lost my baby, so well done you. Only you couldn't stop there. You had to impregnate me and what better way than to do some sort of devil's pact with my husband, drug me and rape me. Did it feel good, big man? Is that the only way you get hard? Was it exciting to shag someone who was out of it and couldn't fight back?'

Nausea rises as another memory flares in. Ursula and Fabian's low voices ... And yes, her, in person. 'Not quite so out of it not to know your parents and "cousin" Meryl were there, watching the rape ceremony. What is wrong with you people? On what planet is it OK to do any of these things, threatening my mother and my grandparents, let alone killing anyone who happens to get in the way?'

Though I glower and pant from my spat monologue, Jerome doesn't move or reply or even react. His pupils black dots, he stares at me blankly.

'Don't you have anything to say for yourself?' My throat is raw from my anger, my dismay, my shouting. 'Not an acknowledgement, let alone a sorry. And what now? Am I expected to move in here and become some sort of wife? Give birth to my babies and encourage them to love you?' Tears pelt from my eyes. 'You made me feel special. You made me like you. I thought you were nice, I really did. Whereas you're actually insane.'

Without a hint of emotion, he squares his shoulders and steps towards me. 'I have to go. I have an appointment.'

I finally take in his attire. Yes, he clearly has. Wearing a spruce suit and tie, he's clean-shaven and his hair's groomed, business-style. Suddenly fearful for my safety, I step aside to let him pass. I shudder to think what his 'appointment' entails, but he's no longer a man I remotely recognise.

78

I dumbly stare at the textile weaving for several moments. Signed off by that same elaborately sewn 'Cognati', the embroidered letters give me no clue to what's really going on behind these closed gates. Or why me and Mum were duped into being part of it. Frustration and anger thrash inside me and, when my vision becomes as small as a pinprick, I stumble outside to drag in some air. It's actually another godforsaken cloudless day, the sun benevolently smiling on Pavilion Gardens again. Grimacing at how horribly misleading appearances can be, I make for my 'home', managing to stop a split second before crashing into Ursula.

'Hello, Francesca!' she says in her usual song-song tone. She peers more closely at me. 'Are you all right, dear? Mummy and babies well? You look a little pinched and pallid. Have you eaten?' Her gaze is loaded with her usual fake bloody concern. 'If you hadn't caught me short, I'd have rustled up something for you myself. Having twins takes a toll even as early as—'

'I'm fine.'

I actually want to punch the damned woman in the face. Yet I've exhausted every iota of my remaining energy on yelling at Jerome. If he'd responded, I might have had something to work with, but his lack of a vehement defence, let alone any reaction at all, has sapped me, so I push by her and traipse to my door. Once I'm on the other side, I silently scream. Pinched and flaming pallid are the very least of my worries. She does have a good point about food, though. Other than the banana my mum insisted on, I haven't had anything since breakfast.

Tears prod my eyes. My babies need sustenance; I mustn't lose sight of that. At the heart of all this darkness and trauma, I have to look after myself for them; they have to be my focus and priority.

Despite the balmy afternoon, I'm shivery cold. Intending to fold my achy body into a winter dressing gown, I plod up the stairs. At the top, Ursula's unusually stylish outfit occurs to me. No apron, smell of baking or flyaway tresses today, but a floral dress with a navy blazer, matching handbag and heels. A snort of derision escapes. Perhaps the chapel has reclaimed its original religious purpose for a wedding or a christening rather than a cover for some sort of satanic baby-making cult. I move to the window and peer out. There are no lights on in the building, or other signs of activity from the penthouse above, yet prickles beneath my skin make me rotate to the lawn. A tall couple are climbing out of a chauffeur-driven Bentley in the car park beyond.

I squint as I watch them draw near. In their seventies but wearing well, the straight-backed pair have a tangible air of royalty about them. A blend of intrigue and fear fires through me. Bloody hell, it's *him*. And though I can't see the colour from this distance, I have no doubt his eyes are sapphire-blue.

79

Certain I'll have visitors at some point this evening, I pass the time by making myself pasta sauce from scratch. I slice onions, tomatoes and aubergines, slide them into a frying pan with a slug of olive oil and wait for them to slowly caramelise. I add fresh basil and seasoning, biding the long minutes until the salsa reduces. Once the fresh fusilli comes to the boil, I drain it and pour it into a bowl belonging to Julia, the poor woman whose husband fell foul of these wicked people and paid the ultimate price.

Like Greg and Marcus. Like my first baby.

I sit at the table and spoon in my creation, churning within from apprehension and nervous energy, but mostly from fury. Though I struggle to swallow the food down, I eat for my twins. As Mum put it, I have to be smart for them; I have to control my temper, my knee-jerk tendencies. My rage will not go away; good God, I don't want it to, ever. I must use it to fuel me rather than blindly lead me.

When the doorbell finally rings, I check my appearance in the mirror and lift my chin to practice the look I want to portray. I'm terrified. I'm also weirdly fascinated. I've briefly seen him before – smiling from the front page of the Hundred Club pamphlet, appraising me at the water park, and in my own reflection – but today I'll meet the man who sired me in person. I allow myself a twitch of irony: I always did want a father and the moment is here. With Meryl, the devil stepmother, to boot.

I open up and eyeball my callers for several moments without moving.

'Oh, it's my dearest father and his wife. How very lovely to have you pop by,' I eventually say. My boldness and sarcasm feels good. 'Do come in and get comfortable. You must both be exhausted after all the excitement, especially at your age.'

Though Meryl doesn't reply, Raymond's lips curve. 'Thank you.'

I gesture them into the lounge and observe them sit; him sinking back into the sofa with ease, her stiffly perching on the edge.

'So how was the inauguration?' I ask. 'Who'd have thought Jerome would scrub up so well. Do I get a crown too? Maybe an orb?' I gesture to my jogging bottoms. 'If you'd given me a warning, I'd have made more of an effort.'

Raymond just smiles. 'I've had the pleasure of glimpsing you over the years, but it's so lovely to speak to you at last, Francesca. We met thirty-one years ago, of course. In fact, I was the first living soul to hold you and we spent some quality time together whilst your mother ... recovered.'

'I prefer Frankie.'

Recovered ... God, twilight bloody sleep; I'd almost forgotten about that. I grimace at the thought of those shackles in Fabian's clinic. A genuine attempt to give women a more pleasant birth experience or clear evidence of patriarchal control? I know which way my vote would go. No wonder my militant Mum didn't 'fess up' about it.

'Did the drugs make me a quiet, compliant little baby?' I ask. 'Because that's how "the family" elders seem to prefer their women.'

He chuckles. 'Not at all. You made your presence known from the moment you came into the world.' He nods approvingly. 'You clearly started as you meant to go on. Strong willed, a leader rather than a follower. I like that.'

I want to ask why the fuck he thinks I'll be a 'follower' now, but he speaks again. 'Do you play chess, Frankie? You should. It's a game which needs passion, mental strength, a fighting spirit, the will to win. And patience, of course.'

His wife clears her throat and holds out her hand. The frostiness Mum described oozes from her. 'Hello, I'm Meryl.'

I don't take it. This is the bitch who recruited Mum to be some sort of surrogate, who lured Toby into a devil's pact, who watched me being raped. I'd like to pin her against the wall by the throat and squeeze until she coughs out why. 'We have already met,' I say instead. 'You didn't deign to introduce yourself to me. You only had eyes for my husband. I can't possibly imagine why.'

'And indeed before that, albeit briefly.' She smooths a strand of blonde hair behind her ear. 'Though my daughter will be more familiar to you.'

That throws me. 'Will she?'

A minuscule twitch around her lips shows she's pleased with her curveball. 'Yes. Petra. Doctor Gauss to you. I believe she took care of your most unfortunate miscarriage.'

Shock hits my chest like a bullet and I struggle to hide it, so when Raymond stands, takes my elbow and guides me to the armchair, I comply. 'Why don't we all sit?' he says smoothly. 'I believe you've had a long day.'

My heart thuds in my ears as I try to process this new information. Doctor Gauss is their daughter ... How far have these people inveigled themselves into my life? What does her involvement mean?

Raymond continues to speak, his rich voice lyrical, soothing. 'Nature softens and loosens all your joints, muscles, tendons and ligaments when you're pregnant, and if you're carrying two ... Well, it pays to be extra kind to yourself.' He studies me pleasantly. 'So how are we doing? Any quickening? Perhaps it's a little early yet, but some describe the flutters as butterflies dancing across the bottom of the tummy. Others say it's like a tiny machine gun blowing bubbles.'

His genial manner almost brings tears to my eyes. Whether a father or obstetrician, his assuring warm tone is how it should be. I set my jaw and reinstate my abhorrence. I mustn't let Meryl throw me, or him pull me in with his deceptive charm. This man isn't my dad in any sense. He never will be.

'Excellent,' he says, even though I don't reply. 'It's an exciting time, especially when proper movement kicks in, but don't be surprised if tummy troubles come along. There'll be more crowding in the area, more strain on your GI tract, which can lead to digestive discomforts like heartburn, indigestion and constipation. It's nothing we can't manage with medicine and a heathy diet.'

I snap up my head. 'What are you saying? That I'll be under your care?'

'Goodness, no. I meant the proverbial "we".' Obviously delighted at the notion, he spreads his large hands. 'However, now I think about it, there's no reason why I—'

'Raymond is retired,' Meryl interrupts brusquely. She fixes her mouth into something resembling a smile. 'So whilst that would be very lovely, it's best we leave it to the younger generation.' She opens the clasp of her handbag and brings out a small diary. 'In fact, another appointment with Petra is long overdue, so let's arrange one now.'

There's no way I'm going near Doctor Gauss again. Meryl is clearly deranged, but the suggestion that another woman is complicit in this madness is terrifying. 'I think what's best is up to me, not we,' I hiss. 'You know, as the mother of my twins. It has zilch to do with you, Meryl.'

Fury flashes through her pale gaze. 'Check your tone when you're speaking to me.'

'Oops, touched a nerve, did I?' I squint in thought. Her hatred of Mum, despite being her handler, her pimp. Her desperate need to take control here ... My mouth slides into a smile. 'Oh, I get it. You're jealous! What should we call me? A love-child?' I can tell from her blanched cheeks that I'm on the right track. 'So the plan was to impregnate Nina with your hubby's supremacy sperm, but by *artificial* insemination rather than the personal touch?' I guffaw. 'So I am a *love*-child indeed! Poor old Meryl, no wonder you're so bitter. You must have found out that Daddy went far beyond his remit. Romantic dates, I believe, kisses and cuddles, sweet whispers, fun and laughter. Gosh, you must have been incandescent!'

I know I've lost it, that I've gone too far, yet my rage needs an outlet. 'And what about the family heirloom? I've got the sapphire necklace somewhere. I bet it would have looked lovely around Petra's pasty neck, but Daddy chose to give it to special me.'

Meryl strides over and leans in. 'I suggest you behave,' she spits, an inch from my face. 'You have family you love. How sad would it be if Colin dies from complications after all? And what about Sylvia? A bit overweight and getting on. I'd say she's ripe for a heart attack. Then there's dear old Baba. He's got a secret or two he'd prefer to keep to himself.' She prods my throat. 'So from hereon in you'll do as you're told; you'll set an example by attending your antenatal appointments with Doctor Gauss and going on the Sunday walk with a smile.'

Horrible realisation pumps through my veins like hot lava. The distinctive aroma of Meryl's perfume. Her size, her shape, the width of her shoulders. And her words: '*And indeed before that, albeit briefly.*' Yes, we had met before. Only it wasn't briefly enough.

'It was you. You were the burglar. You broke into my flat and threatened me with a knife.'

That same smirk of victory about her lips, Meryl pulls away and gracefully sits down. 'As if I'd go to the bother. Whoever it was, let that be another lesson to consider.'

80

Sleeping soundly despite all the trauma, I wake late on Sunday morning, check in with my mum on the phone, then drag myself out of bed for some sustenance before the walk.

Not daring to make my own way there in case I'm being watched, I accept a lift to the water park from Scott and try to converse with Pippa, squashed in the back seat between her two kids. The moment we arrive, I'm commandeered by Minta, and though it goes against every fibre of my being, I fix a smile and attempt to amiably chat as we meander around the glinting lake.

Hearing familiar voices behind us, I glance over my shoulder. Perhaps it's paranoia, but more of the neighbours seem to be out here today – and flanking me like flaming bodyguards. As I take in groups of normal, happy people enjoying the breezy summer's day, there's an urge to run over to them and say: *Help me! These people might look normal but I'm effectively imprisoned in a cult. They are all insane, incestuous freaks and I'm growing two more in my belly to add to their number.*

And yet I wouldn't change that part for all the money in the world. Aside from the vicious bile Meryl hissed in my ear yesterday, that's why I'm stuck, why I have to comply.

Wondering how much my companion knows about what's really going on within – and beyond – Pavilion Gardens, I study her smiley features. Perhaps Minta is the same as me. Maybe baby desperation has fudged her sense of reason, too. She has Dominic, though, and they seem genuinely happy, whereas my husband traded both me and his soul for his ambitions, and the father of my babies is ...

With a stomach-turning jolt, I catch Jerome in my peripheral vision. Bloody hell, he's here and chatting to Pippa as if nothing's amiss. Is this the part where I'm expected to cosy up to him? To bat my eyelashes and pretend we're becoming an item? I grit my teeth. No way am I doing that. The thought of even being civil to him sticks in my throat.

I revert to Minta's guileless expression. 'I need a wee, but don't wait for me. I'll stroll home along the riverbank to make the most of the sunshine.'

She looks panicked. 'Are you sure? It's quite a walk and we have the car. You wouldn't want to overdo it.'

'I'm positive, thanks. Gentle exercise is the thing and I'm half-way through a podcast I want to finish. I'll see you back at the ranch.'

Hoping they'll move on, I spend far more time in the sour-smelling toilet block than is needed. When I finally emerge and breathe in the fresh air, Jerome is waiting by the fence.

'Timed me, did you?' I snap. 'Because it wouldn't do to keep the vehicle for your precious commodities out of sight for more than five minutes, would it? What if I absconded? That would upset the apple cart big time. All that frigging planning for years to no avail.'

He's wearing sunglasses, so I can't see his eyes. 'I'm going the same way as you, so I thought I'd join you, if that's OK.'

'If that's *OK*? Are you fucking joking?' He doesn't reply. 'Ah, of course. Armed escort. Though I suppose I should be honoured to be ushered back by our newly crowned leader.'

Unshaven and with messy hair, he appears more like the vet guy today. That simply makes his deception all the worse; I now know he's the dead-eyed stranger from yesterday, and that this is a wolf-in-sheep's-clothing disguise.

The blend of anger and disappointment sputters out of my mouth. 'Did you enjoy your coronation ceremony yesterday? Or maybe it was an inspection and a few medals as a reward for your heroic fucking efforts?'

Rather than respond, he sets off, so I follow. Although walking companionably like we're friends is the last thing I want to do, there's a desperate impulse to shake him or strike him, to pummel him with my fists to get an acknowledgement of what he's done.

I manage to hold it in until we reach the riverbank. 'Did no one teach you that it's rude to snub people when they ask a question?' It's laughably banal in the context of the darkness between us, but the shouting didn't work and I need to understand how I got him so very wrong.

'Yes, obviously. Ursula and Fabian were – are – good parents, good people.'

I stop. 'Are you actually serious?'

'Within their circumstances, yes.'

My cheeks burn with anger. 'They watched you rape a semi-conscious woman for some sort of medieval desire to extend the bloodline.'

'It wasn't like that.'

Disbelieving, I glare. 'How else would you describe drugging a woman, then having sex with her? It was rape, pure and simple.'

'Yes, yes it was. I'm not denying that.' He rakes his hair. 'It was also a ceremony the elders are required to witness. They briefly saw what was needed to attest to paternity and left.'

I should be incredulous, but life has become so skewed over the last forty-eight hours, nothing will surprise me ever again. 'Oh, that's all right then.'

He removes his sunglasses and peers at me intently. 'It wasn't all right, Frankie. None of it is. You can't begin to imagine how disgusted I was with myself; how much I still am. I liked – I like – you very much. I abhorred having to defile you, humiliate, hoodwink you. I honestly didn't think I could ... perform. I had to go to some other place and force myself. I'm so, so sorry. I had no choice; I have no choice for similar reasons to you.' He looks over his shoulder. 'Come on, we'd better move on.'

I have to firmly block the desire to believe him. 'Well that's a mightily convenient thing to say.'

He spreads his arms. 'It's the truth.'

'Is it?' I picture the stranger I tried to talk to yesterday. That unrecognisable man who had an 'appointment' with Raymond and Meryl; evil people who manipulate – and kill – to get what they want. 'I don't believe you.'

'Fair enough.' He drops his head. 'The truth is all I can offer.'

81

Though Jerome walks on, I fold my arms and don't move for some time. I'm fighting a bloody battle in my head. Yes, I have to play it smart and be careful; I have to protect myself and my sanity by not trusting anyone except my mum. I've already been horribly, horribly blindsided; I can't risk doing it again. Yet I saw the slump of Jerome's shoulders just now, the look of sheer defeat and devastation in his eyes. Suppose what he says is true?

Searching for him in the distance, I set off again, dodging the jagged stones along the arid towpath. I finally spot him half-way up a grassy bank, so I accept his proffered hand and scramble up beside him. 'Why did you have no choice?' I bark.

His sunglasses raked back, he watches the rippling river. 'I know the outside world wouldn't even begin to understand our family ... idiosyncrasies. To us they were normal. Stefan was born ten minutes before me, so he was the eldest and he grew up knowing he'd study medicine, have a wife chosen for him at some point, sire a son and continue the family line.'

Remembering Fabian's 'private collection' of sperm, I shake my head. 'Only it wouldn't just be siring one child, would it? It'd be sowing the family seed far and wide.'

'Yes.'

'That isn't *idiosyncratic*, Jerome, it's insane.'

'Traditionally—'

'Don't blame fucking tradition, rituals, bloody ceremonies. It's simply wrong. It's totally unacceptable on so many levels.'

'I agree. Dad knows it too, which is why he did what he had to do in a limited way, and for purely altruistic purposes, and not for—'

'For what?' I picture the 'regal' Raymond and Ursula. 'Control, supremacy, power?'

'Yes.'

I pause to absorb what he's saying. 'Then if Fabian and Ursula are the "good people", as you put it, who the hell are the bad?'

'Cousins, second cousins, third, from other chapters.' He grimaces. 'Don't they say we're all related in one way or another?'

The thought makes my skin crawl. 'So Raymond and Meryl. Are they your cousins too?'

'Yes, second or third, possibly. They're higher in command, so Dad – we – answer to them.'

'Hmm, really?' I frown. 'Funny how your dad shares rooms with Petra Gauss in Manchester.'

'Yes, when they ask for a favour, you don't say no.'

I turn to his profile. 'Who are *they*, exactly?'

He stares into the distance and doesn't reply.

'For fuck's sake, Jerome. You've made me part of this.'

'I'm sincerely sorry I did. I didn't have a—' He sighs. 'They call themselves the Cognati.'

I pause in thought. That capital 'C', Raymond's smiling face, the Hundred Club. They must hide behind a children's charity. But why? For money? Respectability?

I go back to Jerome. 'A tapestry was hung in your hallway. Something in Latin followed the word.'

'Yes. There of all places.' A spasm of grief passes through his tired eyes and, somehow, I know Stefan became another name on the Cognati's hit list.

'What happened to your brother?'

'I shouldn't have left him. I should have stayed, protected, helped him.' He looks up to the sky and doesn't speak for a while. 'There were two problems,' he says eventually. 'Well, at least two that mattered living our particular life. Firstly, Stefan was infertile. That wasn't fatal as Dad covered for him by providing the specimens.'

I shouldn't feel shock, but I jolt. 'What? They tested his

fertility?'

'Yes.'

'Bloody hell.'

'The second was insurmountable. He was gay.'

I swallow. 'So they ...'

He looks away. 'Pushed or jumped; what's the difference? They killed him either way.'

'God, I'm so sorry; it must have been dreadful to lose him and especially like that.'

'It was.' Plucking spears of grass, he falls silent for some time. His brow creasing, he finally rotates to me. 'Look, there's something I want to say. When I was allowed to ... I don't know ... to see you and give the nod to the arrangement, I—'

'Arrangement.' My stomach lunges at the notion. 'When was this? In February at Folk?'

'Yes. Well, just outside. You bumped into me, as it happens. Then we followed you in and sat at the next table. Until I heard the exchange between you and your friend, I had no idea you were pregnant. I tried to backtrack, but the match was already set in stone and there was nothing I could do to persuade them otherwise.'

I feel myself bristle afresh. 'So your mother did know. Not such a good person after all.'

'I'm not following.'

'She was there, your date, your enabler, whatever.'

'Ah.' He sucks in some air. 'No. My mum loves babies. She'd have fought tooth and nail not to go down that route. My warder that evening was Meryl.'

The woman's turn of phrase about her daughter filters in: 'I believe she took care of your most unfortunate miscarriage.' Was she really suggesting my baby hadn't died in the womb – or was, perhaps, hiding another twin? Then there were the sonographer's words of condolence about the loss coming from 'a higher power' as she touched the 'C' around her neck.

Rage twists inside me. 'Right. Of course she was.'

Jerome squints at the glistening water. 'Carry on walking or go home?'

'What, "home" to the bloody Lodge?'

'Yes, if you like.'

'I don't like any of it, Jerome. It sickens me.'

'I know.' He rubs his weary face. 'I can't apologise enough for my part in this ... this living hell. I can't turn the clock back either. I failed to save my brother and I love my parents; I have to go on and play the game for their safety.'

I nod. I felt the sharp swipe of Meryl's power only last night and, in truth, I'd do the same to protect Mum and my grandparents. My anger finally shrivels and dies. This man is as imprisoned as I am.

He offers his palm to help me up. 'Shall we spot the heron at the weir for good luck, then turn back?'

'Sure. We need some of that.'

Lost in our thoughts, we amble for ten minutes without speaking. I bring myself back as we approach Northenden Bridge. 'I wonder if we can get through on the path beneath the arch yet. Otherwise we'll need to cross the road.'

'Oh, has it been—'

'Yeah, the walkway by the weir has been closed for ages.' I gesture to the girder of the huge viaduct above us. 'Repairs to the motorway foundations, apparently.'

Jerome doesn't comment. His attention is fixed on the high concrete structure, which he squints at with a frown.

'What is it?' I ask, following his scrutiny of the guardrail.

He gasps. 'Don't look,' he wheezes, a moment too late.

I already have, my terrified eyes like magnets as I watch the rag dolls flap and tumble through the air, then smack and crack against the rocky ground.

82

As if I'm still two years old, Mum kneels by the bathtub and gently squeezes the warmth from a sponge onto my back.

'Tell me when you need me to top up the hot water. Or when you've had enough,' she says.

'Not yet. It's nice, comforting.' My lips twitch a touch. 'It must be a recreating-the-womb type of thing.'

She kisses my hair. 'That's what mums are here for.'

I've finally stopped shaking. It was uncontrollable shuddering and chattering teeth when Mum and Col first arrived at the riverside this morning. They were on their way to the countryside for a Sunday roast in a pub when I phoned, so were able to turn back and collect me within fifteen minutes. The police and ambulance arrived even before them, so someone must have spotted people climbing over the motorway safety rail and called 999.

'He told me to stay put,' I say again. The whole thing was so unexpected and shocking, my concentration is zilch and my mind keeps hopping from one moment or thought to another. 'He said the Mersey was full of chemicals, boulders and bottles, let alone unexpected currants, so that's why I didn't wade in after him.'

'I know, and he was right.' Mum smiles thinly. 'I'm very glad you did as you were told for once. It could have been dangerous.'

I turn to her. 'And we know about dangerous, don't we? Look at poor Col. He still has a limp.'

'True, but he's getting there. He's not one to let a "little mishap" get in the way of his determination to make the most of every second of his life.'

Her eyes shine at the mention of his name. Despite all this darkness, I'm happy she's met someone who clearly adores her. 'He's really nice, Mum. Pretty fit too.' I go back to my erratic contemplation. 'He doesn't know the real reason someone drove into him?'

'Not exactly. I haven't said anything for obvious reasons. He isn't stupid, though. I guess he knows not to ask; that I'll share things with him if, and when, I ever can.'

'He must have missed you when you were in Spain.'

She purses her lips, Gran-style. 'The poor sod was on traction in hospital for three weeks, wondering why I couldn't even manage a visit. It was horrible reading his texts as they arrived. Then when he was mobile, someone messaged him and suggested I might appreciate a visit. After isolating myself for so many weeks, seeing him was a godsend. I wanted to confess everything, but I couldn't risk it for—'

'Hold on. Who contacted him?'

'I don't know. It was from an unknown number. I'm guessing the same person who occasionally texted me to say you were OK.'

'What the hell, Mum? Why didn't you tell me?'

She sits back. 'A lot's been going on, Frankie ...'

'OK, fair enough.'

'Clearly someone with inside knowledge, though.'

'True.'

A horrible notion occurs to me. I bite it back, but Mum's eyes are sharp. 'What is it?'

'Nothing.'

'Tell me. The brutal truth, remember?'

'OK. Something Meryl said yesterday. God, I don't know; she might be playing mind games ...' I cringe. 'Maybe they got to Baba.'

'Baba? No. There's no way I believe that.' Clearly struggling with the notion, she pauses. 'Why, what did she say?'

'Something about him having secrets he'd prefer to keep to himself.'

'No, she's just being spiteful. Isn't she?'

I don't reply. Look what happened with Toby. They found his deepest desires and vulnerabilities, homed in and exploited them.

Mum's brow crinkles. 'Baba gave me the fifty thousand pounds to buy this place. He wasn't by any means flush afterwards, but looking back ... Well, I suspect he earned more than a part-time postman. Money; that was his weak spot.'

'Like Toby's ambition and my need for safety.'

'And my desperate desire for a baby.'

'Their precious package ...' I turn on the tap and watch the warm water tickle my toes. 'Why though? That's what I don't get. Why go to all the effort to create me? More to the point, why did Meryl choose you?' I glance at her and guffaw. 'She was jealous, though; she clearly loathed the idea of your liaison with Raymond, and thus hated me by association. I might have just goaded her about it a little.'

'That's my girl.' Her smile falls. 'But seriously, you mustn't. We know what wickedness she – and, undoubtedly, he – are capable of.'

'I know, I shouldn't have provoked her. The real her hissed out like a banshee. It was frightening. Then as if things couldn't get any worse – today.' I cover my face. 'It keeps flashing in. They held hands and sort of fell forwards, as though the sky would support them, make them buoyant. It didn't, of course.' I try to blink the image away. 'Neither of them made a sound. It was dreadful, I just stood there and watched them flap down like sacks, then ... well, snap against the rocks. Jerome's howl broke the surreal, horrifying moment. Until then I didn't realise who they were.' My heart loudly thuds. 'Were they good, were they evil? I have no idea. I just feel horribly guilty. Was it because of me? Something I did or didn't do? My altercation with Meryl, for example?'

Mum looks at me solidly. 'Don't go there, love. From what you saw, it was their decision to do it.'

I'm not sure any more; they were clearly on something hallucinogenic. 'Pushed or jumped; what's the difference,' I mutter.

'What do you mean?'

'Something Jerome said about his brother's death.'

'So much tragedy in his life. I know he's ... well, one of them, but it makes you wonder how much a person can take.'

I finally let out a sob. 'When he dragged her out of the water she was still alive. Ursula. He cradled her and she tried to speak. Only blood came out of her mouth. She was trying to say she was sorry.'

Mum's tears fall. 'I'm so sorry too. I positively welcomed the relationship with Raymond, whereas you ... well, you didn't ask for any of this.'

'This isn't your fault, Mum. You were groomed by them both.' I picture the sheer hopelessness etched in Jerome's features. 'It isn't his fault either.'

'Whose?'

'Jerome's.' Anger surfacing, I scowl. 'I bet they made him put down his dog. I can see Meryl passing that judgement down with a smirk. And Raymond is just as bad. He might play the charming good guy, but he lets her do whatever she wants.' I pause. 'He didn't like the way she spoke to me, though; I saw his flash of annoyance. So maybe his offspring come first ...' Remembering their smiley family photographs in Ursula's gallery, I frown and mutter to myself. 'They had two kids in the portrait. A boy and a girl. We know Petra became a doctor and joined Fabian's practice, but what about the son? Where's he, then?'

Mum shrugs.

'A boy. Precious son and heir to the entail. Why have they given the crown jewels to Jerome and not him?' I mentally home in on the Hundred Club pamphlet for several long seconds. An answer snapping in, I revert to Mum. 'Did you ever find out where they lived? Raymond and Meryl?'

'No, I only ever met him at his rooms and, of course, I didn't even know he was—'

'Right.' I stand. 'Pass me a towel. I need to do some research on your laptop. Then we're going to give Baba a visit.'

'What, at this time?'

'Yes. Is Col still downstairs?'

'As far as I know.'

'Good. He can come too. I'll need a joiner.'

83

Tightly holding hands, me and Mum travel from Withington to Hale in the back seat of Col's Ford E-Transit van.

'Are you OK?' I ask her.

'As OK as I can be,' she replies. 'How about you?'

I grimace. 'I suspect we're both running on adrenaline for now.' I smile a wonky smile. 'We'll swap notes when it's over.'

'Oh, love,' she says. 'I wish I had your confidence.'

She looks away and I know she's hiding her tears. Though we'd discussed Baba's possible perfidy earlier, I don't think the penny really dropped until we turned up at my grandparents' house. Once Col had distracted Gran by flashing a grin and asking for a peek in her famous baking tin, Mum folded her arms and just came out with it.

'Have you been paid dirty money, Dad?' He coughed and spluttered, but she was having none of it. 'So that's a yes. I haven't got time to go into my deep, deep disgust with you right now. Our Frankie's got a request. I suggest you come up trumps.'

Though Mum held out a flat palm to show she didn't want to hear it, he hurriedly explained it was only a 'few extra bob' to write to Raymond twice a year and keep him posted about the precious package. My health, my happiness, my schooling, my progress. My degree, my job, my love life.

'It was obvious he was a married man with kids of his own, who required, you know, discretion,' he said. 'And we were on the same page about wanting the best for our Frankie, so I saw no harm in it.'

He didn't need to say that was until reality struck him like a

294

sledgehammer in April. His drawn features and red eyes said it for him.

I now go back to Mum. 'Do you think you'll tell Gran?' I gently ask.

She blows out a stream of nervy air. 'Who knows. Brutal truth is all very well in theory, but ...'

Her words trail off because she's scared. Scared that Gran was in on it too, I imagine. That's the sheer terror of these people. Their deception spreads unseen beneath the earth, then cracks the surface, destabilising lives. And so much worse.

I set my jaw. Poison. Those fucking roots need poisoning.

*

As one would expect, the house is huge. Located on an exclusive road in leafy Hale, the grounds are inevitably protected by imposing electronic gates but, when Colin does a second drive by at midnight, we decide the walls either side aren't insurmountable with a strong helping hand.

The helping hand is now peering at the sprawling property online.

'Bloody hell, they bought it ten years ago for a snip at £3.25m,' Mum comments over his shoulder. 'Probably doubled in price by now.'

'It goes to show how intimidation, control and the bloody rest, pays,' I reply dryly.

'I'm surprised at the layout. I thought it'd be like Fort Knox.'

'Me too. Another illustration of how important, how invincible the pair think they are. It'll be fun to show them they're not.' I look at Col, the man I hope to call 'Dad' one day. 'So, what do you think?'

He studies the extensive back lawn, duly mowed in neat stripes, then enhances the photograph and taps at the glassy exterior. 'No problem,' he says. 'The bifolds either side are all the rage and look nice; they're also a burglar's dream. As for the balconies above ...'

'OK,' I reply. 'I'm ready.' I turn to Mum. 'I think you should stay in the van. You know, keep an eye out for foot soldiers or whatever.'

She honestly looks petrified, yet she arches her eyebrows. 'And miss all the fun, as you put it?'

I'd rather she remain here where she's safe. 'Look, you're—'

'Old?' She pulls a sour face. 'And you're pregnant. I think that makes us physically equal.'

Though I doubt physicality will come into it, I nod. This is as personal for her as it is me. 'Right. Come on, Mother. Let's do this.'

84

Although my heart madly whips as Colin applies tools to ease open the patio door, I'm paradoxically disappointed the alarm doesn't shrill and scare the shit out of the residents upstairs. Yet in a way it fuels my resolve. These people don't think they need protection, nor cameras or warnings; so used to welding their power, they believe they're above both criminals and the law.

'Thanks, Col,' I whisper. 'Wait in the van. We'll try to keep you posted by text. If we're not back in an hour, call the police and say you've come to collect us and that you're worried we haven't emerged from our visit – or some such malarkey.'

'I'm perfectly happy to stay with you two.'

'Nope. I don't want to get you into trouble or put you at risk again. I'd rather Mum leave as well.' I smile through my jangling nerves. 'Seems I've inherited the stubborn gene from her.'

'Ha.' He lifts the crow bar. 'At least let me leave you with this.'

'Thanks, but it's not my weapon of choice right now. I think adopting theirs will be more effective.'

I inwardly nod. Using psychological ammunition rather than bodily: mind games, confidence, lack of fear. Menaces with charm. Poison. Christ, I hope so. This potential act of self-sabotage is way more than my usual knee-jerk reaction to stress, but I need to do this for Mum, Gran and Baba. I put a gentle hand on my belly. And especially for my babies.

Once I'm sure Colin has scarpered, I flick on every light switch from the showy chandeliers and matching wall mounts, to the plethora of standard lamps, then I saunter around the spacious living room, doing the Felicia 'touch test' along its elegant contents. Not surprisingly, there's an inlayed lacquered chess board, the brass and wood pieces lined up to make their move.

Passion, mental strength, a fighting spirit and the will to win, I remember. And, of course, my Achilles heel, patience.

I finally sweep my fingers over the textured wallpaper. 'Lovely, isn't it? Though too much grey for my liking,' I say without lowering my voice. I flop down onto the plush velvet sofa and pat the cushion beside me. 'Take a seat, Mum. We may as well get comfy whilst we're here.' Settling my tired legs on the pouffe, I point the remote at the TV screen. 'Fancy a film?'

We watch *Get Out* for a few minutes, and though I increase the volume, there's no hint of movement from above. 'Well, I need a strong drink,' Mum says, standing. 'Can I get you anything?'

'Something soft would be nice,' I reply. 'Careful not to spill on the carpet. I can't decide if it's white or cream.'

'Cream Axminster, I'd say. Yes, it wouldn't do to stain it.'

When she returns with a large glass of red for herself and an orange juice for me, I tut. 'Maybe I should have gone for the big balcony entrance. I didn't want to lower myself to their standards, though.' The memory of the burglary, the sheer terror I felt, infuses me. '*Her* standards.'

'Quite right too.' Mum gestures to the television. 'Maybe turn up the sound again? Losing their hearing, I should think.'

I do as she suggests. It has the desired effect, yet neither of us turn when the door creaks open.

'Who's there? What the hell do you think you are doing?' Raymond growls from behind us.

Meryl darts over to peer at her visitors. 'It's them,' she squawks. 'It's both of them.'

Despite her tremulousness beside me, Mum's voice is strong. 'Really, Meryl?' She makes a show of looking her up and down. 'That nighty's a bit brassy for someone your age. Don't try too hard, is my tip. Puts a bloke off his stride, if you get my meaning.' She smiles sweetly as Raymond appears. 'Never had any problem in that department with me, did you, big man?'

'Don't you dare ...' Swiftly pulling something from behind her,

Meryl jabs it towards her and sneers. 'Not so chirpy now, are you?'

Black handled, engraved and with a curved tip, it's not only a knife, but *the* knife from the burglary, my night terrors, waking dreams and post-traumatic stress. Though my pulse starts to race at the memory and my debilitating fear, I remind myself its strength is symbolic. It's just an athame, only dangerous to me if I let it be.

I lean in and read the Latin wording out loud. '"*Non ducor, duco.*" Sadly, I didn't have the benefit of a classical education, so I'll have to guess what that means.' I give Meryl a withering look. 'Super sperm?'

'Only a fool laughs.' She swishes her weapon to me. 'It means "*I am not led, I lead.*" Today you saw in person what happens when rules aren't obeyed. You'd be wise to heed it.'

I shelve her loaded comment for now. 'Oh, for heaven's sake, put it away, Meryl. We both know you won't use it.' I rotate to Raymond. 'Will she, Daddy?'

He smooths back his thick fringe. 'Why are you here, Francesca?' He corrects himself. 'Frankie.'

'To tell you and your cult chums how things are going to be from now on. Only I'm not a coward like she was. I'm not hiding behind a mask.' I yawn and stretch. 'So what were we talking about? Oh yes, super sperm. Where's Peter?'

Visibly flinching, Meryl glares at her husband.

'Don't worry, it wasn't Daddy who told me. As if he'd share the dark Gauss secret.' I adopt a bright beam. 'All the Ps. Peter and Petra. Cute names for twins.' I glance at Meryl. 'Get with it; it simply involved a search of birth records online.'

I return to the man who sired me. 'So back to beloved Peter ... I always thought that women got it worst, what with periods and hormones, not to mention giving painful birth, but poor little chap. You know, having to wank at what, the age of thirteen or so, and have his semen tested by the Cognati? How dreadful for you both to discover he was "firing blanks", as they say.'

Meryl brandishes the knife. 'Shut up. Just shut up.'

I laugh dryly. 'Uh oh. The supremacy plans were going wrong, weren't they? Too many cousins, too much inbreeding resulting in all manner of homozygosity-related issues. I'll admit, albeit only for qualifying *family*, your Hundred Club charity is commendable. Sadly, there's not a lot even the most talented medics can do for the one thing that matters for world domination. Is there, Father?'

Seeming to evaluate my performance, he doesn't reply or even blink.

'Fertility, of course! How else can you spread those roots far and wide? That's where Nina came in. You couldn't risk accidentally choosing a random Cognati relative, so someone who was a different colour and class was the thing. But looks, youth, athleticism and intelligence were still key to breed with the elite, naturally. Gosh, I bet you couldn't believe your luck when someone so desperate to conceive – as well as ticking all the boxes – fell into your lap.' I eyeball Meryl. 'She scrubbed up far better than you anticipated, didn't she? I bet you were quite put out when you saw how beautiful she was without her red nose and swollen eyes. Then when Raymond became smitten, and decided on a *personal* donation—'

'Stop or I'll cut you. I mean it.'

'No you won't.' I genuinely chuckle this time. 'Apparently "Cognati" means: "Persons related by birth; specifically, the descendants of the same pair." I looked it up. Ironic, no?'

Thank God the 'why Nina?' answer finally dawned on me as I studied my toes in the bath: simple genetics. Supremacy bloodlines and superior genes were all very well in theory, yet in practice the flood of recessive alleles were leading to a severe inbreeding depression, in particular a decreased biological ability to procreate amongst the Cognati. Like poor Stefan and Peter, and undoubtedly many more male 'cousins' as well. Ironically, my blue eyes descend from a single genetic mutation which means me, Jerome, Raymond and Fabian are descended from one common ancestor. But so are every other blue-eyed human being. And thankfully for my protection, invincibility and survival – and that of my twins – I'm part Nina too, thus genetically diverse and all the more 'precious' for it.

My smirk falling, I set my resolve. I've had my 'fun'; it's now down to the business of spreading poison. 'You don't scare me, Meryl. I'm a "precious package", as are my twins. After all that planning and effort, it would be a tragedy to lose them.'

I abruptly stand and bare my teeth. 'And if you or your cult maniacs go within another inch of my grandparents, my mother or anyone else I love, like, or happen to meet in a shop or on the street, that's what will happen. Today, tomorrow, when they're born, when they're helpless babies, when they toddle ...' I jerk my head towards Raymond. 'I will decide whether his legacy, his bloodline, his fucking fee tail continues.'

I snatch the knife from her hand. 'Get me? Because this belongs to me now.' I bring the point to her throat and gently press. A gravelly voice I barely recognise emerges from my mouth. 'And I will use it. Understood?'

85

'Nearly there,' Mum says from beside me. 'Come to mine tonight? The bedding is clean on.'

Though she tugs me from the cusp of sleep, I'm certain she's been watching me – her eyes loaded with a question I hope she'll never ask – since I joined Col in the van ten minutes after her.

I look at my freshly washed palms and consider my reply: *I was having a last word. I needed a pee. I forgot my mobile. I didn't believe Meryl really had 'understood'. Her 'what happened today' sneer. Stefan's tragic death. Her pimping my mum. Toby. Jerome's poor dog. The burglary and D&C. The loss of my first baby. The rape.*

That isn't Mum's query, at least not for now, so I drag myself back to practicalities. I'm so exhausted it's a struggle to keep my eyes open, but things have irrevocably changed. Though I didn't realise it when Fabian and Ursula fell to their deaths from the sky, I belong at Pavilion Gardens now.

'No, thanks. Drop me at home, please.'

'OK. If you're sure?'

'I'm sure.'

I look out to the black night. *Home.* It feels as though I've travelled a full circle in terms of place, yet I'm no longer the Frankie who set out in April. Or maybe that Frankie was always there, hidden in her genetic make-up, waiting to be acknowledged and released.

I shudder. Or perhaps unleashed.

'Here will be fine,' I say as we pass my railings.

'I'd rather see you to the door. And it's drizzling now, so we'll drive through.'

I climb out at the gates. 'No need to wait. They take ages to open. You two get to bed!'

I stride to the keypad and input the code. When I turn to wave, a fluttering in my stomach stops me short.

'Frankie?' Nina winds down the window. 'Are you OK?'

Praying my babies know I would never, ever harm them, I put a protective hand to my tummy. Just like a reply, the gentle swish comes again. It's the very sensation of 'quickening' Raymond described. Blinking away his approving eyes, I focus on the wonderful 'first' moment. Movement, life, the future, Jerome. Good flowering from evil. And, of course, my guarantee of safe passage.

'Yes, I'm fine. I think they're telling me it's time for sleep. Night, Mum.'

Looking away from The Gatehouse and all the tragedy it entails, I trundle towards number three. A sudden tapping sensation on my shoulder makes me stop and spin around. No one and nothing is in the vicinity, but when I glance up to the penthouse, dim light seeps through an arched window. An icy shiver scuttles through me. Who would be in Fabian's clinic at all, let alone at this time of night?

Certain that something is very wrong, I belt to the chapel, clatter up the steps and yank down the handle. The door that's never locked is locked today. Jerome; it has to be Jerome. My heart pumps with alarm. I should have stayed at the river and offered him comfort instead of thinking of my own needs. However traumatic I found the appalling scene, it would have been a hundredfold for him. And even before then, on our walk, didn't I sense he was defeated and lost, on the brink of quitting like ... God, yes, like Stefan.

It's a struggle to think, to work out how the hell I gain access. Smash the ancient window panes? But with what? The reflection of headlights in the glass brings me back to my senses. Colin and Mum haven't left, thank God.

I madly beckon them over. 'Bring the crow bar,' I yell. 'Quickly. I need to get in here. It's urgent.'

Praying I'm not causing damage to the ancient building without cause, I watch Colin efficiently split the portal ajar, then I run up the stairs until I'm on the shadowy landing.

I stop at Fabian's surgery, quickly steady myself and stride in. 'Christ.'

His dark head lit by the dull beam of the desk lamp, Jerome is collapsed in the chair. My eyes dart around the table top surrounding him. There are several scattered drug vials and ... oh, God, a syringe.

'Mum? Call an ambulance,' I shout over my shoulder.

As I peer at the handwritten labels, I swiftly change my mind. They are clearly Fabian's 'perfected combination' of drugs. It involves a heavy dose of morphine, but God knows what else is in there. 'No, go back to Hale and fetch Raymond instead. Drag him here by the hair if you have to.'

Clearly perplexed by my decision, Mum pauses. 'Are you sure? We can do that, of course. Shouldn't we call emergency services too?'

Understanding I have to make an executive judgement already, I glance at the open medicine fridge. Though time is of the essence, I have the reputation of Fabian – and more particularly my community, my people – to consider. 'It's fine, I'll do that. Tell Raymond it's an urgent "twilight sleep" situation, then bring him here with whatever antidote medicines he needs.'

Mum's gaze slides away and I know that despite our 'brutal truth' pact, she'll never ask me about that missing ten minutes. 'OK,' she says. 'We'll be back as soon as we can.'

When they've gone, I kneel down by Jerome's side and lay a hand on his back. Though shallow, he's breathing. Puffing out my relief, I gently shake him. 'Wake up, Jerome. Wake up. Please.'

He stirs and half opens his eyes. Same as when he was suited in The Lodge, his pupils look like two tiny black dots. He'd clearly imbibed or injected drugs then to help him through the ordeal of his 'appointment', and I feel a surge of *something* for not understanding him better.

Now isn't the time for sentimentality. 'What have you taken?

How much have you taken?' I briskly ask.

He seems to unstick his tongue. 'Still here,' he croaks. 'So not enough.'

'You don't mean that.' I gather my strength. 'I understand how devastated you must be. It was awful, appalling. This isn't the answer.'

'It is. Their evil, their regime, their ... requirements, locked in these gates. And you. What you've suffered. Your baby. Toby. Abhorrent rape.' He taps his temple. 'It's in here. Tormenting me.' He swallows. 'An animal would be put down for doing less. Rightly so.'

My chest floods with panic. This isn't the plan. Yes, I do want the power, I do. I also want the paddling pool, the slide, the colourful cushions, holiday mementos and thumbed paperbacks. I want my nuclear family.

I peer at him intently. 'Yes, it was abhorrent, but you were under duress and we can't allow it to happen ever again. Right? And your parents, they were proud of what they had done here. In the most difficult circumstances, they were philanthropic and tried to do their best, bringing joy to so many. The last thing they'd want is this.'

'No, you're wrong.' His gaze becomes glassy. 'Spent hours working it out. They freed me. That's why they jumped. Now they've gone, there's nothing the Cognati can take away from me.'

I want to share what Meryl said earlier. That they – or even he – unknowingly broke her 'rules' and were 'pushed' rather than jumped. That Ursula's attempted final words were 'sorry, *they made me.*' But he's in such a delicate state, I'm fearful of tipping the balance.

'If that's true, then walk away and leave. Take back your autonomy. Be a vet again.'

'Wait for the day they come for me? Tragic fire; heart attack; hit and run?' With a clear effort, he straightens up. 'No, thanks. Do it on my terms.'

I snatch the hypodermic and move back. 'No. I'm not letting you do it.'

'Empty,' he says. He opens his fist to show a second syringe. 'Fell asleep before ...' He sighs. 'Go. Please. Let me finish. It's honestly for the best.'

A blend of pique and distress winds me. 'What about me? What about our babies?'

'You're protected; safe, I promise. If I thought—'

'That's not what I mean. Don't my feelings count?' I glare. 'What about filling The Lodge with children? That's what you said.'

'A beautiful dream I don't deserve. I see a monster in the mirror. You see it too; always will.'

'Not any more. I truly won't. I *forgive you*, Jerome. Total honesty and a clean slate from this moment.' I hold out my palm. 'Please give it to me. I need a partner, a lover, a friend. My twins – *our* twins – need a father.'

His brow creases. 'How can you possibly ...'

'Isn't that for me to decide?' I set my jaw. 'It's time to look to the future, and I want you by my side.'

Tears seep from his eyes. 'You're incredibly—'

'No, Jerome. I'm not good or virtuous or kind. I was willing to benefit from other people's loss; I was selfish and single-minded about what I wanted. I intend to do better. Good will emerge from the bad. The fertility clinic will stop, but we'll help this community in other ways. We'll be the best parents to our kids when they come. They won't be judged by their ability to breed or grow up with the pressure of bloodlines hanging over them like a dark cloud. They will live a normal life.' I will him to understand. 'It's down to us now; we won't use intimidation, blackmail or violence. But we can change things.'

He smiles a small smile. 'Love your spirit. Love you. We're tiny, Frankie. Here is part of something much bigger.'

'I know it'll be a battle. However ...' I pull the knife from my bag and bring the engraved words to the light. '"I am not led, I lead". It's ours now.'

He frowns, perplexed, then draws away. 'A Cognati athame doesn't equate to—'

'It's just a symbol, Jerome. A token to demonstrate that we are determined and strong.'

Although the heady surge of adrenaline floods back from earlier, I look at him with solid reassurance. 'An athame's traditional use is to channel and direct psychic energy rather than harm or draw blood, and that's how I intend to utilise it.'

I blink away my father's sapphire gaze and his nod of approval, even as the cream Axminster carpet was spattered red. 'I promise, Jerome. No more evil. Let's live and love and do this together. Are you in?'

Hoping he can't tell I've already used the knife to avenge our loved ones, and that I'd do it again in a heartbeat, I hold my breath and wait for his reply.

Finally, finally, he speaks.

'OK,' he says. 'Yes, I'm in.'

Epilogue

Mum never did confess to her twilight sleep birth experience, nor did she ask me about that missing ten minutes. Quite honestly, I wanted to shred Meryl to ribbons that night, but *play it smart, Frankie* rang in my ears and I limited the incision to the hollow of her throat, sinking the curved tip of the blade into her skin as though I was performing a tracheotomy. An astonishing amount of blood spurted out, yet my eyes were on hers, watching the terror she'd inflicted on me, my mum, Jerome, Stefan and so many others.

I suppose the cut might have been life threatening had she not had a doctor at hand, but 'smart' was the right move just then. Cowing rather than killing her, bringing her to heel and using her as a messenger to the Cognati cousins: this new leader means business, she'll lead and not be led.

When my labour came around in the December, I chose not to have my twins medically extracted from my body, opting for the traditional method of giving birth instead. I had gas and air to help me with the undeniable agony, but I wanted to be there, fully conscious for every last searing moment of finally bringing my beloved girls into the world. Yes, girls! The two beautiful bouncing babies Ursula so eloquently described. They're blue-eyed, of course, as bright as buttons and with mops of the curliest hair. Jerome loves them dearly and I couldn't ask for a more doting, affectionate daddy, yet I still see a spasm of pain in his gaze. I've forgiven him completely; my fear is he'll never quite forgive himself. He has fulfilled his promise of filling The Lodge with children, though, as we have a toddling boy and another baby on the way. As I watch them splash in our paddling pool, hurtle around the quadrangle lawn or fly to the sky on the communal swings, there's always the flash of fear that homozygosity of some form will worm its insidious way in, so I focus on the brilliant qualities our offspring will inherit from the people we love: feisty principles and *joie de vivre* from my mum, kindness and benevolence from Ursula and Fabian, tender thoughtfulness and humour from Jerome. And me? Strength, dedication and passion, I hope, not those hot-headed impulses I'm always striving to tame.

As for my father ... Now Meryl has 'passed', he's superficially a shrunken version of himself. Though others might not see it, his mental endurance is still there, shining through his brilliant eyes. I visit him every Sunday and play a round of chess like a dutiful child. I listen and nod when he directs me or speaks, but we both know I'm eking out information and intelligence, the what, who and where I'll need to bring my enemies down. He doesn't want to die, so he's measured and clever, making his moves strategically. Yet he can't help his conceit, that unswerving pride in his 'achievements', so I patiently play on that.

It's a slow game, for sure, but this is one I will win.

A letter from Caroline England

Hello lovely reader,

Thank you so much for reading The Return of Frankie Whittle. I do hope you've enjoyed following Frankie's journey, living alongside her in Pavilion Gardens and discovering its dark, disturbing secrets!

If you'd like to read more twisty, chilling tales about ordinary, relatable characters who get caught up in extraordinary situations, dilemmas or crimes, or who unearth deeply hidden, dark secrets, please check out my other Caroline England psychological suspense novels, *Beneath the Skin*, *My Husband's Lies*, *Betray Her*, *Truth Games*, *The Sinner* and *The Stranger Beside Me*. Or my CE Rose gothic-tinged psychological thrillers, *The House of Hidden Secrets*, *The House on the Water's Edge*, *The Shadows of Rutherford House* and *The Attic at Wilton Place*.

Book reviews are extremely helpful to authors so, if you have the time, I'd be hugely grateful if you'd pop one, however short, on Amazon, Goodreads, Waterstones, social media or any other forum you prefer.

If you happen to choose any of my Caroline England or CE Rose titles to read in your book club group, I'd be delighted to join you by Zoom towards the end for any questions you may have. If you'd like to hear my latest news or see photos of my moggies and other random things, my website and social media links follow on the next page.

Thanks again!

Best wishes, *Caroline*

Website: http://carolineenglandauthor.co.uk
Twitter: https://twitter.com/CazEngland
Facebook: https://www.facebook.com/CazEngland1/
Instagram: https://www.instagram.com/cazengland1/
TikTok: https://www.tiktok.com/@cazengland1
Linktree: https://linktr.ee/carolineengland1
LinkedIn: https://www.linkedin.com/in/caroline-england-35888064/

Acknowledgements

Huge thanks to:

The Bullington Press team — the charismatic boss, Guy Hale, my fantastic and insightful editor, Samantha Brownley, and the super talented Will Templeton.

My loving, supportive and brilliant family — my daughters Liz, Charl and Emily, and hubby Jonathan.

Our gorgeous Poppy, who sat on my knee as each chapter appeared on the page. My lap feels empty without you.

My wonderful friends — too many to name — but thank you for keeping me smiling.

Every single fellow author, blogger, reviewer, reader, online book-group admin and member, who has taken the time to champion my books.

Last, but not least, you guys — the fantastic reading public! Thank you so much for buying my novels, investing hours of your life reading them and posting such heartwarming reviews.